SILHOUETTE AND THE MONSTER

DELANEY ANDREWS

SILHOUETTE AND THE MONSTER

ALSO BY DELANEY ANDREWS

Silhouette and the Shadow

For Zack.
This story has been with me for a long time, but I didn't know the ending
until I met you.

CONTENTS

CHAPTER
ONE

Halloween was a weird night to be a superhero.

For once, my mask, hood, and fitted black suit weren't out of place, but I stuck to the rooftops anyway. I was one with the darkness, black curves hidden among the night's blanket. As heat gushed through my suit made of dark gray, flexible plates like mismatched scales, I stared down from my hiding spot. A few blocks prior, I'd left behind the parks with their hay bale mazes and trunk-or-treats mobbed by kids. Crown City, a haven for spectacles of all kinds, had some of the most epic haunted houses in the country. Hell, there were a few parties I wanted to attend, but this was more important.

The gangly man with the electric blue eyes and ill-fitting suit stood rooted to the sidewalk, a grocery bag dangling from one pale hand, the hazy, not-quite-rain blurring his edges.

Ian Dove was right hand to Dr. Kaylen Kavoh, my family's oldest nemesis and, we believed, the biggest threat to our city in ages. Kavoh was responsible for our incredible powers, though she didn't know we had them. My grandpa had managed to conceal that from her, at least.

Back then, she'd been Eleanor Kavoh, a brilliant geneticist hellbent on attaining immortality. A goal she seemed to have achieved, considering she was in her late eighties now but looked not even half that as she paraded as her own granddaughter who'd returned to honor her grandmother's work.

In the months since her arrival, we'd discerned fuck all.

No outright crime. No suspicious activity. Nothing.

She hadn't made public appearances more than a few times, and Dove stepped out only a little more often than that, so he was my continual target. It was the first time I'd been able to catch him in weeks.

The unfocused disinterest in his gaze sent a shiver down my spine. Using a button on the wrist of my suit, I clicked up the temperature inside. The powers Kavoh had bestowed upon my family were temperature dependent. The warmer my body was, the stronger I was. My uncle Bane's powers operated on the opposite scale; he was most powerful when cold. Inside my suit was like a furnace, but it did nothing to dispel the buzzing beneath my skin as I stared at Dove.

He glanced up and down the mist-darkened street before reaching into the bag he'd just exited the convenient store with.

My eyes narrowed. "What're you up to, Dove?"

He pulled out a marshmallow and tossed it in his mouth, closing those eerie, intense eyes as he chewed.

"Bummer," a voice said in my ear.

I yelped and rolled backward, my suit scraping against the roof's uneven surface.

"You scared the shit out of me," I hissed, pressing a button at the side of my mask.

Lenses popped down over my eyes, and a muscly Filipino man's soft smile lit the small screens. Vennie Ello waved, looking like he was video chatting me from a dingy bathroom stall.

"Sorry, Silhouette," he said. "Thought you might want some backup."

I hit a second switch, and vented panels shot out of the

parts of my mask on either side of my mouth, covering my lips so I could speak to Vennie across our comms line without risk of anyone in my vicinity hearing. "I thought you were out with friends tonight."

"I am," he replied, adjusting his earbuds, "but this movie they dragged me to is boring."

"What movie?"

"Uh, *A Seventh Component.*"

I hummed knowingly. The early reviews were mixed.

Lifting my head above the roof's edge, I eyed Dove through the transparent image of Vennie projected on the lenses. Dove's head was slightly cocked; his attention was fixed on the next building over. He scanned, his face slowly turning toward my hiding place.

Harsh buzzing from his pocket interrupted his attention.

"Hold on a sec," I said.

Below, Dove withdrew a phone from his pocket, his face somehow paling further as he brought it to his ear.

"Yes?" His voice was weirdly hollow, his eyes blank as he listened.

With my suit's heat enhancing my senses, I could hear the person on the other line.

"Dove." Even from far away, the voice strangled me. *Kavoh.* Her tone was as melodic as in her interviews on the local news. "I have a task for the Vine Unit."

Dove swallowed. "Okay."

"Nicklai is en route. He knows where you're going. Bring this one in. You're ready for another."

"Understood."

A pause, then Kavoh's voice slithered through the speaker. "I can't wait to hear how your project with the bacteria is coming along. Update me after."

The line went dead, but Dove kept the phone to his ear for a breath, his shoulders high and tight.

"This is it," I hissed. "They're up to something tonight."

The other times I'd surveilled Dove, he never went anywhere interesting or suspect. I'd watched him pay visits to bodegas, pharmacies, indie bookshops, and once to a pet store. Not exactly the haunts of an evil scientist.

"Want me to call Shadow?" Vennie asked.

I chewed my lip as a nondescript car halted with a screech before Dove, the passenger side door swinging open before it completely stopped. With a long sigh, Dove got in.

"Nah," I decided, letting the vehicle gain a few blocks before following. "Let him enjoy his evening. He deserves it."

Brisbane Leo, my uncle and the other half of our crime fighting duo who took the alias "Shadow," had a date. My mouth curled into a smile at the thought. It was his first since he'd taken me in, as far as I knew. Calling him now might make him think twice before taking a night to be social again, instead of roaming Crown City's streets with me. Work-life balance was neither of our strong suits.

Well, more like vigilante-work-school-love-life balance. Whatever. We were bad at it.

"They're on the move." I sprinted across the rooftops, keeping the car's taillights in my sight. "Someone named 'Nicklai' picked Dove up. How much do you want to bet Mayor Keep's ex-lackey found new work with Kavoh?"

"It's possible," Vennie mused. "If he gets out of the vehicle we can confirm."

The car moved at a steady pace, heading from one of Crown's smaller downtown neighborhoods to the less populated shipping and receiving ports along the river. I continued my chase, thankful for the cramped and often abandoned buildings in this area that made for easy tracking from above.

They made an abrupt turn onto a dead-end street, headlights illuminating a wall of corrugated steel blocking the space between two derelict buildings.

They'd turned down the opposite side of the road from my hiding place. With a curse, I eyed the distance. To get closer, I'd have to expose myself and sprint through the dimly lit street and silently scale the other building. It was too much risk, especially without Bane watching my back.

Instead, I moved to the middle of the roof across from where they'd stopped to gain a direct line of sight. I clicked up my suit's heat. As warmth from the veins lining it increased against my bare skin underneath, my vision sharpened so I could make out as Dove, with his telltale height and night-dark hair, stepped out.

The car's engine cut off, and a shorter man emerged from the driver's side. Light from the dashboard illuminated a mask of scars across his face, alongside a permanent scowl. My stomach clenched, instincts screaming for me to run. It was Nicklai—part of the team that had abducted me under Mayor Keep's orders not long after I came to Crown City.

"It's definitely him." A sneer contorted my face as I recalled fighting with Nicklai—rolling across a grimy warehouse floor, ferociously grappling to beat each other unconscious.

I'd won, barely.

Vennie nodded. The sound of a toilet flushing echoed across the line, and he winced. Someone must have been in the stall adjacent to his, limiting his options to provide me whatever helpful information he could pull up on his phone.

Nicklai prowled to a door hidden in the buildings' shadow, taking up a relaxed stance against the wall just beyond its frame. Dove stood further away, arms crossed. Though he faced away from me, I could see one long finger tapping an erratic beat against his suit's worn sleeve.

They waited, still and foreboding as tombstones as night stretched on. Nicklai picked his nails, every so often shooting Dove a mocking look. Dove didn't react. Not to Nicklai, not to the cold breeze ruffling his moon-brightened hair, not to the echoing sounds of rambunctious Crown citizens celebrating deeper in the city.

I tried to stay just as still, shifting only to pull my trademark hood closer around my face to fight the chill breeze coming off the lake. Vennie broke the silence once to let me know he was able to track my location and determine Nicklai and Dove were stationed at the rear of a gym.

Finally, the door opened with an indignant shriek. A woman backed out, clad in a tank top, leggings, and a bulky backpack. She'd just put a key in the lock when Nicklai pounced. He grabbed her around the shoulders and shoved her to the ground. With a screech, she kicked at him, but Nicklai dodged her flailing sneakers and straddled her torso, aiming punches at her face.

The woman shielded her head with her arms, still shouting, but her cries melded with the holiday ruckus echoing throughout the city.

"Don't be difficult," Nicklai hissed through gritted teeth. "We've got an incredible opportunity for you."

Dove strode toward the pair, his feet dragging, as Nicklai pinned her arms on either side of her head. She spat in Nicklai's face. His only retort was to laugh quietly as Dove crouched beside them, pulling something from his jacket.

Cloud-diffused moonlight glinted off silver. Dove held a small pistol loaded with a glass vial that sloshed with glowing, orange liquid.

"What is he—" I started.

Vennie's silence echoed my confusion.

As Nicklai held her down, Dove pressed the barrel to the woman's arm and pulled the trigger.

The woman thrashed. The vial drained. She gasped for breath, her captors seemingly content to observe her panic.

After a long minute, she began to scream.

Her petrified howls pierced the night like lightning. They wouldn't bring the police running, though. Not with her cries blending with the distant screams and laughs from a dozen haunted houses.

Dove stepped back. As he receded, her cries grew more intense.

"Please!" she begged between shrieks. "Please, make it stop!"

Nicklai braced one of her arms beneath his knee. Freeing a hand, he clapped her mouth. Dove turned away, his face ashen like he was going to be sick.

"Listen," Nicklai shushed his prey.

My gloved fingers dug into the roof's cement barrier, digging small trenches as I leaned forward.

"We think you've got great potential. We're gonna help you unlock it. No need to cry. By the time our boss is done with you, you'll be more than you ever imagined."

Starlight glittered on tears crawling down her face.

Dove darted forward and somehow rendered her unconscious. He shoved Nicklai off her and into a puddle. Nicklai spat an ugly curse at him, but didn't retaliate.

Nicklai righted himself and hauled the woman's limp form over a shoulder. He shoved her into the car's back seat before settling into the driver's side.

Dove took measured steps, pausing only to roll his head back and gaze upward, his expression impossible to read. His eyes nearly glowed as they searched the sky.

He cleared his throat, blinked, and straightened his tie. He stooped to get into the car. "Let's go," he commanded. The door's closing slam sounded like a coffin's lid.

As Nicklai reversed, I ducked behind the roof's raised edge, arms wrapped around my middle. "What the hell was that?" Vennie asked, his voice quiet and tight.

"We were right," I managed, breathing deep to avoid being sick. "They're making Extrahumans."

I buried my face in my hands, the heat from my gloves a small comfort.

"Lions," I gasped, not comforted at all that I'd finally

found a solid clue in the mystery of Ian Dove. "He's a *monster*."

🔥🔥🔥

Vennie and I debated the merit of pursuing them, but the car had long gone by the time I regained composure, and we agreed it was a bad idea for me to investigate further alone.

On my video feed, Vennie checked his watch. "I'm pushing the timeline of a believable bathroom break. Are you okay to get home?"

"No sweat." It was early enough. I could stay out, stop some crimes, help some Crownies. But I was badly shaken and craved the comfort of a pile of blankets and a romantic comedy to make me forget what I'd seen for a little while. "Thanks for checking in. See you later."

Vennie signed off with a salute. I took deep gulps of Crown's night air, attempting to soothe my unsettled shivering.

What did Dove do to that woman?

Bane and I had to find out, and stop it.

I raced toward home, jumping between buildings and admiring Crown City all lit up, seeking comfort from the familiar skyline. As I passed one of the livelier nightlife areas, I slowed. Taking a detour, I stopped on top of a movie theater situated across from one of the most popular college bars and scanned the writhing crowd for a head of brown curls and a megawatt smile.

I leaned against the giant, neon-lit "M" that topped the sign reading "Movies" and rested my head against the warm metal. Max Keep practically radiated light as he wove through the dancing and drinking crowd of costumed guests leaking onto the patio—weather be damned—offering smiles and charming comments. He wore suspenders and a goofy red hat, a plush dalmatian safety pinned on his shoulder.

He'd invited me to this party, but I'd ignored the text,

something I was making a habit lately. I knew if I'd said yes, he and I would end up pressed close together along the bar, making jokes and sharing whiskey.

With a groan, I peeled my eyes from him. Sometimes Max felt like home, and other times, a cold, impenetrable castle where I'd never be comfortable. The more time we spent together, the more good memories we made, the more I realized we'd never work for long as anything but friends.

My ribcage squeezed painfully. Despite our shared interests, Max and I each loathed half of the other, and I was the only one who knew. Max hated Silhouette and the Shadow. He helped his father, Mayor Keep, with a city-wide project bent on taking us down. He loved working on armor designs for the Gold Guard, and I loved being Silhouette. Whenever we got close to uncovering whether or not we loved each other, we ended up taking our clothes off instead.

I blew out a shaky breath. One of these days, I'd have to end it.

That didn't mean I couldn't spend a few minutes watching him dance and appreciating how he hadn't worn a shirt beneath his firefighter suspenders.

Gentle beeping in my earpiece interrupted the plan.

The alarm signaled someone logging into our comms channel from our basement headquarters we called the Den.

My uncle Bane's face burst onto my screens, his blue-gray eyes that were twin to mine wide with concern, his usually disheveled brown hair smashed under a red beret.

"Silhouette!" he burst out. "What happened? Why are you out?"

"I'm okay." I stalked to the other end of the roof, which faced a near-empty parking lot. "Our cameras caught Dove out, and since it's been so long since we've caught a glimpse of him, I decided to check it out."

Bane nodded as he listened, and with each bob of his

head, a whooshing sound came across the line. I studied him closer, noting thin, jagged plastic ringing his T-shirt's collar.

"Wait—" I demanded. "What are you dressed as? Step back from the camera so I can see."

Bane did as I asked, spinning and striking a pose, his face expectant. He wore a clear trash bag stuffed with small, colorful balloons over his top half. On the bottom, he wore silver shorts and sneakers. "You can't tell?"

"Are you . . . a cupcake? A ball pit? Gay space ice cream?"

Bane deflated and dropped his arms, popping some of the balloons. "I'm a gumball machine." He pulled the costume away from where it clung to his shirt. "Dancing got a little staticky."

I snorted. "Very clever. What was your date dressed as?"

"He went as—never mind. Tell me about Dove. Did you learn anything?"

My mood dropped, and I filled him in. "They're kidnapping people to make them Extrahuman, Uncle Bane. Taking them right off the streets. What if this woman wasn't the first? How many came before her?"

Bane got close to the camera again, his expression resolute. "Don't worry, Mel. We'll stop them. Soon."

FOUR MONTHS LATER

CHAPTER
TWO

Sometimes I'd forget I have superhuman strength and nearly bite off one of my own fingers.

My Leo Optics tablet—no longer the family company's newest model, but still my favorite because it was a gift from Bane—sat before me on the desk in my grandfather's old office, plugged into my laptop and neatly displaying my cache of problems in glorious high definition. I'd recently replaced the standard cat eye logo wallpaper. Now it was a digital collage featuring a photo of me with my new family at a Crown City Mallards game, and another of my mom from before she died.

Her loss was a more subtle ache now—a permanent part of me, like a well-exercised muscle in my chest. It was sadness coated in a gentle buffer of gratitude for the time and memories I had with her.

I unclenched my teeth from my thumbnail and tucked that hand into the sleeve of my sweater. With the other, I clicked through the internet tabs I sometimes minimized but never completely closed.

The first was an older article from the *Crown City Chronicle* regarding the sudden disappearance of Eleni Brooks. No one had seen her since her last fitness class on Halloween, and the trail had long since gone cold.

After that night, Bane, Chezza, Vennie, and I dove into finding her. We spent weeks of long nights scouring the city in a grid pattern, searching for buildings Kavoh could be using as a base. We carefully reviewed every missing persons case reported to the local police, searching for hints of other abductions that may have been performed by Kavoh's people.

I ground my teeth. Eleni's broken screams and begging played in a quiet, constant loop at the back of my head.

I'd been there and done nothing.

Not one whisper of her in all our months of searching. We'd caught glimpses of Dove, Nicklai, and Cellina, Nicklai's partner in for-hire crime, but every time Bane and I got close to where we'd spotted them, they disappeared. They were like a swarm of warped, vicious fireflies infesting the city, never illuminated long enough to hint where they kept Eleni and any other captives.

The next tab featured a headline from around the same time stating that Dr. Kavoh was taking an extended research trip to South America. From what we could tell, she truly was away from the city, doing lions knew what.

Which left Dove in charge.

My fingers tapped a frustrated rhythm along the desk as I frowned at the final tab, the beat growing more frenzied the longer I stared into its subject's piercing gaze.

When we discovered Kavoh's return to Crown City, Bane had asked me to keep tabs on Dove and leave tracking Kavoh to him. I was happy to take on Kavoh's mysterious, dark-haired second-in-command, especially since he appeared in public at least marginally more than she did. Ever since Halloween, my responsibility had turned into an obsession. I wasn't proud of how many times I'd entered his name in my browser's search bar.

Dove wasn't from Crown City and hardly had an internet

presence beyond news items featuring his research. A prolific scholar, apparently, he'd graduated from medical school in his early twenties before being recruited by Kavoh for her "plant genetics" projects.

His mother had died when he was sixteen, his father a few years after. I snuffed the twinge of sympathy that bloomed within me whenever those facts reappeared in my research.

I flipped from webpage to webpage, issue to issue, until my head throbbed.

"Grandpa," I called softly.

Sydney Leo's AI apparition appeared on the near-invisible Hologlass screen in the corner of the room. My family's patriarch and the reason for our Extrahuman abilities had died before I could meet him, but maintained a legacy through the slightly eerie digital persona he left behind.

"Melbourne! There's my favorite relative. What do we know?" He always appeared in the same expensive-looking suit and red pocket square, his cornsilk hair that matched mine neatly combed back from his gently lined face.

I groaned, lolling my head against the back of my chair. "Nothing new."

My grandfather's image frowned. "Come on, now. You're one of the most powerful beings on the planet! Surely, you'll find them soon."

"The ability to bench press a rhino isn't helping me find people who don't want to be found." I nearly started biting my nails again, but caught myself and sandwiched both hands beneath my thighs. "Have there been any more reports of Extrahuman-ish behavior in the news we might have missed?"

Sydney's image froze, indicating his program was running a search. I was thorough, but he could carefully review every piece of media circulating the city in an instant.

All four of us that lived in the Leo House were devoted to stopping Kavoh. While the others used their precious few free hours to sleep or date or see friends, I holed up here, trying to utilize Sydney's resources to find a single additional lead or clue. I was the only one who could, since only I knew about Sydney, and I had no intention of sharing the knowledge.

"It doesn't appear so. One resident claimed on their blog to have spotted a werewolf by the lakeshore." Sydney chuckled. "Seems unlikely. And, *ah*. The mayor's office released a statement this morning that they will be investing further in the Gold Guard program."

"They can't be serious," I whined. "Only so many citizens can believe all the property damage the Guard is causing is mine and Shadow's fault."

Sydney frowned apologetically. "Such is the nature of politicking—"

"Mel!" Chezza's voice carried up the stairwells. She raised her voice just loud enough for my enhanced hearing to register.

Ever cautious, at least in digital ghost form, Sydney winked at me and shut himself off, fading to invisibility in the corner.

"More and more like your uncle every day. You're going to be late!" Chezza continued.

I released a stream of curses that ended in a vehemently hissed, "lions," as I scrambled to my room for my backpack and a coat. In a whirlwind, I dashed down the stairs, hopping awkwardly as I tied my shoes.

"Thank you, thank you, thank you, Chezza!"

Her head appeared around the kitchen corner, one unimpressed eyebrow raised. "Do you need a ride?" She and Vennie shared the same light brown skin and dark, almond shaped eyes, though Chezza was tall and sinewy to Vennie's stocky, compact muscle.

I shook my head as I stopped at the bottom step to give my sneaker the attention it needed. "I've got it. Can I pick you something up from Hardwired on my way back? A croissant, a coffee? You saved me—I didn't realize what time it was."

Chezza gave a dramatic sigh and flipped her long black hair, showing the dyed layer underneath the color of overripe cherries. "I guess I could accept that bribe. I'll take one of each, if you insist."

"I do," I crowed, and I bolted out the front door.

My backpack bounced, textbooks knocking my spine as I picked up speed. Though I wore a coat on top of a full unit of Tempatches, hidden adhesive units set to heat my body under everyday clothes, the air's chill gave me shivers. I frowned at the snow as I zipped past, assuring the fat flakes melted as they touched the ground, leaving puddles between fallen leaves.

"This better not stick," I grumbled, leaping over the tall border wall around the Leo property.

Delicious heat, my oldest friend, flooded my limbs as I pumped my arms, washing away my frustration. Twigs snapped beneath my rushing feet, and I batted snowflakes from my face as I hurtled through them. After quick glances in either direction, I dove across the blessedly empty streets and slowed.

After a pause to smooth my hair and make sure I hadn't worn a hole in my jeans during my mad sprint across town, I hitched my backpack higher on my shoulders, took a breath, and crossed onto Camden College's campus.

I mounted the steps of the closest building and careened into a lecture hall, shoving the door wide. Most of the class was engrossed with their phones, not noticing my near-tardiness.

Max glowed at the front of the room, his light-brown skin flawless, his pristine face unreadable.

I didn't drop his mahogany stare as I breezed to the front of the classroom, feigning nonchalance. Professor Gray-Phoenix, looked up from his notebook, eyes flicking to the clock. I'd made it with a minute to spare.

"Good morning," I said stiffly.

"I could have given you a ride," Max said between gritted teeth. "I'm amazed Bane didn't drop you off even later."

I bit my tongue. "Technically, I'm on time."

Max's lips drowned into a glower. "Cutting it a little close for comfort when this presentation affects both our grades."

I forced a steadying breath, reigning in my temper. I hadn't accepted a ride to campus from Max since I'd ended our romance a few months prior. It had been a tense and painful time since, and our breakup didn't excuse us from being presentation partners in the class we shared.

Still friends.

The words echoed in my head as I riffled through my backpack. I couldn't remember who had suggested it, between the two of us.

"Aren't you hot?" Max asked, eyeing my thick sweater and jacket I made no move to take off, even though heat cranked throughout the lecture hall.

"Yes," I said absently, scanning our presentation notes.

Max was overdressed, per usual. A crimson sweater with brass tips on the collar underneath, not a single wave of hair out of place. Meanwhile, mine misbehaved, with strands tangling across my face.

"You look nice today," I threw out. A peace offering to soothe his ego before we dove into this presentation.

His gaze washed over me, too close to how it used to when we spent time alone together. "I always look nice," he countered.

I snorted and offered him our index cards. "Are you ready for this?"

He waved them off. "Of course."

I think we did well, but I was too distracted, my muscles pulled taut, by Max's proximity and the glaring headline I spotted at the corner of a desk halfway through our presentation. When we finished and received an approving nod from the professor, I darted for the paper as my classmates shuffled off to lunch.

ANOTHER "MUTANT" SIGHTING REPORTED IN BLIGHTMOORE

I scanned the article. A ride-share driver claimed he saw a hulking figure at least ten feet tall prowling the streets, an unconscious person being dragged by one of its clawed hands. Was this the same beast my grandpa had found mention of? Was this what Kavoh's team had made of Eleni Brooks?

But where in Blightmoore? I ripped the paper open to search the next page, hungry to see if this instance's location overlapped with any of the other "mutant" sightings, which had been spread widely across Crown City, but the reporter hadn't named any cross streets or landmarks.

I sensed Max fiddling with his watch next to me. The fluorescent lights glinted along Crown's skyline etched into its massive gold face. Max ducked his head close to mine, reading over my shoulder.

"Terrific," he huffed. "Another aberration stalking the streets. Silhouette and the Shadow certainly aren't trying very hard to get rid of any freaks that remind them of themselves, are they?"

I turned to stare him full in the face, despair twisting my insides. When Max got rolling on one of his anti-Shadow-and-Silhouette rants, which was often, I could never find words to react that didn't bare my loyalties. Max was my closest friend. If anyone could surmise my secret identity, it was him, and I had enough catastrophes on my plate at the moment.

His sculpted brows smoothed, and the disdain melted off his face. The contrast of his easy smile and the curve of his cheeks against the commanding adult formality with which he carried himself . . . Max Keep was the handsomest juxtaposition, with one smooth side and another like a serrated blade that twisted in my heart every time I saw him.

"Want to hang out tonight?" His finger caught a ribbon of my hair that clung to my neck. His hand floating a breath from my skin, he settled it neatly into place behind my shoulder. "We could watch a movie. My dad just got some new screeners in the mail."

The offer was tempting. Partially because I missed Max as a friend, partially because I missed him as more. But he hated a part of me he didn't know existed, a part I could never tell him about. He'd only gotten deeper into the Gold Guard project. He consulted for the small army, determined to end Bane and me by any means necessary.

Not to mention every reference to Max's father was like ice water over the embers of affection I harbored for Max. Even though he was a pain in Silhouette's side, Mayor Keep thankfully left my public persona alone. Ever since I'd made it clear I knew he was behind my abduction the prior summer, he steered clear of Bane and me. We were happy to keep that tactic mutual.

I shook myself and offered an apologetic smile. "I can't. I have plans with my uncle."

Max's pout belonged in a glossy magazine. My heart throbbed as his hand dropped away.

He kneaded his forehead, seeming torn. "Alright then. Have a nice spring break."

"Maybe another night, though," I offered quickly.

Bad idea, BAD IDEA, my instincts shrieked, but some part of Max had a stranglehold on me—the part that couldn't forget that amidst our ill-fitting romance, he was still the best friend I'd ever had. "I'll text you . . . And you're right. I could use a more reliable mode of transportation. Want to start bringing me to campus after break?"

He brightened a little and shot me in the face with a grin. "Of course I do. Tell Bane I say hello."

CHAPTER
THREE

"Wʜᴀᴛ?!"

Bane's shout sounded over the clamor of shattering glass. A storm of bullets pierced the windows of the truck he crouched behind. He grasped it under the fender. Squatting with a groan, he lifted it a foot off its driver's side wheels.

I sprinted from my hiding spot behind a light pole's thick concrete base to help. The night air was crisp, fogging out from beneath my mask and hood.

"It's Silhouette and the Shadow," one of the men grunted to his cronies. Diamond watches and lengths of gold chain dripped from their pockets. Slightly fearful sneers curled out from beneath the ski masks they wore.

"Max says hi," I repeated, crouching near Bane.

Together, we heaved the truck into the air and toward the trio of sours—our term for bad guys—whose jewel heist we'd interrupted. They scattered as the truck flipped through the air and landed in the middle of the street.

"How are things with him?" Bane asked. Though the tight-fitting helmet he wore as Shadow concealed his identity, I could hear him easily through the vents hidden in the front.

I huffed noncommittally and pointed down a side street.

The patter of fleeing footsteps echoed from it. Bane didn't push against my silence, leaving me to think as we pursued them. The avenue was lined with boutiques full of luxuries. The fairy lights carefully strung from the small trees out front of each rebounded off Bane's helmet and set the emblems on our chests glowing. Bane's was an angular blue shard, like a frozen version of my fierce flame emblem.

We rounded the corner, and instead of fleeing backs, we were met with the trio, regrouped. There was the snick and flash of a lighter in their midst.

"Get down," I commanded, shoving Bane behind me as one of the men launched his weapon into the air.

A Molotov cocktail. Of course they had vodka in their pockets. Following it with my eye, I caught it easily in one hand and crushed the bottle in my grip. With a flare and loud crack, it exploded, sending delicious flames licking up the side of my suit. The heat kissed my face, nuzzling me like a contented cat.

"Care to try something else?" I asked, my modified voice coming out deep and foreboding thanks to the brilliant technology in my mask.

Brushing stray ash from his shoulders, Bane clapped me on the shoulder as the sours stared, stunned with disbelief. "You want the two on the left? I'll take the one on the right."

Bane would want to handle the sour that had a gun drawn, even if the man was struggling to load the pistol with shaky hands. He liked to keep me away from firearms as much as possible, but in the vigilante line of work, it was pointless. Still, I let him have it.

I gave a sharp nod, and we shot off like cannonballs. I didn't need to watch him as I tackled my own targets, barreling one into the other. We rolled across the ground in a flurry of flailing limbs—mostly mine—as I aimed to knock them both senseless as quickly as possible.

Though I could hear the scuffles of Bane's own battle, his voice sounded steadily in my ear through our comms system.

"It's not too late to book a spring break trip, Toasty. Why don't we get out of Crown, go somewhere fun?"

Maybe he had noticed how much time I spent in front of the computer, looking for Eleni Brooks.

"Eh." My dark hood flared around my face as I shook my head.

One of the men managed to roll on top of me, scrabbling for purchase against the hard matte finish of my suit. I withdrew my legs and kicked him into a lamp post. I stood and found my second prey attempting to crawl away through a puddle.

As I stalked him, I continued to Bane. "I'd rather be here. I have schoolwork to keep up on." *And research to do on Kavoh and Dove*, though I didn't voice the latter point out loud.

Calmly, I walked up to my sour and pressed a boot between his shoulder blades, rendering him immobile as I searched his shoulders and waistband for a holster. I found nothing but a lighter. This one was the cocktail maker.

I tilted my head as I bent to retrieve the stolen jewelry from his pockets. "You idiots planned to rob a high-end jewelry store with one gun and a lighter?"

"Your distraction is running late," he spat against the gravel.

A storm of unease roiled through my gut. "Shadow, something's up."

Bane looked up from his spot straddling his sour's chest, the man's pistol pulverized between his hands. "What do you think—"

The space between us exploded in a cacophony of neon light. I rolled, attempting to use my body to shield the sour from flying chunks of asphalt.

"Gold Guard's here," Bane stammered. He'd made it away on the other side of the explosion, safe.

Rolling upright, my world continued to spin. I scrambled for the sour's neck, detecting a pulse.

A dark menace in his Shadow suit, Bane burst through the drifting smoke and helped me upright. "Time to go!"

As I got my feet beneath me and ran at his side, Bane shouted into the comms. "Beacon, Braveheart, where the hell are you?"

There was muffled cursing, then Vennie's flat voice came across the line. "Sorry, sorry, sorry. We're here."

"I never thought I'd say this." Chezza's smooth voice came next. "But you two know what you're doing. You had it handled, so we were playing QuickCart 7."

Another projectile blew past us, careening into a park bench and bursting into shards of light, sending warped metal flying.

"The sours called the Gold Guard to keep us busy, and somehow, they have laser rocket launchers now?" Bane said.

"I see that," Vennie said evenly, his fervor only belied by the sound of rapid keyboard clicking. "There's a parking garage for rental cars two streets over. Might be your best bet."

Bane led the way, Vennie no doubt having pushed the location to a map projected inside his helmet.

"Is anyone hurt?" Chezza demanded.

"Just our pride," I hissed, weaving through the street's deepest shadows. "Muting my mask," I added, hitting a switch on the side that made the bottom half expand to cover my mouth. This way, I could speak with the team on our channel without the Gold Guard hearing anything. A whir over the line told me Bane was locking down the vents on his helmet, too.

We sprinted into the depths of the darkened parking garage and split ways. Bane darted toward the back of the garage, while I slid into the shadows between the small fleet of minivans lined up near its entrance.

Bane's voice crackled in my ear while we settled into the silence. "You don't want a break from all this? To spend a couple days just chilling on a beach?"

Even hiding here, listening for the sound of our armored pursuers, my muscles were loose and a contented smile curled my mouth. This was my favorite time. Even with the danger, nights out with Bane as Shadow and Silhouette were my deepest peace.

"What would you do in the smothering sunshine of a beach?" I demanded. "Be miserable the whole time?"

"Of course not. I'd live in the pool with a margarita. Make use of the floppy hat you got me for the holidays."

I snorted. "Really, Shadow, I'm fine."

The sounds of slow, heavy footsteps encased in metal halted his next argument.

Our current strategy with the Gold Guard was twofold. First, we prioritized eliminating threats to Crown City innocents as quickly as possible, because the minute the mayor's people realized Silhouette and Shadow were out, they'd send the Guard to hunt us down. When that didn't work, which was often, we led them to unpopulated areas full of property belonging to Crown's biggest corporations. If anyone could influence Mayor Keep, it was the other business bosses in town—we hoped.

From my hiding spot, I watched the foreboding figures of two Gold Guards march into the garage. They were covered in bulky black armor with gold detailing, and a stylized gold crown that Max had drawn was painted on their helmets, glaring over their tactical goggles.

The Guard's weapon of choice was a sort of laser projectile we didn't fully understand beyond that they could be used to kill us. We hoped the hubbub created over any damage they did to corporate property was enough to make them take shots very carefully, which meant less risk for us.

After conferring with sharp hand signals, the Guards split

up. One walked past my hiding spot, while the second crept deeper into the garage, toward Bane.

"On three?" Bane asked.

"Bet I can take mine down faster than you."

"Watch and learn, impudent spawn." Bane growled. By his voice, I could tell he was bracing himself to sprint head on toward his target.

Chezza groaned. "I've told you a hundred times, that nickname doesn't make any sense."

"Silence, spurned lover!"

Chezza grumbled in our ears. "Please. I dumped you."

I laughed as Bane charged. I opted for the quieter route, easing up on the unsuspecting Guard.

I grabbed her from behind, but she twisted out of my grip and bashed me in the face with the butt of her rifle, knocking me airborne. With a grunt, I rolled to regain my footing and dashed back, not giving her time to get the weapon between us.

I had to focus furiously for a minute. This woman was well trained like the rest of the Guard, but fast enough to give me a tougher fight than her bulkier counterparts. We traded swift blows, and when I finally sensed her strength failing, I sent her gun flying with a well-aimed kick.

Bane's own fight migrated near us, and I watched out of the corner of my eye. It was exhilarating to see him at work. He ducked a ferocious punch and shifted his weight against the Guard's middle to hurl him over his shoulder.

I got my Guard in a headlock and snaked my hand beneath her combat helmet until my gloved fingers felt the bare skin of her neck, then released one of two taser blasts my suit held for emergencies. She crumpled, hitting the ground a split second before Bane's Guard did.

Bane withdrew the bottom half of his visor to reveal a wild, brilliant grin.

"I guess you win . . . " he started, slightly breathless.

His Guard twisted on the ground, showing dexterity I couldn't imagine possible in a man of his stature. He flung a hand out to grab Bane's ankle and pulled.

With a yelp, Bane went down.

Shock trapped me. Froze me to the concrete floor, my mouth open in despair, arms limp at my sides as I watched the horror unfold.

The Guard's other hand fisted around the material at the nape of Bane's neck and dragged him along the pavement. They rolled over the ground, Bane struggling to avoid getting trapped beneath the much larger man.

The Guard got his arms beneath him before my uncle could. Bane struggled to get up, the wind knocked out of him. I started into a sprint. The Guard leapt to his feet. He surveyed my uncle on the ground, then me, a snarl contorting his face.

"Shadow!" The cry echoed from my mask.

Bane made it unsteadily to his hands and knees. The Guard took two heavy steps toward him. Bane rolled onto his backside and scrambled backward, his gloves and boots scraping in desperate hisses along the ground.

I wasn't fast enough. I was still ten yards away when the Guard made his choice. He turned a sinister stare on Bane and took a final step closer, then lifted one foot high and brought it down.

Even without my heat-enhanced hearing, I'm sure I would have heard the crack echo through the entire garage. Bane and I roared in unison, both of us howling in pain. I nearly saw red as I ripped across the remaining distance between us.

"You couldn't evade us forever," the Guard said, looking satisfied as he glanced up from Bane's contorted shin.

His expression morphed as he beheld how quickly I barreled his way.

I savored his terror as I leapt over Bane's prone form. I couldn't decipher whatever Chezza and Vennie shouted through my earpiece, only Bane's pained groans and the ghost of the sick snap of bone. My bloodlust narrowed to a fine point as I launched my fist into the Guard's chest. He crashed into the cement wall, cracks haloing around his body. His armor sported a small, fist-sized divot in the middle of his chest.

I spun and dashed to where Bane curled on the ground.

"Damn, Silhouette, you might've shattered his sternum," Chezza breathed.

"I don't care," I hissed, crouching near Bane's head. I pressed the button to withdraw his mask.

Underneath, his face was coated in a sheen of sweat, his eyes pinched in pain and teeth clamped tight.

"Something's broken," he grunted.

I moved toward his shin, my shaking hands hovering over the broken shape of his leg as I realized I couldn't do anything to help.

"Are you bleeding, Shadow?" Chezza asked, all focus.

Numbly, I heard Bane reply that he didn't think so. I spiraled down into the thought of how useless I was in this moment. I hadn't been able to prevent catastrophe.

"Don't walk on it. I'm coming to get you. Silhouette, get somewhere safe." Chezza's voice was clear and commanding.

I tried to focus my breathing and keep an eye around us, making sure no one else showed up.

Barely holding in sobs, I dragged Bane across the ground and into a musty stairwell at the back of the garage. "Braveheart, can you put out a fake report that Silhouette and the Shadow were seen heading away from here? In case more Guards come looking for their friends."

"On it," Vennie said, voice tight with concentration. "Silhouette. . . Did you kill that guy?"

"Kill what guy?" Bane's question was a stunted moan.

"No, at least, I don't think so. That's not what I—"

"She nearly impaled him on her own arm!" Vennie said.

"She did this flying leap thing. Oh, man, you gotta see it on the mask's cam footage."

"Unhelpful," I growled.

"It's highly unlikely," Chezza reprimanded, the sound of an engine revving through her side of the comms channel. "Now you know for next time to not lose your cool when Shadow gets an ouchie. Can you keep from getting discovered for ten minutes?"

"Yeah," I said weakly, glancing down at Bane again. He wore a contorted mask of pain, not a trace of his usual aloofness anywhere.

"You okay?" he managed.

I nodded, sure I couldn't speak without bursting into tears, which would have Bane focusing on me rather than his own distress.

"Good. That's good." He allowed a low moan to escape past his teeth, and the minutes seemed to stretch forever while we waited for Chezza to show up.

Huddling in the stairwell with just the drip of a leaky pipe to accompany my racing thoughts and Bane's hisses of pain, I knew for sure a spring break trip was the wrong choice. I needed to be here to deal with these threats to my family, and deal with them now.

CHAPTER
FOUR

Back at the Den, I sulked the entire time Chezza took care of Bane. She shot me angry looks in between moments of assessing his injury.

"I can't focus with you prowling," she finally snapped. She scrubbed a hand across her sweaty forehead and addressed the room in general. "This is beyond my abilities. We need Korey."

Bane had mentioned his personal doctor before, one who was in on the secret of our Extrahuman abilities, but I'd never met him.

While Vennie made the call, I pulled Chezza aside.

"Sorry, Chez," I said. "I'm freaked out."

Chezza pursed her lips. "I get it. You haven't seen him hurt like this before. He'll be fine. We've gotten through worse, and will again, I'm sure. You can make it up to me by taking notes on all Korey says about Bane's recovery. I need to get to bed. I can't make mistakes at work tomorrow."

"Absolutely. I'll write everything down."

She offered me a tired but optimistic smile and backed up the stairs with a wave. Vennie stayed quiet at his station before the LUMA, massaging a spot above his prosthetic as he worked through convoluted code crawling across the massive floor-to-ceiling screen. Bane was quiet on the exam table, his discomfort eased by some painkiller Chezza gave him, his blinks slow as he stared at the rough stone walls. I touched his shoulder.

"How are you feeling?"

He made a valiant effort to smile, though it was strained. "I have a sneaking suspicion at least one of the bones in my shin is in more pieces than it should be."

"I—" I started, but a ding echoed through the Den.

"Doc's here," Vennie muttered, buzzing a sleek sports car through the front gate.

"Don't ask him any personal questions," Bane said, shifting upright. "It's part of our deal."

I fidgeted beside the exam table as the garage elevator lurched into motion. How often did Korey have to make house calls to the Leo residence?

An alarmingly attractive man with gray-streaked brown hair strode into the den in faded jeans and a sweatshirt, looking entirely bored.

"What act of superior stupidity did you complete this time?"

Bane's face was apologetic as Korey strode over. "I pissed off someone twice my size."

Korey glared down from his own considerable height as he sifted through the large pack he'd brought. "Wouldn't be the first time."

"Or the twentieth," Bane said, gesturing to his leg, bared beneath the obscenely short shorts Bane preferred, especially in chilly weather. I still wore my Silhouette suit, too anxious to change and too attached to the steadiness its heat provided me.

Korey went silent as he performed his examination, leaving me to stand awkwardly.

"Are you grievously injured as well?" he asked as he worked.

I jolted and stammered. "Ah, no. I'm fine."

"Only a matter of time," he said, hands steady and eyes glued to his patient.

Bane frowned. "Back off, Korey. She's smarter than me."

"Now *that* I do believe." Korey eyed where I paced back and forth. "This is going to take a while."

Recognizing the dismissal, I headed to our cubbies and methodologically removed my suit, sanitized the inside, and hung it neatly. With a remorseful glance over my shoulder at Bane's twisted face, I hurried to my room to shower and change as well, hoping the more I moved, the less I'd freak out.

After what felt like hours, I receded to the Den, where Korey was lecturing Bane, who looked significantly less in pain than when I'd left them.

Korey waved me over to listen as he finished with his instructions. "With how fast you tend to heal, I say you need to be in a boot, off of it entirely for at least three days. Five would be better. Have Chezza send me scans, please, and we can discuss."

I nodded dutifully as Bane scowled.

"Completely off your leg, Bane. I mean it," he repeated. "Or you might make it significantly worse. You could be out of commission for months." He closed his bag with a snap and stalked back to the elevator. "Think of all the muggings that could be pulled off with the Shadow gone for that long."

Bane waved him off. "I'll behave."

"And I'll become a world-renowned opera singer," Korey snorted as the elevator closed behind him.

I cleared my throat as Bane frowned and prodded the stiff boot wrapping his leg from just below the knee. "Is he always so . . . abrasive?"

Color washed across Bane's cheeks. "We have a history."

"Lions, have you slept with everyone who could be our ally?"

"Just him," Bane said, sheepish. "And Chezza. And Roger."

"Don't forget that fling you had with the pop star lady," Vennie added without looking away from the LUMA.

Bane's eyes went glassy, "Oh, she was incredible, wasn't she?"

"And then like half of Clare's assistants—" Vennie continued.

"Moving on," I muttered, gesturing at Bane's leg. "That's it? No Shadow stuff for a week?"

Bane swung his legs gingerly over the side of the table. "Guess so."

I snagged the crutches we kept on hand and helped Bane to the chair lift at the base of the stairs, staying two steps behind him as he rode it up. My hand hovered protectively behind him as he got his bearings and hobbled through the kitchen to the foyer.

"Tonight was tough, huh?" Bane asked, leaning heavily against the wall of the hallway leading to his rooms.

"I should have stopped the Guard before he got to you," I said quietly.

"Hey," he started, drawing my eyes from the floor to his. "Occupational hazard. I'm okay."

I didn't trust myself not to cry, so I clamped my lips together.

Bane's face fell. "But . . . Mel. Were you trying to kill him? The Guard who hurt me?"

I shuddered and wrapped my arms around my middle. "Of course not. I just saw red after what he did to you. I couldn't think. So, I just. . . hit him with all I had."

Bane pulled me in for a hug, but I didn't miss the concerned downward tilt of his mouth.

"Just be careful—more mindful—next time."

I nodded; my eyes unfocused at the darkened rest of the house over his shoulder.

"Have you ever killed someone?" I asked quietly. My stomach felt rotted. I never wanted to lose control like that again.

"Not directly, and never on purpose," Bane admitted. "Though there have been casualties as a result of some things I've done, and some I'm sure I don't know about. We have to commit to avoiding it at all costs, and try to make it count when we do. Honor them, take care of their families, do more good than they did harm in their lifetime."

I clasped my hands together, my gaze catching on the bulky brace around his leg. I winced.

"I know that face," he said. "I've seen it on myself too many times. Don't blame yourself for this."

My stare bored into the carpet. Bane whistled quietly, drawing my eyes up.

"Mel. Toasty. Seriously, my injury is not your fault. Preventing it was not your job. Stop ripping into yourself. I mean it. Promise me."

"I promise," I muttered.

He flashed me that goofy uneven smile of his, and I didn't fight mirroring it. "Good. This is one of those rare times I'm right. Don't waste your energy tormenting yourself. You'll need it because I'm a nightmare when I'm injured. I'll want a five-course breakfast tomorrow." He stretched, nearly dropping his crutches. He deftly caught them and lifted one to poke me in the leg. "Now get some sleep. I'm serious. You're in for a full day of couch and snack duty with me."

"As long as I get to pick the movies."

"Obviously."

"Good night, Uncle Bane." I watched to make sure he made it to his room without injuring himself further—he only caught a crutch on the carpet and nearly fell once—then trudged up the stairs. Blame crashed over me like an icy wave the minute I closed my bedroom door. I didn't sleep. Images of the Gold Guard stomping on Bane's leg battered me all night long.

🔥🔥🔥

"YOU LOOK—OH, WHAT'S THE EXPRESSION? 'RODE HARD AND put away wet.'" Gem had a wicked gleam in her wide hazel eyes.

I glared, and she sipped innocently at her latte.

"What happened?" she asked in a gentler tone.

I deflated into my chair, hands braced around my own steaming coffee cup. "Rough night at the side hustle. I'll explain fully the next time you come over."

Gem blinked knowingly. After I made the choice to reveal my secret identity when we were abducted together, Gem became a part-time fifth member of our team. She helped strategize, bringing insight from her role in Crown City's journalism scene, and was the best at making us all laugh.

She offered me a piece of chocolate croissant. "Anything I can do in the meantime?"

I shoved aside the notes from one of my college courses, which for once I couldn't care less about, and grabbed the pastry gratefully. "Distract me."

"How did your presentation with Max go?" Gem asked, twining her long brown hair into an elaborate braid. "Do I even want to know?"

I scowled. "About as well as expected."

"Hard to be friends when he oozes sex appeal out of every pore, huh?" she said with a wince.

I dropped my head into my hands with a muffled groan. "I'm so angry at him. All the time. And we can't talk about it because I can't tell him my secrets, and there's still a part of me that's so attracted to him. Physically and emotionally."

"That part might just take time," Gem said sagely. "What

about seeing someone else? Are you going to ask Sophie on another date?"

Turns out the rainbow apple didn't fall too far from the bisexual tree, and I'd been exploring my own sexuality since breaking it off with Max.

I slumped further with a sigh, "I don't know . . . She's so nice and smart, but we don't have a lot in common, you know? She doesn't like watching movies very much, and did you know she's an avid skier? I can't work with that. It's not fair to her that I can't partake in her favorite hobby."

"Plus, you're intimidated. She's so hot."

"She's *so* hot!" I shrieked. "Lions, I'm glad it's spring break. Are you excited for your trip?"

Gem leaned back; her eyes focused on some far off beach. "Yes, Cancun . . . This time tomorrow, I'll be knee deep in tequila sunrises, flirting with bartenders left and right."

"How does Brynn feel about that?" I cast a smile in the direction of Gem's girlfriend and Hardwired's fastest barista.

"I didn't tell you? I convinced her to take the week off work. She's coming with." Gem's starlight grin nearly overtook her entire face.

"Good for you two," I said in earnest. "Enjoy the sunshine. I can't wait to hear all about it. Please get into some trouble."

Gem flicked her expertly manicured nails at me. The tips were painted fluorescent green, and they popped against Hardwired's orange walls. "You too." She leaned forward with a conspiratorial whisper. "Please try to do something other than fight crime this week."

I took a long sip of coffee rather than make my friend a promise I couldn't keep.

CHAPTER
FIVE

Besides thwarting crime lords' master plans, Bane and I were also excellent at making up terribly stupid games.

While I completed a set of training exercises and Vennie worked on one of his many freelance gigs, Bane sprawled across the Den's battered blue couch and played sudoku, tearing out each page and crumpling it into a ball when he finished a puzzle. Whether that meant he successfully completed them or not, we weren't sure.

By the time I finished, this devolved into Bane and I chucking the paper balls at various targets around the Den and made-up rules we argued over for impressive shots.

"Really, I'm fine," I insisted for what felt like the hundredth time. I sat on the hideous floral loveseat, while Bane stretched across the full length of his couch, his bad leg raised over the worn arm.

"Are you sure?" he mused. "There's gotta be a movie out you want to see. You can't be the only Camden student staying in town for the break. Maybe you could get a group together and go to the mall?"

I rolled my eyes. "No one goes to the mall anymore."

Bane clutched his heart, feigning distress. "Where do people meet their newest crushes?"

"Speaking of crushes . . ." I hedged. "How's your man?"

The maneuver to change topics succeeded, as Bane was immediately distracted. "He's not 'mine,' yet, exactly." His face screwed up as he attempted to describe their situation. "We're both extremely busy, so we're taking it slow."

"Have you seen him recently?"

"It's been a few weeks, but I'm not making plans until this"—he gestured at his leg—"is all healed. I'd rather not lie to him again, besides all the other lying I have to do."

"Shadow can't have a boyfriend?"

Bane sighed. "He can, but we need to be a lot further along before that. Bringing someone else into this is dangerous."

Before I could ask another question—I wanted more hints about who this mystery man might be—Bane turned the conversation back on me. "But I gotta tell you, Mel, it's nice to have an additional person to talk to. Even if it's only non-vigilante stuff. I don't care if you have a partner or anything, but it's us and Max and Gem. Who else do you go to? Who else do you talk to?"

A sudden and sharp trilling alarm from the LUMA saved me from having to formulate an answer. Or even consider the question. There'd be time for more friends, or more-than-friends, after we stopped Kavoh.

I dashed to Vennie's side, where he'd pulled up security footage he'd hacked into from a spot along the docks. The grainy video showed a woman in sweats with her hood up looking over her shoulder before rounding a corner. LUMA's software matched her features as belonging to Eleni Brooks.

"Suiting up," I called, already halfway across the Den. I whipped my suit pants out of the cubby and began changing.

"Coordinates sent to your mask," Vennie confirmed.

Bane wrung his hands. "I don't adore the idea of you heading out there by yourself."

I stuck my head around the cubby's side to gape as I zipped up my suit's jacket. "What do you mean? We haven't had a lead like this in months."

"I know. But we don't know what Kavoh has done to her. You could be facing down an Extrahuman on your own, or she might have backup around."

"I'll be careful," I promised. "This can be solely a recon mission. I won't engage her unless I have to."

Bane chewed the inside of his cheek for almost a full minute, then nodded.

I turned to the wall made of mirrors, fixed my mask to my face, and pressed the hidden buttons that sealed it tight to my skin. The tough black material covered my forehead, across my nose and cheekbones, and finished with wicked downward spikes on either side of my mouth.

Bane's worried face reflected in the mirror.

I sighed. "You'd rather me stay here when I could be out there, saving someone's life?"

He tugged his unruly hair. "If it's in your best interest? Absolutely. But it's not my choice to make. You know I don't tell you what to do. I'm being selfish. But don't forget I worked all day on a new cheesecake recipe. White chocolate pumpkin. It's in the fridge. Come back soon so we can try it and watch *Date Wars*."

Pulling my hood up, I veered back to the couch to ruffle his hair. "Save me a piece, Uncle Bane. I'll be back soon."

🔥🔥🔥

THE PUDDLES NEAR THE LAKESHORE WERE ESPECIALLY ICY AS the snow turned to light rain, the cold trying to combat the heat radiating through my boots. As if in protest, a wave of extra warmth flooded my feet.

"This intuitive temperature boost upgrade is incredible, Braveheart."

Vennie had earned the nickname after accidentally exploding cyan ink all over his face trying to set up a printer in the Den.

Pride swelled in Vennie's voice. "Thanks, I think you'll like the rear-facing camera, too."

"What, no cup holder?" Bane asked in my ear.

Chezza chuckled. She'd come down to watch my progress alongside Vennie and Bane.

I made a careful circle of the warehouse outside which we'd spied Eleni. The road and walkways were one giant puddle, so I had no luck finding her footprints. Not a sound existed beyond my quiet breaths and the lapping of the lake. "No sign yet. Did any other cameras around here catch a glimpse of her?"

I scanned my perimeter while Vennie searched, but it was hard to discern movement in the murky darkness through the soft curtain of icy rain.

"Hmm . . . no."

"Maybe she went inside?" I mused. "What does this warehouse store?"

Vennie pointed another camera away, so I could climb a dumpster and see if the small windows beneath the roof could be easily opened. I wedged my fingers beneath the edge and used just a touch of Extrahuman strength, but no simple locks popped. I stood on my tiptoes so I could peer through the window. Through the glass' grime, I spied a spacious storage facility, filled with neat rows of shelves holding boxes emblazoned with a variety of Crown City business logos.

"Temporary commercial storage, according to the website," Vennie said. "Kavoh could be storing anything in there under some fake company name."

I rubbed my chin, deciding my next best course of action.

The subtle whoosh of a well-oiled door had me immediately pressing my back against the building's steel wall, my heart racing. Eleni Brooks appeared, gaunt and exhausted-looking, her mouth drawn in misery. She tucked a small package into her pocket, while she checked left and right, but not above, where I was hidden.

"Holy shit," Bane whispered, slightly garbled. He must've already broken into the cheesecake.

Anticipation had me bouncing in my boots. I leapt down from the dumpster, landing silently on the wet pavement. This was it. I could rescue her . . . Or she could lead me to wherever Kavoh's true base was hidden.

How about both? I decided with a satisfied smirk.

"Careful . . ." Bane warned, nearly reading my mind.

I hummed affirmation and followed her. I crept a few yards behind, sticking to the street's deepest shadows.

Glass crunched beneath my boot. A stray broken bottle whose glass was indiscernible from the glinting puddle next to it. I froze, blood roaring in my ears.

Eleni kept walking, too focused to notice my misstep.

I loosed a breath. She hadn't heard me.

But something else did.

A small, scrappy dog that looked like it lived in a sewer popped out from behind a legion of trash cans, black eyes intent on me. He growled a quiet warning.

The hairs at the back of my neck lifted. My head swam. Fucking dogs. My worst nightmare. This one was small, but he looked tough enough to take on a whole pack of dogs twice his size.

I squeezed my eyes shut. The last thing I saw was Eleni's receding back nearing the next intersection. My teeth ground together. *Please go away. Please go away. Please go away.*

Cracking one eye open, I took a small, cautious step past the dog's trash can castle.

He voiced a single, earsplitting bark.

Eleni spun toward me, eyes wide. I flinched and held back a whimper, sprinting past the dog and directly toward her.

Bolstered by fear, I was able to catch up and grab her arm.

With an indignant huff, she ripped out of my grip far more easily than should have been possible.

"Extrahuman," I gasped.

Eleni utilized my shock and sprinted away.

"Wait," I called. "I can help you!"

She hung a sharp left and disappeared into a maze of shipping containers stacked high in every direction.

"Silhouette," Bane cautioned, "she might have backup."

"I'll be careful," I insisted, and dove into the labyrinth.

I crept through the containers, ears perked for any hint at which direction she'd gone. I was moments from giving up when I heard the subtle ring of an outbound call echoing out of a cell phone's speaker, just audible to my Extrahuman senses.

I followed the sound down a narrow gap between containers to where Eleni hunched over, one hand braced on her knee, the other holding a phone.

"I'm being followed," she gasped. ". . . by Silhouette."

A faint, hollow voice responded over the line. "Prioritize."

I slid around the corner.

She spun on me, and I cursed myself for forgetting her abilities could potentially include enhanced senses, too.

Eleni hesitated. I held up my hands and began to speak, but she was on me before the words left my mouth. Her punches were Extrahuman fast, requiring all my focus to dodge. I didn't notice when she shifted her weight, and I was stunned when she kicked me viciously in the side.

I slammed against a shipping crate, air grunting from my chest.

Eleni eyed me warily, her chin quivering, and took off again.

One hand to my aching ribs, I took off after her, the wet

night air whipping by. My pulse pounded at being so close to finally getting some answers, at potentially helping Eleni go home, if she would just listen to me.

It seemed her concern for subtlety had expired, as I easily followed the sound of her wet, rapid footsteps deeper into the freight yard.

After a few turns, I spotted her stock-still before a tall fence topped with barbed wire, a single, spotty streetlamp casting her shadow over the wet ground. We'd reached the boundary of the complex. It was a graveyard of rusty construction equipment that leaked a wide, ugly oily stain. The rain fell harder, drops running down my mask and onto my chin, my emblem.

Eleni was out of options unless she wanted to duck back into the maze and try to evade me all night. Fine by me. I'd been an Extrahuman longer. I had the endurance for that kind of standoff.

I approached her. "Hey—"

She spun, eyes wide as the moon above, and with a voice like bubblegum, addressed me. "You shouldn't have come."

Alarm bells pealed through my head, my feet backing up before I could instruct them to.

"I'm bailing," I declared.

"I would, too," Bane said. "What kind of creepy premonition-ass shit was that?"

I stepped carefully, maneuvering my back toward the nearest shipping container, so I could assess the best route for racing the hell out of this place. I sought the sound of strange breaths or shifting footsteps beneath the pelting rain.

Eleni remained motionless.

The shadows within the aisles on either side of her shifted.

Cellina stepped out of one, Nicklai the other.

My heart stammered at the sight of them—Nicklai's shallow sneer and Cellina's contented cat grin. They didn't know who Silhouette truly was or that we'd met before, but in the moment, it made no difference. Ice gripped my spine in a vice, and I was back in that grimy warehouse, scared and hamstrung by my own panic.

"What the—" Chezza started in my ear. Her final curse was cut off by the hitch in my breath as Cellina prowled forward.

Nicklai shoved past her at the last instant, barreling straight toward me. I ducked and his massive fist connected with the steel behind my head. He howled as I whirled away, right into Eleni's arms. She wrapped them tight over my torso, binding my arms, and lifted me into the air. I gasped as she squeezed the air from my lungs, strong as a python.

Vennie and Bane were frantic in my ears, but I couldn't decipher their words over the rushing howl of my own panic.

With a roar, I twisted, kicking and tearing my arms wide to no avail. Scrabbling for purchase on her skin, I released one of my suit's taser blasts. She hissed but hardly budged, so I launched the second, and finally, she dropped me. I rolled away, trying to create space between us, so I could launch some attacks of my own.

"You got this, Silhouette." Bane's voice was terse.

I straightened, shifting my feet and centering my gravity.

Nicklai and Eleni closed in slowly. Cellina, looking bored, trailed behind them, twirling her long blonde braid around one finger.

In the corner of my eye, I made out the nearest aisle. If I could just get there, I could outrun them, especially with Eleni looking worse for wear after dealing with my tasers. I stepped toward them, like I was planning to engage, while also side-stepping a margin, bringing me closer to my escape route.

Nicklai dodged forward, faking me out before dancing back, driving me closer to the aisle. *Perfect.*

Almost there . . .

A soft but urgent pinging sounded in my ear. A light blinked to life in the corner of the screen on my forearm. I squinted at it. The screen showed only slowly shifting blackness, an odd arrangement of dark shapes I couldn't make sense of.

"What is—"

"New feature. Rear-view camera," Vennie hissed, as the shifting darkness leapt for me.

I ducked too slow. Long arms like steel rebar wrapped around me.

Frantic, I shot my elbow back, and rough breath huffed around my hood, but the grip didn't lessen. I writhed, shifting in the tight grip as the sleeve slid past my vision. A large, pale hand clamped around my forearm. I cried as my shoulder wrenched, and my attacker twisted my arm behind me. I thrashed like a creature caught in a net, desperate and uncoordinated. The toes of my boots desperately scraped the slick pavement. My captor lifted me. My kicks backward did nothing. With my free hand, I battered the arm squeezing my chest, eliciting a curse from a voice that sounded stereotypically male.

My feet met the ground again, and the arm shifted from my waist to band across my throat. My wrenched arm was freed but ached furiously, nearly useless. More frightening than the pressure against my windpipe was the slim, silvery pistol my assailant brandished before me.

He pressed the muzzle to the inside of my forearm and pulled the trigger.

Pain shocked through my arm as something sharp burst from the gun, like a wide needle, shredding through my suit and arm. An icy prick was followed by the gross sensation of liquid being shoved into my body. I gagged at the autonomous force of it. Then I saw it, the glowing liquid from Halloween, draining into my arm.

My captor flung me away and I rolled, disoriented across the dirty ground.

"What the hell was that?" Bane demanded.

"Syringe, I think," I choked out.

Chezza spoke, deathly quiet, "Oh, no. What do you feel?"

I groaned. My blood buzzed through my veins too fast, my heart racing to match. The world spun in a disorienting blur, keeping me from finding my feet.

"Maximum heat. NOW," Bane said.

"She's basically there," Vennie argued, but he complied.

A hint more fire raced through my suit, but it hardly made a difference when I was too freaked out to move. A sick sensation dribbled up my throat, and my arms shook. Wispy shadows curled around the edge of my vision.

"Something's wrong," I rasped.

The dim light from the moon and lone streetlight dissapeared.

Or rather, my vision did. It flickered to pitch black and back to the dim night. "I can't see," I whispered.

"Get out of there now," Bane hissed.

As my vision flickered and I struggled to get my arms beneath me, my attacker moved out of the shadows. I knew who approached me. My stomach was a panicked riot. I couldn't breathe.

Dove was even taller than I'd built him in my mind. He moved with slow confidence, his dress shoes scuffed. Black hair curled around his ears, the nape of his neck.

But his face was worst of all. It emerged from the shadows like a knife, his cheekbones gaunt, a sharp, thin nose holding up glasses. He could have been handsome, were his expression not entirely detached, uncaring, near-dead. Except for those fractured eyes. Blue like lightning's core.

My vision flicked in and out again, fragmenting his leer like flashes in a storm. He stopped and tilted his head, the movement so calculating it sent goosebumps across my body like a growing tide.

A click of boot heels echoed off to my left, along with a voice that frequently narrated my nightmares.

"What a prize," Cellina crooned.

"She's weak for at least fifteen minutes, yeah? Is she seeing things yet, Doc?" Nicklai's voice curdled my blood and had it racing to hide behind my spine.

I realized the wild, broken keening in my ear was Bane.

Dove tore his electric stare from my face to eye his watch. "Any moment now. But yes, I think she's weak."

I hissed, pushing myself onto my knees. I had to get upright. Had to make a plan.

Nicklai snorted. "How about you make sure?"

Dove stepped toward me. His legs were long, but whatever he injected me with screwed with my depth perception. It was like he took ages to reach me, and I was paralyzed and damned to wait and watch. My strength felt far away, somewhere underground.

In my mind's eye, the logical outcomes spread before me. They flickered out, one by one in quick succession until a single path remained.

I was beaten.

That left only the opportunity to set myself up as best I could for whatever terrible thing was about to happen.

"Braveheart," I said, forcing my voice even and sure.

Bane, to his credit, stopped shouting for a minute.

"Yeah," came Vennie's even response. Military drilled calm.

"Lock down the mask. Closed circuit on whatever power's in it. Can you do that?"

Half a second of dead air. Another step brought Dove closer.

"Yes." A flurry of clattering keystrokes. "I'm not sure how much your remaining battery will translate to, timewise."

"I'll figure it out."

The only way to remove my mask was by pressing the correct hidden buttons in unison, and I'd be damned before I shared their location. This would be my identity's only chance at staying hidden in the short term.

Bane realized my plan and started railing again.

"ABSOLUTELY NOT! You have to get out of there! *Fight!*"

I brought a fist down on my suit's screen, smashing it beyond recognition and ripping it from my sleeve.

"Genius," Chezza murmured.

"Stop it right now!" Bane demanded.

Vennie paused; he'd listen to Bane if it came down to it.

"Beacon, please. Hold him back," I whispered.

Chezza knew. She knew what I had to do. What we all would do in my situation—protect our family.

I reached between my shoulder blades. Dove was so close I saw the sweat beaded on his furrowed brow.

"Remember to breathe," Chezza said. "You have to hang on as long as possible."

"Don't do this to me . . . *Mel!*"

Bane's pleading cut out as I tore out the brick that provided power to my suit and smashed it on the pavement. I brought my fist down over and over to assure it was decimated into tiny, irreparable pieces. Whatever happened, I had to make sure Kavoh's people couldn't trace anything back to my family.

The last thing I heard was Vennie cursing, and the sound of furniture breaking.

Then their voices disappeared, and I was alone.

CHAPTER
SIX

Heat ebbed from my suit, drifting away like a life raft in a disgruntled sea. It left me numb. I made myself as small as possible as Dove took his final steps toward me and crouched.

Utilizing the strength I had left, I hauled back with all my might and punched him in the face.

He grunted and gripped my shoulders, shaking off my blow to haul me upright.

Without power, the electromagnetic weights holding my hood up failed, and it fell away from my face. Dove's eyes widened at the sight of my mask, his incredulous face the last thing I saw before my vision went dark for good.

Shadows swam before my eyes, undulating violently. I jerked back, let out a whimper, and thrashed in Dove's grip.

"Shouldn't she be out by now?" Nicklai grumbled.

Dove replied quietly, his voice close. "She's incredibly resilient to high levels of trauma and psychological distress." He almost sounded impressed.

The shadows formed themselves into the dripping jaws of a pack of rabid dogs that lunged for me. I screamed.

"Dove, put her under." Cellina's voice rang through the shadows, riling them. "We're going to draw attention."

I was shifted, and another needle jabbed me, this time at my neck. The shadows slowed and drooped, woozy. I slumped, and the doctor fumbled to get me to the ground without smacking my head.

"Why bother," I demanded weakly.

Whatever he injected me with didn't knock me entirely unconscious, but I faked it, going limp against the ground. Strong arms scooted beneath me, lifting me gingerly. Whatever sedative they used kept the damn shadows at bay, so I kept my eyes closed and listened as I was set in the backseat of a car. Someone slid in after me, my head pressing against their knee.

Nicklai mused from one of the front seats. "You're losing your edge, Dove. That took longer for your bugs than it should have."

"I think we should leave her," Dove said nearby. He was the one seated next to me.

"What, are you scared?" Nicklai scoffed. "She's half your size."

"Did you see how quickly she moved before the bacteria? Crossing her is a death wish," Dove said blandly. "And the Shadow may retaliate."

"That's why we sent you in first," Nicklai crooned. "Plus, that freak couldn't find us if he wanted to."

"Enough, or you can be the next test subject. I'm sure the boss wouldn't mind." Dove's voice had frozen to a violent promise.

No response came.

"Did you have any trouble securing the other one?" Dove asked.

Nicklai snorted. "She was happy enough to be tranquilized again. She's in the trunk."

My stomach lurched. Eleni was still with us, coerced to go along with the schemes of Kavoh's team.

"Maybe you should swap places," Dove said drily.

"*She* will want to see Silhouette when she gets back in the country," Cellina cut in as the car smoothed into motion. My spine iced further. Kavoh.

"We don't mention this to her yet," Dove said. "You know she doesn't like to be disturbed."

My breath hitched at Kavoh's mention, and I twitched. My vision returned for just a moment.

Long enough to catch Dove glancing down at me with an unflinching cold stare. He frowned, and warm fingertips pressed against my neck—the very right spot—and rendered me unconscious.

🔥🔥🔥

I AWOKE STIFF AND FREEZING, COLD FROM A TILE FLOOR leaking into my back.

My eyes snapped open to dim fluorescent light, yellowed walls, and a bruised ceiling with a bulbous black security camera settled in its center.

I shoved upright. The movement was slow and painful, the cold having sapped the strength from my limbs. Without warmth for however long it had been, I'd gone from a powerful Extrahuman to weaker than a newborn kitten.

I was on the floor of a small, square room. A metal cot and sad-looking mattress lined one wall. A matching low table sat before it.

My hood was a crumpled mess behind my head. I reached behind it to the jagged remains of my power brick, then felt my mask to ensure it was still tight and immoveable against my face. It radiated a faint hum; there was still some power there. I hoped Vennie was able to discern something from it, like my location or at least that I was alive.

The mask distorting my features and my wits were the only things protecting me until I figured out an escape, or Bane launched a rescue mission. I didn't like the odds of the latter timeline; though he healed fast, he still relied heavily on his crutches.

My vision snagged on my arm. My suit's material had been ravaged and torn back, and a thick plastic band fastened around my wrist inches below where Dove had injected me. Someone had carefully cleaned and wrapped a bandage over that wound.

I twisted my wrist tentatively, and my stomach roiled at the feeling—there were prongs on the inside of the band, slivered directly into me. Blue light glowed softly from the band's center, innocuous. I ran a finger experimentally along the material, shuddering as the prongs moved beneath my skin.

"I recommend being careful when touching that."

I froze at the strained voice emanating through a tinny speaker hidden somewhere in the ceiling. *Dove.*

I gulped, itching to fire a barb back, but I barely had my bearings.

"There's some privacy through the doorway to the bathroom," he continued. "And a shower if you want it. Discard your suit. There are other clothes in there for you. Take any longer than sixty seconds, and I'll be forced to activate the wristband."

"What does it do?" The faint glow stared at me like a wicked eye.

"You remember," he said simply.

The creeping, stalking, attacking pack of shadows. My racing heart rate. Disappearing vision.

I glared directly at the camera. I was in no shape to retaliate yet, so I needed to play along. Gather information. Make a plan.

Take a shower.

If the bracelet could activate whatever Dove had injected me with, these people could incapacitate me easily. Stiffly, I stood, my head one solid ache. With no windows in the room, it was impossible to tell what time it was or how long I'd been out.

I limped through the open doorway to find a cramped shower stall and a metal toilet stuffed in the tiny space. I cranked the knob and shucked my suit, moving slowly. I'd forgotten how heavy it was without my enhanced strength. I stepped into the shower in my sports bra and compression shorts. No way was I getting naked anywhere near these people.

The water was freezing. Foolish of me to assume these creeps would support their captives with the luxury of a hot shower. There'd be no warm water to help me.

With a muffled curse, I bore the brunt of the chill water to swirl some in my mouth and make a quick turn to rinse off the stale sweat. I leapt back out, scrabbling for the threadbare towel on the floor as my head spun. I dried hastily, fruitlessly willing heat into my extremities, and donned the clothes in a pile on the floor.

They were a pair of stone-gray scrubs, sterile and powdery against my skin. I shivered as I drew them on, the water leaking from my hair and underclothes into the fabric.

"Fifteen seconds," Dove's voice rang from the ceiling.

I flipped off the lens and hobbled to the cot, hauling my suit with me. A single sheet covered the mattress, and I pulled it around my shoulders, swallowing back my fear every few seconds.

I tried to inhale deeply, to build any semblance of heat in my core to stave off the wooziness lurking at the corners of my consciousness. It had been so long since I'd fainted from the cold. I couldn't let it happen here.

A heavy lock whined open. I barely subdued my jump of surprise.

Dove entered the room in the same ill-fitting suit he'd captured me in.

My scalp prickled at the sight of him up close.

His crow black hair was tousled, a few strands falling over his glasses. I stared at his towering form. He didn't look much older than me, though the shadows beneath his eyes suggested he was as familiar with trauma as I was.

"Hello, monster," I spat.

Dove hesitated; his large hands spasmed around the notebook and nylon bag he carried.

After a moment of stillness, his head cocked sharply to the side. "You're quite the terror yourself. Not everyone in Crown City has nice things to say about you, you know."

I snorted, hiding that he'd struck a nerve. "Keep telling yourself that." I waved my arm around in false bravado, brandishing the glowing bracelet. "Is it torture time again already?"

He sat at the edge of the low table before my cot, the only other furnishing in the room. "I need to assess your injuries."

My brows tried to meet beneath my mask. "You inflicted most of them. You're not familiar?"

His face was impassive as he unzipped his bag, withdrawing tools. None of which were sharp, unfortunately. Smart man. I watched every movement, assessing.

He lifted the end of a stethoscope. I stiffened.

Dove sighed. "You'll be doing yourself a favor if you let me work peacefully."

I eyed the slim remote peeking out of his breast pocket. "Or you'll activate whatever the hell was in that orange goo?"

A terse nod. I scowled, but I held still as he pressed the cold metal beneath my collarbone.

After a few beats, he frowned. "Try to breathe normally."

"I've just been abducted."

Dove's eyes flicked to mine. "Fair."

He sat back and made a note in his book, then withdrew a bottle from the bag and spilled sharp smelling liquid onto a cloth. He offered it and pointed. I swiped it from him and dabbed the slice beneath my jaw he indicated, glaring daggers the entire time.

"How's the mobility in your shoulder?" he asked, handing over a bandage for my jaw.

I rotated it with a wince. His eyes tracked the movement, the rest of him still.

With deep satisfaction, I noticed the glorious black eye developing across one bladelike cheekbone.

"How's your face?" I crooned.

That riled him a fraction, finally. Though his face remained stoic, I didn't miss the faint tinge of red rise to meld with his bruises.

He clicked his tongue. "What's your name?"

I clamped my mouth shut.

Seconds passed. It seemed we were in a staring contest.

"Are you serious?" I asked, exasperated.

He blinked and shook his head, his left hand sweeping in beautiful script across the page. "Fine. It doesn't matter. How old are you?"

"Twenty-five," I lied easily. "Got any whiskey for me?"

He continued writing. "If only. Height . . ." He eyed me, his gaze flicking from my head to my bare toes. "Miniscule."

I scowled, eyeing his long legs. "Compared to you, maybe. Genetic anomalies, both of us."

His hand faltered, dragging a splash of ink across the page.

He cleared his throat. "How does the suit work?" he asked without looking up.

I glanced at the remote in his pocket. "You're going to torture me when I don't tell you."

He swallowed. "I prefer not to. Does the lining stimulate your muscles in some way? Like an electric current or something similar?"

It was tough to keep the shock from my face, but I

managed. These idiots didn't think I had superhuman abilities, just a really fancy suit. Finally, something in my favor.

I sat back with a shrug, using the second it bought me to think up a lie. "I guess so. I don't know how it works exactly. I wanted to be super strong. I did some searching. I put in an order to a lady in Vancouver. You can find anything on the internet."

He sighed doubtfully but scribbled the city's name anyway, then pulled the suit from my hands, eyeing the material. Without the brick to power it, he wouldn't find much but empty veins.

It pained me to part with it, but it wouldn't do me any good in its state anyway.

"I'm playing so nice," I said blandly. "Can I get a blanket? It's freezing in here."

"No," he said, examining the suit, lifting and exploring it with gentle care.

"Why not?"

"You would try to strangle me with it."

"I would succeed at strangling you with it."

His mouth twitched. The rest of his face remained dead.

"I'm going to gather some data on how you experience the effects of the FR-10 bacteria."

I balked as he pulled tiny electric nodes from his bag. "This nightmare is caused by bacteria?"

"A bacteria-technology hybrid, yes," Dove explained, and held out the nodes. "One on the side of your neck, please, and the other on one of your temples."

Biting back indignation, I affixed them to my face and neck. Dove withdrew a small tablet with data already populating across the screen.

"What do you see when your vision goes out?"

I sneered as the sensors sent data to his tablet. If I could get my hands on it, maybe I could send a message . . .

Dove addressed me without looking up as he studied the

images. "It wouldn't do you any good. It's on a completely private network. Nothing in, nothing out."

He almost sounded sad.

I swallowed my dismay.

Rage built in my chest. Dove scrolled through a few charts, zooming to examine a graph more closely, making notes.

"I'll ask again. What do you see in the shadows the bacteria show you?"

My mouth remained a flat line. With a dismal sigh, Dove reached for the remote in his breast pocket. I braced myself. I could handle this.

Dove pressed a button, a deceptively simple prompt to cause me ultimate distress.

The prongs in my wrist vibrated. I glared at the bracelet, whose light had turned orange. After a moment, my vision shuttered, my heart rate ratcheted, and shadows roiled before me, forming into pointed snouts with jagged fangs.

I gritted my teeth as they dove, snapping just before my face then dissolving into mist, drifting back, and reforming. One clamped for the space where my arm would be, if I could see it. Pain rocked up my arm, like it had indeed wrapped its jaws around the muscle and bone.

"Dogs," I gasped.

The sensation faded abruptly, my vision coming back to Dove before me, remote in hand.

"Dogs," he repeated.

I nodded mutely, ashamed at how quickly I'd been bested by the terror bugs flooding my system.

"You're afraid of dogs?"

"Clearly," I said, hoarse, then tried to regain my composure as he delicately pulled the node from my temple.

He remained quiet and studious in packing up his supplies.

"What does the bracelet do?" I dared to ask, tugging off the node at my neck and tossing it into his lap.

A sigh through his nose. "When you're first injected with the bacteria, they're agitated, or 'active', as we say. They cause the reactions in your body, but calm down eventually. The bracelet's prongs reactivate the bacteria when necessary."

"'Necessary,' huh? Interesting spin you're putting on the situation." I gestured to my scrubs and the miserable room we sat in.

Just a flat look in response, his eyes went dead again as he repacked the bag.

"How about a movie or something?" I scoffed; my voice weaker than intended with his face so close to mine. "How do you kill time around here?"

Dove seemed to consider it, eyes flitting to the door. "I can get you something to read."

Ugh. Better than nothing.

My answering tone was smug. "You don't think I can hurt you with a book?"

He tilted his head to the side as he stood, but he said nothing.

I scrunched my nose. "Preferably something with a film adaptation."

He was silent for another moment, then—"I'll see what I can do." With that, he hauled my suit into his arms and left, leaving me on the icy cot.

A flash of movement through the closing door caught my eye. In the dim hallway, Cellina, stony-faced, dragged a limping Eleni Brooks past my room. Eleni glanced up. Her tired eyes caught mine. No emotion touched her face, and her shoulders drooped in the distinct posture of someone who'd given up their fight. She wore a wristband identical to mine.

As soon as the door closed, the room went dark, the only light left coming from my wristband, which shone blue again, and the blinking camera light letting me know I was constantly watched.

Brimming with dread, I curled on my side, uncaring if

sleep found me. Instead, I wrapped my arms around my middle, trying to generate heat. Instead of working as a bellows, my breaths barely beat back the panic lurking in every corner of my body. I tried to catalog what I knew, what I'd learned, the resources I had at my disposal, but my thoughts returned over and over again to the shadow wolves and pounding heart brought on by the bacteria slumbering inside me. The temptation to tear out the bracelet was nearly unbearable, as was the urge to cry.

Somehow, I managed to stifle both urges and sleep, just after I promised myself I'd make a plan tomorrow.

CHAPTER
SEVEN

THE HARSH LIGHTS CLICKED ON WITHOUT WARNING SOME hours later, yanking me from fitful sleep. It was nearly a relief. Whenever I closed my eyes, the bacteria's aftershocks caused echoes of the attacking shadow hounds to flicker behind my eyelids.

I blinked at the ceiling, trying to orient myself. The cell was so cold my teeth clacked. The faint heat from my mask kept my head clear, but didn't extend its helpfulness below my neck. Eventually, I sat up and scowled at the wall, tugging numb fingers through my snarled hair.

Dove entered my cell, looking like someone had squeezed a lemon in his eyes. He balanced small cups and a lumpy parcel in one hand, his clipboard and medical bag under the other arm.

"Good morning, monster," I purred.

"Terror," he said weakly.

I drew my knees under my chin and mustered false cheer. "You look like shit."

My barb solicited no reaction beyond a bland blink. "You're telling me you look rested and at ease under that thing?"

I fingered the side of my mask. "Must be hard to sleep after a long day of torturing captives, huh?"

He ignored me, and I ignored it. "What's my schedule for the day? Light torture, lab tests . . . Please tell me I'll be done in time for afternoon water aerobics."

Hopefully, they'd take me out of this cell, so I could find some source of heat and a potential exit.

Dove set a small paper cup of water on the floor by my feet and tossed a wax-wrapped sandwich on the bed, then leaned against the wall, sipping from his own cup as I took unceremonious gulps of water.

He checked his clipboard. "You're not scheduled to leave this room today, if that's what you're asking. No chance to search for an escape route."

I rolled my eyes and studied the questionable sandwich. Suggesting: *Please. You know I'll find a way out.*

An awkward pause yawned between us.

"Your shoulder looks better," he said finally, gesturing toward my arm from his spot on the wall. "Swelling's gone down."

Even sitting down, the difference in our heights was laughable, but he still leaned down a little to hear me when I opened my mouth.

"You don't actually think of yourself as a doctor, do you?" I sneered. "I worked with a doctor recently. He helped people. Healed them. That's not what you do."

His mouth tightened, but he otherwise ignored my comment and ambled to sit on the edge of the table with a sigh, as if folding his long legs was an effort.

"I need to take your vitals," he said in that hollow voice as he withdrew a blood pressure cuff from his bag.

I considered fighting him, but thought better of it and ruefully extended my arm. Dove went to work silently, his eyes unwavering from his task behind his glasses. His midnight hair curled around his ears, mixing with the steam wafting from the cup at his side. Black coffee.

Finally, something hot! My thoughts raced. If I could talk Dove into bringing me a cup the next time he had his . . . It wasn't much—nowhere near a complete plan, but it was a first step.

"How did you end up here?" I ventured as he affixed the cuff around my arm, careful to keep his fingertips from my skin.

"A series of incredibly prestigious academic accomplishments and once-in-a-lifetime opportunities," he said flatly.

I squinted. "And how did someone like you get a name as angelic as Dove?"

"My guess is it's the universe's idea of a terrific practical joke."

He placed his fingers gently on my wrist, and I shivered. His eyes flicked to mine, and I played up the shaking. Maybe he would find me a blanket, or at least a shirt with long sleeves.

My mind wandered as he worked. My family was surely mounting a plan to get me back, but had they even discovered my location yet? Could I afford to wait for them? Drove dropped his hand from my wrist to jot down numbers.

"What's the plan?" I asked suddenly.

Dove froze in his writing.

"What are you going to do with me?"

He frowned. Set down his pen. Glanced upward, before finally speaking. "There's no plan yet."

"Right, because you didn't plan to abduct me. I was a lucky catch." I fiddled with the band on my wrist, the twisting of the rods beneath my skin a tether to reality.

Dove snapped a hand out to cover mine. His palm was warm. We both froze.

"Seriously, don't," he said quietly, and he dropped my hand like it was on fire.

"Why?"

He ran a hand through his hair with a sigh. "If you disturb or attempt to remove that without the correct key, a failsafe code activates the bacteria extremely and . . . indefinitely."

I gulped.

"Yeah." He tugged at his collar.

"Why do you do this?" I ventured.

Dove studied his clipboard. "Every other captive here committed a violent crime against an innocent."

I pursed my lips. *Even Eleni Brooks?*

"Every one," he repeated.

Until me. And even then, a vigilante's reputation was hardly sterling, regardless of good intentions.

"So, we deserve this?" I prompted.

His face remained blank. It was deeply unsettling how quickly Dove could scrub his features of emotion.

My fists clenched. "This place has to be on record somewhere. Taxes, fire codes. What does the city think your operation is?"

His focus didn't leave the clipboard. My attempts to rattle him were failing miserably. "A volunteer testing facility developing new treatments for manic depressives and the like using brain stimulation techniques."

I paused. "You're not worried about sharing that kind of information with me?"

Finally, he looked up, and the despair in his voice curdled my blood. "No one makes it out."

I wanted so desperately to hit him. But I was weak from the cold, and even if I wasn't, I didn't want to give away that my strength inherently came from me, not my suit. He took a sip from his coffee, the movement highlighting his too-wide sleeves. Could I trick him into bringing me hot coffee, hot enough to boost my strength, then knock him out and steal his clothes for some warmth? Bust out of here, and grab Eleni on the way. Depending on how many other sours were in the building . . .

I thought back to how he'd bested me in the alley. His wiry frame had to be packed with muscle. With the bacteria on his side, I wasn't sure if I could take him without getting the remote away from him first.

"Of all the people working here, you're the only crony brave enough to deal with me?" I cracked my knuckles, aiming to keep up the facade of being unconcerned.

"The others have their own responsibilities. You're lucky you're stuck with me and not them. Especially Nicklai."

I scoffed. "What part of this situation seems lucky to you?"

He winced. "You know the scars on his face. Did you spot the others? On his lip, his neck, under his ear? They're all over his body. They're all self-inflicted."

I blanched.

Dove continued with a grave nod. "He wants to know what will hurt his victims most, so he learned firsthand."

I had to keep talking or I'd have a panic attack.

"And what do you want?" I asked. What was his role in all of this?

He stared at the wall, like he longed for a window to look beyond. He set his face in iron and signed his paperwork with a flourish. "I want to be finished with this as quickly as possible. I don't get paid overtime."

I stewed in the silence. I didn't want him to leave yet. I needed more information.

"Why are all of your suits slightly too big?" I asked, hoping to cut him down and find a weakness.

"They all fit when I started working here."

"When was that?"

"Five years ago."

He looked uncomfortable. He fished around in his bag before withdrawing something and holding it out to me. A small, battered paperback. The cover was missing, the spine creased with deep wrinkles.

I grimaced. "I meant something published *recently*—never mind. Thanks." I eyed the book in my hands. The small act of kindness from Dove needed to be my leverage.

"Do you ever let people go for good behavior?" I managed. "I'm not a criminal."

He gritted his teeth. "I would recommend you keep being compliant. It can at least . . . buy you some time." He stood abruptly, heading to the door and pulling it open.

"When it all comes down to it, does how I behave matter?" I asked.

His fist clenched around the doorframe.

The answer was so quiet I could barely hear it.

"No."

"So that's it, then?" I demanded. "My life ends here?"

Dramatic, yes, but I needed to break him.

Those electric eyes flashed to hold mine. "No one gets out. I'm sorry."

He was halfway out the door when the words escaped me, unprompted. "I'm not scared."

Dove didn't turn to face me. The back of his neck tensed, shoulders scrunching together high above his back.

"Not yet."

He pulled the door closed behind him with a soft snap. He'd left his coffee behind, but by now it was cold.

🔥🔥🔥

Minutes or hours later—I'd long lost the ability to care or try to keep track of time—I stared, unseeing, at the tenth page of the book Dove had given me. The story didn't stick in my mind. Instead, that mental space was occupied by mine and Dove's last conversation, which I reviewed in a torturous loop.

I swore silently, allowing myself the dangerous thought that perhaps my situation was significantly more perilous than I'd allowed myself to believe. As if in confirmation, the subtle thrum of heat within my mask fizzled as its power reserve ran out.

Quickly losing a fight with devastating panic, I resumed detangling my hair in an attempt to maintain the last bit of warmth in my fingertips. The room was so cold. My 'plan,' if you could even call it that, was laughable. My toes were like ice, even beneath the harsh bedsheet. Chills racked my spine, and a woozy headache leered at the front of my head, threatening to pull me under. I couldn't faint here. I couldn't afford Kavoh's team any further advantage over me, or a hint at what I really was.

I drew low, quiet breaths, begging my body to stay calm.

When that technique failed, I paced, taking careful steps back and forth across the tiny space.

"Can I at least have some fucking socks?" I growled at the ceiling. "I'm freezing."

No answer came, so I crossed my arms and continued to shuffle around the room. The movement did little for the dying core of warmth in my center.

My back faced the door when it creaked. I spun to find Dove halfway in the room, his face a mirror of my own surprise. He lobbed something in my direction. My reflexes slow, it took both arms swung wide to barely catch the small ball. I stared down. Cradled against my chest was a thick pair of knit socks.

I frowned. "Are these yours?"

Dove stutter-stepped, still half outside of the room, like he was delivering contraband. He opened his mouth, but the buzz of a phone rang out before he could answer.

He withdrew the device from his pocket, and his face paled as he checked the screen. He sidled out and shut the door. I crept to it, hopping to tug on the socks as I did. With the subtle build of heat from walking and the addition of socks, I could just make out the conversation happening beyond my door's tiny window.

"Hello," Dove said evenly, belying none of his physically apparent unease. He rubbed a hand over the back of his hair, mussing the ends. The dark waves were bordering on shaggy.

I pressed my ear against the seam where the door met its frame, straining to hear the response.

"Hello, Doctor. How are our patients doing today?"

My stomach plummeted. The faint preening voice was unmistakably Kavoh.

"No changes since last week." Dove kept his tone casual. "Resident E has been compliant, though less energetic with Resident R no longer with us." He turned, catching sight of me through the window. His brows lowered, but otherwise, he ignored me.

"Hmm," Kavoh mused. "That's to be expected, I suppose. Moving R to Thorn Unit was necessary, though they have their hands full enough with a new subject. Tell E her good behavior will correlate to the quality of her scaled friend's care. He'll be mostly in confinement while they work on their new addition, but she doesn't need to know that." Kavoh's silence stretched for long enough I wondered if she'd hung up, but Dove waited. Eventually, her cheery voice cut in again. "What about Resident I?"

Dove closed his eyes. "No problems."

"Prepared for the next excursion?"

His throat bobbed once. Twice. "Of course."

"Excellent. This is why you're always employee of the month. I should have a plaque made." Kavoh sounded as satisfied as a wealthy retiree sipping Malbec on a private beach.

Dove gave a weak laugh.

"Anything else to report since we last spoke?"

I drew back, hands planted on either side of the window,

staring in horror. If they hadn't spoken since last week, I was breaking news.

Dove's eyes found mine, then darted away.

"No."

A sniff from Kavoh. "I still expect updated reports. Keep making me proud."

Dove ended the call and walked quickly down the hall.

I slouched against the wall. Socks. Secrecy. Dove was my best chance to escape.

🔥🔥🔥

SOMEHOW, I MANAGED TO SLEEP AGAIN, BUT THE PEACE WAS short-lived.

The harsh downward shift of the door's handle was my only warning.

I scrambled upright, my hand finding the book abandoned in the sheets. I stood, brandishing it. My cell's door opened. Smoothing a bored stare over my worried eyes, I drolled, "Does this story ever pick up or—"

But it wasn't Dove who stood there. It was Nicklai, scarred face gleaming in the dim light.

"Hello, hero," he said, lips curling wickedly. "I was checking our files, and it seems Dove is running behind on your testing. I'm happy to catch you up." He clicked his tongue and tossed something up, then caught it. The remote to my wristband.

I dropped the book and spread my feet to a fighting stance. I couldn't take him. Not like this. But every fiber of my being demanded I face him on my feet.

"Don't touch me," I spat, raising my fists.

Nicklai laughed, a jagged, angry sound. "Don't have to. Not yet, at least." His finger hovered over the button that would activate the bacteria inside me and initiate my suffering. "Let's get you warmed up first."

My stomach roiled, a pit of writhing terror.

Nicklai took a step closer.

The strangest sensation rolled through the room. My reality shifted, blending my bland cell with shifting scenes of quiet city streets, then a dark forest flying by.

"What—" I was breathless, unable to form words. Nicklai remained frozen, poised on the edge of terrorizing me. The lights flickered, or was I blinking?

My legs ached. My chest burned in the way I liked.

I was standing, then suddenly sat again, somewhere else, Dove on his knees before me. Fear was written across his murky face.

Sensations whipped through my body in quick succession. Terror. Pain. Shock. Hope. Despair.

Orange lights and shadow wolves and very real smoke and deliciously hot fire.

Then I fell.

My world stopped shifting as the toe of my boot caught on a piece of uneven pavement. I recognized my tumble quickly enough to curl and catch the collision on my side, my suit taking the brunt of the impact.

My suit?

I groped at my chest. It exuded no heat and definitely didn't fit quite right, but the red flame emblem grinned up at me like a lost friend.

With a long groan, I pushed to my hands and knees and lifted my head.

A familiar wood gate stared back, the lion emblem in the middle imperious as always, as if wondering why I'd been out so late.

Home. *Home!*

I scrambled to my feet with a sob and ran to the gate, rocking it on its hinges. My shaking hands searched for the call button on the speaker box. I glanced over my shoulder, but the forest surrounding the Leo property was quiet, like all its creatures had just been disturbed.

Like I'd just run through it.

I found the button and pressed. There was the dull buzz of a comms line opening.

"Uncle Bane!" I shouted into the night.

"Mel?" His voice was there immediately, glorious and disbelieving.

A strangled noise caught in my heaving chest.

He started shouting. A dozen exclamations from him were quickly joined by Chezza and Vennie.

The questions started my head spinning. I couldn't keep up.

"I think I'm fine," I assured them, a haze enveloping my thoughts. Maybe relief was making me delirious. "You better have saved me a slice of cheesecake," I croaked, and I collapsed against the gate.

CHAPTER
EIGHT

When Chezza opened the gate, I toppled into her arms, coming to as she gently guided me to her car. I gripped the dash as she drove to the house, the Lion statue out front swimming in double across my vision. By the time she ushered me into the elevator, I was able to stand on my own and the walls had stopped spinning.

The doors opened, and Bane threw himself at me, nearly concussing Chezza with a crutch. I clutched Bane, wide eyes staring over his shoulder at Chezza and Vennie, too afraid they weren't real to close my eyes.

"Mel," Bane choked. He drew back, and his fingers pushed my hair from my face. They came away bloody. "How did you escape?"

I stiffened. "What do you mean?" A wave of frosty panic crested over my head like a tsunami. A strange blankness had taken up residence in my head. "You guys didn't bust me out?"

Bane frowned, waving a hand toward the LUMA. "We were getting close to having a plan!" Vennie gave a small shake of his head. The screen was covered in sketches and schematics and haphazard notes. One in Bane's handwriting simply read: *CANNON???*

Weird desperate gasps emerged from my throat, and I began shaking all over.

"You're okay now. Breathe," Chezza commanded, taking my elbow. She helped me onto her exam table as Bane followed on his crutches. "We'll figure this out. Let me start with a few questions. Can you tell me your name?"

"M-Melbourne Elizabeth Leo."

"Great, and can you tell me who runs Crown City?"

"Travis Keep," I said. "He's an asshole."

Chezza's nose crinkled. "Well, that's promising. Are you hurt? Beside your face?"

My face? I reached up and winced, feeling tender stickiness on my temples. I racked my brain. "I don't think so. I don't know."

Bane squinted from the folding chair he hauled over. "Were you followed?"

Chezza helped me remove my suit jacket, and relief melted her posture as no major injuries were evident.

"Followed . . ." I started. "From where? The facility?"

Bane asked his next question slower. "Where were they keeping you?"

"No movement in the house's immediate perimeter," Vennie called from his station. "I'll comb footage from throughout the city and see if we can get an idea of your route to us, Mel."

"Hold on." I held out a hand, halting Bane's questions and Chezza's ministrations. "Give me a minute."

I pressed my palms to my eyes, blocking out the light. My head pounded louder the harder I searched for answers. There was a void in my mind. A dense wall I clashed against but couldn't find a way past. How did I escape? Memories sifted through my fingers like water, a select few remaining clear.

Nicklai prowled toward me, his appraising gaze sliding down my body like sludge. This close, I could see some of the other scars Dove had mentioned at the edges of his dark clothes.

Dove. The doctor. We'd spoken at length. I remembered that.

My eyes caught where Chezza unwrapped a bandage from my wrist, revealing two nasty punctures along its underside. I knew those. They were from my bracelet, the one that activated the FR-10 bacteria.

This knowledge felt concrete, like I could count on it being real. It showed the line where my memories felt normal then disintegrated into nothing at all. With my free hand, I removed my mask, wincing as it nudged my scrapes. "How long have I been gone?"

Bane's face contorted. "Two and a half days."

"There's no way . . ." An edge of hysteria crept into my voice. My chest and shoulders rose and fell in quick jumps. I swallowed a few times before I could speak again. "Some of my memories are missing. The most recent ones, I think. It doesn't feel like I was there for long."

I searched Chezza's face for confirmation. "Amnesia is far outside my area of expertise." She looked over her shoulder at Vennie. "We can find out as much as we can, though."

Vennie was already furiously typing. Articles and videos began populating half the LUMA as he swiped the camera footage he was analyzing over to make room on the massive screen.

"I remember getting caught and smashing my suit's brick . . . I woke up in a cell. The doctor was there. The tall one . . . Dove." I glanced down at my wrist. "They're using some sort of mecha-bacteria to torture people."

Bane blanched, but caught himself before asking more questions. "Let's deal with one thing at a time, yeah?"

Vennie joined us, the comforting tap of his prosthetic

against the cement floor reminding me I was home. "There could be a few explanations for the memory loss. I think the two most likely for this case are severe trauma, or someone dosing you with a substance to make you forget. Chez, you're planning on a blood draw?"

She nodded. "That's the next logical step, since you don't appear to have other injuries. We can try to see if there's something there messing with your memories and learn more about this bacteria."

Vennie shifted his weight from his foot to his prosthetic and back. "It's that or you experienced trauma so intense your mind's repressing it."

The seat of Bane's chair whined in protest from where he gripped it, knuckles white.

The ghost of a memory swirled in my mind. Strong fingers on my wrist. Someone's collarbone in my line of sight. Bottomless fear and impenetrable darkness.

Bane's movement broke my reverie. He offered me a glass of water. "We'll figure out what happened. I promise."

I stared at the glass. It felt important.

Vennie handed me some Tempatches, then hauled my suit to his work station. "While Chezza does her thing, I want to see the damage you did to my baby."

I frowned, sipped the water, and passed it back, so I could smooth the Tempatches over my aching body and feel their welcome heat. I laid back, letting Chezza take my pulse and flash a pen light in my eyes. The actions stirred the murky memories in my head.

"I destroyed it to protect all of us," I said stubbornly.

"You did wonderfully," Bane confirmed, shooting a glare at Vennie. He tossed me a blanket, which I gratefully pulled over myself.

I wore the horrendous scrubs I remembered being given, but the gray shirt keeping me warm was unfamiliar.

"I'm safe." The end of my sentence sounded like a question.

Bane nodded, his voice hoarse. "Yeah."

My eyelids drooped. It felt like I could sleep for a week.

"This is going to take us a little while. The best thing you can do right now is rest," Chezza said, tucking the blanket around my legs.

After shooing Bane off to help Vennie, I ticked up the heat coming off the Tempatches all over my body, sighing with relief as they thrummed heat into my limbs. I forced myself to close my eyes and believe that when I woke, I'd still be safe at home with my family, and together we'd find answers to the emptiness in my head. Gradually, I fell into troubled sleep with the faint scent of mint and smoke swirling around my cheeks.

♦♦♦

I JOLTED UPRIGHT, BLINKING WILDLY AT THE PUNK LION MURAL adorning one of the Den's familiar walls. It seemed to laugh at my disorientation.

"*Shitting* lions." Chezza jumped from her spot on a stool next to me, where she'd been examining images on a tablet.

"How long?" I asked, pressing a hand to my racing heart.

Bane hadn't moved from his spot on my other side. He scrolled his phone and was halfway through a bag of gummy bears.

"Couple of hours. Your bloodwork's done."

"I looked at the blood under your nails too," Chezza added. "It looks like the wounds on your face are self-inflicted."

I examined my grimy hands. I was so relieved to be home I hadn't realized how desperately I wanted a shower. "Did my blood tell you anything?"

"The bacteria you mentioned," Chezza said, pointing to a

microscope's image depicted on her tablet. A clump of tiny round organisms with eerie spokes jabbing out of their membranes crowded the slide. "I've never seen anything like it."

Chezza's day job was as a lab tech at a hospital, and blood was her specialty.

"You're the smartest person I know, so that concerns me," I said.

"Even I learn new things sometimes," she teased.

"There's another substance causing an anomaly," Vennie piped in from his spot by the LUMA. "I'm pretty sure it's responsible for your missing memories. I bet you saw something Kavoh's people didn't want you to while you were planning your grand escape. Whatever the solution was, it's already being filtered out by your system. Can you remember anything more now that it's been a few hours?"

I squinted through the dull pain at the front of my brain. Trying to specifically sort through memories was a difficult task, like trying to gather murky pond water and searching the swirls of brown for a specific grain of sand. "Something about dogs," I muttered.

They all looked as lost as I was.

Vennie scooted over to join us. Bane rested his elbows on the side of my table.

Chezza zoomed in on the bacteria. "Mel, you mentioned this bacteria is malicious. When I messed with it, it was . . . easily excited, I guess is the best way to explain it."

"I remember that part," I rubbed my wrist absently. "It's in that orange fluid Dove injected me and Eleni Brooks with. They put a wristband on us that agitates them somehow."

I shuddered and urged myself to go on. "They make your whole body freak out. They cut out your vision and make your heart race . . . and mentally stimulate you. So, in the dark, you see things that frighten you."

No one spoke. Repulsion slithered among us like a heavy, noxious cloud.

"But why?" Bane asked.

I kneaded my forehead. "I'm not sure."

Vennie cleared his throat. "The second thing in your blood has to be a memory loss . . . potion, for lack of a better word, that caused you brief and recent memory loss. I say 'pretty sure' because there are memory altering solutions of that kind that exist, but the composition of what I found in your system doesn't match those. There are similarities, though, as if what you were given was homemade."

Vennie held out a hand. In it, there was a small vial filled with fluorescent blue liquid and a folded, smudged slip of paper. "I think," he said. "This is the cure for one of those problems."

I took the vial from him, cradled it in my lap, and unfolded the paper. It was the title page of a worn book, the one Dove had given me. Beneath the print, a few words were written in a slanting, elegant hand.

Antibiotics—side effect is immediate and severe nausea.

"It was in your suit's chest pocket," Bane said. "Any idea how you got it?"

I examined the sparkling liquid. "I don't know when, but Dove gave this to me, I'm sure of it."

Bane rested his head on one fist. "Kavoh's second-in-command? Like, you became allies or something?"

I worried my bottom lip with my teeth. "Maybe. He seemed torn up about having me there. He said they usually only abduct criminals, as if that makes it okay."

Brow furrowed, Vennie typed rapidly on his tablet. "Huh. Eleni Brooks did a stint in jail for assault a few years ago. Did we know that?"

"Can you find out what happened?"

Vennie clicked some more. "Huh. No. Unless it's buried. It

looks like when Sprinkles has pieces erased from one of his lackey's records."

Was Eleni tangled with Crown City's biggest crime boss before Kavoh's people got her?

I groaned. "Too many questions. Not enough snacks."

"Agreed," Vennie said. "We analyzed the antibiotics. They look safe enough, though if the side effects are as bad as your doctor listed, I'd maybe wait on the snacks till morning."

I bristled. Dove wasn't my doctor. I had half a mind to shatter the vial on the floor.

"Was there a cure for missing memories tucked into my suit anywhere?"

Chezza shook her head sadly. "No luck there, but"—she glanced at her brother—"we have a theory."

Vennie rubbed his chin. "The composition of what erased your memories—whatever you ingested—was simple. Meaning it just suppressed your memories, most likely. Made them fuzzy, rather than literally erasing them. So, they're still there; they need to be brought back. Something needs to trigger them."

"Like what?"

"Something momentous that happened right around when you drank it should work."

My stomach clenched again, and blood rushed to my chest, my cheeks. It seemed whatever my mind had forgotten, my body remembered just fine. I reeled my head back, frustrated, beginning to feel the full effects of several nights without quality sleep. "But I don't remember, so I can't figure out what that would be."

"So, we have to hope she gets lucky and they're triggered randomly?" Bane asked.

Vennie shrugged. "Unless we want to track down Dove and ask him."

Bane opened his mouth, but I was already shaking my head. "Absolutely not."

Vennie held up his hands. "Okay, understood. We can brainstorm memory triggers after you've dealt with the bacteria." He mimed retching onto his lap.

I grimaced at the thin glass vial. It was hardly as long as my little finger, filled to the stopper with an electric blue liquid that bubbled slightly when disturbed.

The color was entrancing. Far too lovely for what it was going to do to me.

"It won't be pretty," Bane said. "This can wait until after you've had a full night's rest."

I shook my head and steeled my nerve, nauseous already.

"Someone get me a bucket."

CHAPTER
NINE

THE LITTLE GLASS VIAL SAT PATIENTLY BY THE SINK, WHILE I waited for my shower to heat up. As steam slowly roiled through my en suite bathroom, I finally hefted the tube, captivated by the sparkling slosh of liquid. The solution's blue color snagged on some incoherent memories in my mind, like a sweater's loose yarn on a wicker chair. With a grimace, I lifted the tube in a mocking toast and tipped it back.

Mercifully, the concoction was tasteless.

A hot shower was the magnificent cure I truly needed. The scent of my favorite citrus shampoo nearly made me cry as it cemented the fact I was truly home. The film of my imprisonment washed away, I felt more like myself, though it did nothing for the gaps in my memory, which I prodded mentally like a loose tooth.

I donned a fresh Tempatch unit and my thickest fleece pajamas, the heat easing my tension a little. Finally, I caught a glimpse of myself in the mirror. Though my hair was clean and untangled, I looked haggard, with circles beneath my stormy eyes and a ring of slowly-forming scabs tracing a phantom outline of my mask from forehead to cheekbones.

The skin there glistened, a residue that hadn't come off in the shower. I touched the tacky substance, which smelled subtly herbal.

A healing salve had been applied to my wounds.

Chezza had sent me upstairs with ointment to treat my scraped face, but I hadn't touched the wounds yet. Someone had taken care of it before I came home.

My eyes wandered to the pile of clothes I'd discarded in the corner. Dismal gray scrubs and a mysterious shirt I'd left the facility in. I grabbed the shirt and ran its softness through my hands, considering. It was far too large for me, and well-worn like it was someone's favorite. Some compulsion made me lift it to my face, touching the sleeve to my cheek. Didn't people say scents were sometimes tied to memories?

Feeling like an idiot, I inhaled deeply. In my mind, the scent there was cold . . . sharp, or was it bright? The faint smell of sweat after a run topped with a comforting herbal flair.

My head spun as a cascade of emotions flooded my body. Intense desire and confusion, concern, a hopeless drop of my stomach, a comforting pressure against my side, a flash, a bang, and smoke.

Nicklai stopped with only inches between us. I didn't look away, didn't flinch. He lifted one scarred hand to brush my neck, then lower to drag a single rough nail along my collarbone. I swallowed back rising bile, and the bob of my throat drew a gleeful smirk across Nicklai's scarred face. Thoughts fuzzy with cold and panic, survival instinct took over. I launched a punch at his face. In my sorry state, he caught it easily, spinning and twisting my arm until I cried out.

"I knew our doctor was weak at heart," he hissed in my ear. "Dove doesn't like to hit a prisoner—sorry—'damage an asset.' But I do." He shoved me away and caught me with a kick to the stomach that launched me over the cot and into a heap on the freezing tile floor.

I gasped against the ground, my head pounding, my breathing hoarse.

Nicklai crouched to my level, eyeing me with his dead stare. Deader than Dove's. He held up the remote.

"Let's see how pretty you are when you suffer." He pressed the button.

My vision went black. Panic raced through my veins, an abhorrent buzzing in my blood.

The mist writhed, sending out flailing tendrils that solidified into fangs and claws. The shadows snarled as they leapt for my face and snapped at my arms and legs. I bit down, thrashing away from the assault, trying to keep quiet. Unless . . . If Nicklai wanted to torture me, would he be satisfied if I began screaming? I couldn't tell if he was harming me already or if the pain was a cruel suggestion from the bacteria. I flailed, and my heel caught something soft.

"You bitch," he grunted. As my vision returned in brief flashes, Nicklai drew a wicked-looking knife from a sheath at his thigh. "Kavoh doesn't know you're here."

He ran a finger across the blade, drawing a thin line of blood from his skin. "I can make it like you never existed. You disappear without a trace, and there's no body? This city will forget you in time."

He flipped the knife in his hand as the barrage of shadows dove for me, taking turns picking me apart. I realized the loud ringing throughout the room was one long, broken scream erupting from my lungs. My vision went dark for good, and Nicklai's voice slithered to me between the ruthless pack of shadows. "Don't worry. I'll remember you and how nicely you bleed."

The memory slipped, and I fell against the wall, breathing hard.

I opened my eyes. In my reverie, I'd held out a hand, reaching for something.

Tilting my head, I pressed a hand to my mouth. Nicklai had tortured me . . . How far had he gotten? I didn't have wounds to suggest much, but how had I bested him?

My stomach gurgled a warning to interrupt my thoughts.

I dove for the toilet. Dove's note had not exaggerated the antibiotic's side effects.

Not long passed until there was a knock on my bedroom door. With all the noise I was making, I didn't blame anyone in the house for checking in.

"Mel? It's Bane," my uncle called.

"Yeah, come in," I managed.

Soft footsteps padding across my room and the bathroom door cracking open announced Bane. I groaned a greeting, and he tossed me a pillow and blanket. He chucked a second pillow into the bathtub and climbed in after it.

"You can't sleep in the tub," I said flatly.

"Wouldn't be the first time." Bane settled in and crossed his arms, staring at the ceiling to give me some semblance of privacy. I left the door that divided the shower and toilet from the rest of the bathroom cracked. "Last time, I was covered in glitter. Roger and I were in Vegas . . . Or was it Cleveland? Either way, this is a vast improvement. While we're pretty sure this 'cure' won't hurt you, someone should keep an eye on you. Better me than Vennie. He wants to make a video journal of it for research purposes."

I made a noncommittal noise and returned my attention to the toilet bowl, though my stomach had begun to settle, giving me hope this ordeal would be short.

After an entire minute, which might have been a record for how long Bane could stay quiet, he spoke. "Have any memories come back?"

"Scraps," I said. "Not pretty ones. Nicklai came after me."

The anger in Bane's voice was hardly restrained. "I think it's fair to assume you kicked his ass."

I laughed. "I don't know, Uncle Bane. It was bad in there. I was so cold."

Bane's voice shook. "So, maybe Dove *did* help you."

Goosebumps flared along my arms. "Maybe," I admitted. "I don't know. Does it matter, as long as I got out?"

Bane was silent for another uncharacteristically long time. "I guess not . . . But don't you want to know what happened?"

"All I want is to figure out where the facility is so we can go back, rescue the prisoners, scare off Kavoh's staff, and burn it to the ground."

"When you're feeling better, we can help Vennie scour the footage, see if any routes or landmarks come to mind for you."

"Yeah," I mused. "We should get Chezza and Vennie something nice. I felt totally useless down there."

Bane nodded, his hair flopping in agreement. "Completely. Any ideas?"

"Spa day? Aren't there packages with massages and pedicures and lunch?"

"Genius." Bane pulled out his phone. "I'll ask them for a good Saturday and arrange it. I'm sure there's a place that will have someone specializing in amputee massage too."

My chance to reply was interrupted by the sudden surge of bile up my throat.

🔥🔥🔥

I WAS SICK UNTIL THE SUN ROSE. IT FELT LIKE EVERYTHING I had ever ingested worked its way through my digestive tract in reverse. The violent heaves left my throat raw, but it signaled that the antibiotics slowly flushed the bacteria from my system. Bane streamed my favorite movies at full blast from his phone the entire night to help muffle my noise, until I felt like a weight lifted from my stomach.

"I think I'm done," I croaked, my voice like glass shards.

I stepped groggily to the sink and stuck my head beneath the faucet, taking a long drink.

Bane straightened from the tub, stretching like he had the best night of sleep ever. "Are you hungry?"

"Ugh. No. I'm going to bed."

"Alright. Shout if you need anything."

Bane left, and I crawled into bed, pulling five blankets over me. I checked my phone from the nightstand, where it had been sitting since the night I'd been abducted.

I had one text from Gem and several from Max.

I fired off a response to Gem, letting her know I would fill her in later, then reread Max's messages from the course of the break. He had stuck around Crown City to work on projects with the Gold Guard.

Heading to Hardwired. Want anything?

There's a party at Collins' apartment tomorrow night. Board games & beer. Low-key. Let me know if you want to join.

Do you need to study? I do and would enjoy the company.

With a frown, I started and deleted several messages before settling on a response.

I've been sick. :(Finally feeling better and should be good for school on Monday.

My phone buzzed immediately.

I'll pick you up at our old time?

I took twice as long to reply this time.

Please do.

I SPLIT THE REST OF MY SPRING BREAK BETWEEN SLEEP AND working out, hoping copious pull-ups and planks would stave off my growing rage. The bubbling anger rose higher inside me every time I pondered my short time with Dove and the resulting missing memories.

I'd thought school would be a helpful distraction, but the

professors were more than happy to ease us back after the break, and all too soon, my first day back was over.

Max lingered when he dropped me off after both our classes had finished. My heart ached when his molten gaze searched my face as we stood on the front porch, his hands shoved deep into his perfectly pressed chino pockets. I constricted my arms around my stack of books, so I wouldn't fling my arms around him instead, reminding myself of the reasons we were better apart.

He frowned at his loafers. "I should've brought you soup when you said you were sick."

It was moments like this, when Max managed to keep his gold-flecked head out of his ass for more than five minutes, I missed him most.

"Vennie's been teaching me some of his best noodle dishes." True. "So, I'm managing. And I've eaten half my weight in ginger in the last two days alone, I'm sure."

Max tried to subtly check his watch, but the sun bounced off its gold face and sent rainbows sparkling through the spray from the lion fountain before us.

"You've got somewhere to be," I accused.

Max tilted his head back. "A strategy meeting for the Gold Guard."

My stomach twisted on itself, extinguishing any embers of desire.

"How's that going?" I ventured.

"Great." He rubbed his hands together. "We almost got them on a recent mission. Silhouette and the Shadow can't avoid us forever."

"Get out of here," I said with a forced smile. "I need a nap."

"Feel better soon." Max blew me a kiss as he sauntered to his car. I averted my gaze from the way those chinos had been perfectly tailored to hug his ass.

As he drove away, I stared into the solemn concrete eyes of

Grandpa Sydney's giant lion statue. "Lions," I said. "Everything is a shitshow."

The lion said nothing.

"Helpful as usual!" I called on my way into the house, kicking the door shut behind me.

<h1 style="text-align:center">CHAPTER
TEN</h1>

After dinner, Bane skipped haphazardly across the kitchen, far too reckless on his freshly healed leg. He patted his crutches affectionately and left them by the stairs to be brought down to the Den. "Sorry, boys, our time together is done."

I clapped, the sound echoing around the otherwise silent kitchen, as Chezza and Vennie were visiting their parents in neighboring Crater City for a few days.

Bane returned to the seat across from me, only tripping once on the way.

"Does that mean you're feeling up to going out?" I asked.

Bane nodded slowly, like he was chewing something over.

"I think we should try to find Kavoh's facility," I said before he could spit out whatever thought he worked through.

Before he'd left, Vennie had discerned a rough location of the building from some security cameras that caught me fleeing.

I closed the textbook at my elbow, careful not to spill pasta sauce on it. Bane somehow had flecks of parsley and parmesan in his disheveled hair.

"I agree," he said finally.

I laid my hands on the table. "Think about it, Uncle Bane. We could potentially find out what happened to me, maybe try and determine their next steps. We might even be able to rescue whoever they've got captive in there." My eyebrows shot up. "You agree?"

"My only concern is if you're up for it—to face this site of your trauma again, mentally. And if you say you are, I have faith in you."

"Thanks." I stabbed a noodle. "We should also try and figure out if they came anywhere close to figuring out my identity. It's a liability if we don't."

Bane rested his chin on a fist, tracing patterns in the marinara with his fork. "I bet we can find the exact building. Your memories will be tickled being back there for sure. I checked the area's feeds earlier and saw Cellina and Nicklai driving a loaded pickup through one of the intersections."

I froze, my heart suddenly thundering. I fought to keep my face impassive. "No one else was with them?"

Bane shook his head. "You don't have to come with, you know, Toasty. You can stay here and keep an eye on me. I'll stick to the perimeter."

But like hell I was going to let him do anything even remotely dangerous alone. I'm sure he felt the same way about me.

I convinced myself that was the sole reason I insisted, "I'm going with you."

🔥🔥🔥

THE FACILITY WAS CLEVERLY HIDDEN, TUCKED AWAY FAR TO the Northeast of downtown in a small string of factories and blocky corporate offices whose architecture screamed 1987. The daytime traffic there was sleepy, just people heading to and from work, so at night, it was an open playground for Kavoh's operation.

Bane and I peered out from a copse of trees we'd taken refuge in while the sun finished setting. Darkness came early to Crown City, with its sentinel ring of mountains blocking the light.

"No wonder Vennie's search took so long," I mused. "Was he hacked into any of these cameras already?"

Bane's helmet glinted as he shook his head. "He cast his net wider after the program couldn't find a trace of you anywhere in the city proper."

I rubbed my chin. The night was crisp but mercifully free of snow. My suit—one of my spares given the hazards of vigilante-ing—kept the chill at bay, but the softest wind kissed the strip of exposed skin at my throat and around my mask. I shivered. "This doesn't feel familiar."

Bane led the way from our hiding spot. "Let's explore a bit. See if anything jogs your memory."

We crept through the shadows. Though it was a pastime we'd practiced countless times before, I had to fight to keep my breaths quiet and suppress an impulsive jump at every small nighttime noise that rose around us.

After a half hour, we turned another corner and I grumbled. "I don't know if I even got a good look at the place from the outside. I just woke up there—"

Movement caught my eye. A tarp's loose corner flapped in the breeze.

Along the side of an otherwise nondescript two-story building, a hole had been blown wide directly through the cinderblock wall. It looked to have been hastily patched with plywood and the poorly secured tarp.

My chest was squeezed tight by a phantom fist, while ice flooded my veins and heat roiled in my belly. My grip on reality wavered, and I was back in that cell.

With threats approaching on all sides, I reverted to survival instincts. I curled as small as possible to shield the most vulnerable parts of me. It was all I could do to endure the barrage of shadows, cringing and whim-

pering as the wolf creatures leapt at me at the same time Nicklai's boots slowly trod my way. I pressed back, my hands scrambling against the freezing tile floor until my back met a wall. The shadows' ripping snarls echoed inside my mind as they tore me apart, bit by bit, disassembling me mentally, surely only a heartbeat ahead of Nicklai doing it physically.

A very real, very close SLAM made me jump, and the shadow wolves grew more agitated.

"Who authorized these tests?" one of the wolves roared over the din.

"Silhouette?" Bane's helmet tilted toward me expectantly.

I swallowed, smoothing the sturdy material of my suit over my stomach with shaking fingers. "This is the place."

He receded suddenly, motioning to join him against the wall of the opposite building. The line of Bane's always-at-ease shoulders was tight.

My mouth quirked. "You don't like me near this place."

Bane crossed his arms. "No. I fucking don't."

I stared into his helmet. "It's okay, Shadow. Frosty. I'm right here. And as much as it gives us the goddamn creeps, we're gonna clear this place out together."

"Alright. You're right," he said. "Let's run the perimeter a few times, see if we catch any sound or movement."

We scoped, snooped, and spent way too long simply staring, but didn't find any evidence of the building being occupied. There was another hole blown in the upper floor on the building's far side, and nothing else.

Bane peeled back the tarp covering the hole on the main floor and pulled on the plywood beneath. The wood gave a single snap as he broke open a space wide enough for us to slip through.

He peered through the opening while I scanned the streets, though I listened carefully for movement within the building, for the sound of anxious footsteps responding to our noise. None came.

Bane shrugged and stepped into the compound. I followed close behind.

Our respective temperatures made it so we could see easily in the darkness. I shivered again as I looked around the devastated room. Flimsy boxes and plastic debris filled the space, tinted with the faint smell of smoke.

"It looks like a storage room," I murmured.

"Anything new?" Bane asked, his helmet swiveling my way. He tapped it to signify he was asking about my memory.

"Not exactly . . . Just murkiness."

"Are you okay to split up? We don't have to."

"I can handle it."

A dip of the helmet. "Let's find some answers then, Silhouette."

Bane took the first floor, leaving me to explore the second story. My heart pulsed in my throat as I traversed the dark stairwell, taking deep gulps of stale air. Grime encrusted the walls and floor, and a spider made its home in an impressively large web in the corner.

"I found their security room," Bane said. "I'm going to see if I can locate recordings of your time here. Find anything of interest?"

"Not yet. Just trash and rat shit."

Bane made a gagging sound. "It's almost creepier that this place is empty."

"Absolutely." I listened at the door at the top of the stairwell for a moment, holding my breath. The building remained silent, though it was hard to be sure with the sound of Bane's keyboard mashing through my earpiece.

"Fuck's sake, are you trying to stab the computer to death?"

"Don't question my methods! I'm not as fast as Braveheart, but I'm a decent hacker."

Shaking my head, I pushed through the door. It creaked angrily. I cringed, shoulders rising to my ears, but nothing moved in the long, darkened hallway, which was lined with steel doors inset with tiny windows.

My scalp prickled.

"I think—" I had to try again, because my throat had gone dry. "I think they kept me up here."

The typing stopped. "Want me to come up?"

"I'm okay. I can do this."

On my third step, Bane cursed. I glanced behind me to find nothing but darkness.

"What? What is it?"

"There's a virus lurking in the mainframe. I think, if I'm reading the code right, it's going to set the building on fire. There must be charges set somewhere."

I put the pieces together. "They moved all their evidence and people, and they're gonna torch the place." I echoed Bane's curse. "How long do we have?"

The clicking grew more furious. I wondered if the keys were flying off the board.

"Ten minutes?"

"Let's hurry then."

"Right."

At the end of the hall, sickly light leaked through one door's window. My pulse ratcheted, demanding I flee.

As I stalked toward it, a small flame of hope churned in my chest against the dread. Maybe something in there would trigger my lost memories. Anticipation roared through my limbs, excitement and fear all tangled together.

My teeth gritted, I kicked the door in.

It crashed against the wall, groaning off its hinges.

I took a step in and was paralyzed.

There was someone in the room.

Eyes wide, his gaunt face bruised and bloodied, was Dove.

Rage surged through me, molten hot. I knew it then. He was the one who had taken my memories, just like he had taken me right off the street in that alley.

Dove seemed afraid to move. Good. His body was far too long for the small cot, and one of his legs splayed at an unnatural angle. His chest rose and fell against the thin cotton of his long-sleeved T-shirt. Flashes of memory flushed through me, moving too fast to identify. I closed my eyes, and my fists clenched so tight the seams of my gloves groaned in protest.

"Toasty?" Bane asked. "What's going on?"

"It's the doctor. Dove," I made myself say, and his eyes widened even further. "He's here."

"Silhouette," Bane said it like he was reasoning with a wild animal. "Don't. Throttle him."

"Why not?" I demanded, startled at my own iciness.

Dove started, perhaps wondering if I was talking to him.

Bane's voice kept me tethered. "He might know something."

"He's in bad shape," I said through gritted teeth.

"Then it wouldn't even be satisfying to kick his ass." Bane swore. "I have more bad news."

"For lions' sake, what?"

"I made the computer virus angry. Fire's starting in one minute."

I cracked my neck as I eyed Dove. "That's not the worst news."

Bane's laugh was dry. "Speak for yourself, Silhouette. I almost have what I need. I've found some things . . . I'll be done soon, but this fire is starting now. What do you—" He cut himself off. I knew what he was going to ask. The choice he didn't want to burden me with.

"I'm bringing him with us."

"Silhouette—" Bane started. "No, you're right. Let's get him out alive, and we can decide from there."

"Yeah. Pick a rendezvous point. We'll see you there."

I took another step into the room, and Dove flinched.

I rolled my eyes. "Great news for you. This just turned into a rescue mission."

He seemed unable to find words, his hollow cheeks taut under the pressure of his clenched jaw. His large, pale hands were translucent at the knuckles braced around the edge of the mattress.

"Did you know your coworkers rigged this place to go up in flames?" I took a careful step forward, and his eyes followed. "Don't misunderstand me. I'm *extremely* pissed, and that's a massive problem for you, but you don't deserve to burn." I jerked my chin at the doorway. "After you."

"I can't walk." His hoarse voice sent my head spinning.

I knew it. I knew it well. How much more had we spoken beyond what I remembered?

Wonderful. I sized him up, not thrilled about the task at hand. Those unsettling eyes searched my face, like he saw all of me beneath the hood and mask.

"I'll carry you," I said dismissively. "Hold your leg steady. I'll jostle you as little as possible."

To his credit, he didn't argue.

I helped him up. He hissed when his leg shifted. I nudged his torso with my shoulder, and I grabbed his wrist. His skin was warm under my hand and . . . familiar.

"Who authorized these tests?"

The voice in my head roared again, causing me to wobble beneath Dove's weight.

A memory overlaid my reality, projecting over the cell. I'd been curled against this wall, screaming and crying.

"Someone has to do your job," Nicklai drawled, as if bored. The faintest whine of metal suggested he slipped his knife back into its sheath. It was a brief, glorious reminder that half of my horror—the wrathful wolves in my head—weren't real. I set shaking hands against the floor, tethering myself to icy tiles beneath them. Air hitched in my lungs as an unreal wolf snapped for my ankles.

Slow clicking, like footsteps somewhere in the room. Nicklai had his finger over the button causing my suffering.

"I leave for an hour and you resort to playing with one of our most lucrative assets like a toy? You better hope you haven't done permanent damage."

I prayed the voice wasn't a hallucination.

"I have just as much rank as you, Dove. I'm testing her endurance. Picking up where you've been slacking."

Nicklai turned up the severity of the bacteria. It felt like I was being electrocuted. Like maggots danced beneath my skin. The shadows grew warped and sporadic. I drowned in darkness. Sounds tore from my throat. I gripped my face and clawed blindly, desperate to escape my own head.

"Enough." Dove's voice cut through my despair.

There was a shuffle, a slam, and a yowl. The shadows receded slightly. Wetness slid down my face, and my wailing lessened to sobs.

"You'll regret meddling. No one's indispensable to her,*" Nicklai spat.*

Dove's response was soft and deadly. "I know that better than anyone, as you're well aware. Now get back to your scheduled work. I'm sure Cellina has someone for you to pick apart."

A grumble, the scrape of metal against the floor, and a spat word. "Have fun with her then." The door slammed.

A long breath out. Then, the horrifying sensation in my body leaked away, and my sight began to return. I looked up into electric eyes.

Dove crouched before me. I flinched, still jittery thanks to the bacteria, my sight fluttering away to blackness every few seconds.

The expression on Dove's face was unlike any of his various impassive masks. He looked . . . frightened. His own hands shook as he held them toward me, like someone trying to reason with a wild animal. He held the remote. My wristband's light was blue.

"It's over."

"Are you alright?" The same voice, as soft as it was in the past, called me to reality.

I shook the passing memory away. He huffed when I ducked and shifted the bulk of his weight across my shoulders in a fireman's carry. His head hung somewhere at my side, where I was pleased I couldn't see his face. He unsettled me.

"Okay?" I asked.

"Yes," he grunted.

We had to look ridiculous. My head only came up to his chest when we were both standing.

"I have Dove," I said. Below us, I heard the familiar roar of racing flames. I gulped. "Where to?"

Bane's voice was strained. "I'm out, heading for a spot in the woods we passed through on the way in. I'll ping it on your map. Be careful; the fire's spreading fast."

I sidled from the room. Dove's weight wasn't an issue, but his height upset my balance. To his benefit, he remained quiet. I headed back to the stairwell, only for a hissing fist of flames to punch up beyond the door's small window.

"Is there roof access?" I asked Dove.

"They probably barred the door. You could handle it, but I'm not sure how long it would take."

I bit my lip. "The others just left you here? Never mind. Where's that hole in the wall on this floor?"

Dove stiffened as he pointed down the hall to a slim door that blended with the walls and led to a tight, dank hallway. I wove us through it, only thinking a few seconds ahead because it's all I could handle.

I moved as quickly as I could, making some effort to not jostle the man across my shoulders. I tried not to let the surge of turmoil rolling through me make me cruel. I carried him to the sole doorway, the heat in my suit making him feel no heavier than a backpack. Placing a palm to the door, I felt no heat. I tried the handle and found it locked.

Releasing my arm from around Dove's legs, I struggled to get the heavy door open, the angle awkward.

"It's locked. I have to put you down for a second," I huffed, setting him on his feet.

He sagged against the wall, a sheen of sweat on his face. He nursed his bad leg, keeping it slightly off the floor. With a stern shove, I shouldered the door open and helped him hobble through. A weak wind greeted us. It must have been doing wonders for the fire below, whose hungry growls grew louder.

"You're running out of time, Silhouette," Bane said tersely in my ear. "One of the walls looks ready to collapse."

As if in response, the building rumbled beneath us. "Which wall?"

"Uh," Bane's voice wavered with uncertainty. "The . . . south one?"

"You are the absolute worst."

"As if you know the orientation of the cardinal directions at any given time . . ."

Ignoring my uncle, I wound an arm around Dove's waist, supporting his chest with my other hand. His heartbeat stuttered beneath my palm. What strength he had left was rapidly flagging. He looked like he hadn't eaten in days. I led him into the room, where remnants of furniture and cabinetry littered the floor. A battered mattress sagged against the wall beside us. I turned my head slowly, peering into every corner.

Finally, my gaze settled on Dove, who leaned away from me as much as he could without falling over. My eyes narrowed, my voice dark with accusation.

"I've been here before."

CHAPTER
ELEVEN

Leaning Dove against the mattress, I stepped to the hole in the wall, unable to look at him. "What is this place?" I demanded, tearing away plastic haphazardly secured to block the hole. Some snow from earlier in the week had already snuck in to stain the floor and papers littering it—the remnants of a small book collection.

Dove didn't answer.

Locking on my full granite face, I scowled. "Bold to withhold information from someone saving your life." My voice was thick with disdain, but still, I extended a hand.

Dove stared at it blankly, his mouth a thin line.

"Come on," I beckoned. "We're going to jump."

He eyed me uncertainly.

I tapped my boot against the dust-covered floor. "Do you prefer your odds with the fire?"

"No."

"That's what I thought."

Before he could balk, I crooked an arm under his back and knees and swung him up before me. Part of me was satisfied to have the tables turned. With my suit fired up and the fear bacteria gone, I was in control.

Dove's leg must have been shrieking. Tentatively, he settled one arm behind my shoulders, and crossed the other to clasp his hands together.

I approached the hole and peered down. No branching flames awaited us below.

Dove eyed the drop, then looked up, his face inches from my own.

"I recommend closing your eyes," I said, and stepped off the ledge.

Air rushed past us. My grip on Dove tightened, and a strangled whine erupted from his throat and was ripped away by the wind.

My knees howled upon contact with the street. I kept my stance wide and legs bent, taking the shock of impact. My joints barked as my feet connected. Our landing carried more force than I could have imagined with Dove in my arms. A small crater of cracks echoed in the asphalt around us. Momentum carried me off balance, and I rolled us forward, tucking my body around his and landing awkwardly on my wrist. We flipped sporadically and fell apart, splayed on our backs.

I groaned, hacking out gravel that had swept into my mouth. Waves of heat emanated from the building as flames burst through the upper floors' few windows. I pushed myself up and searched for Dove. He blinked rapidly at the night sky, his chest rising and falling in great heaves.

His head tilted toward me, dark hair falling across those eyes that seemed to glow in the night. My breath caught.

Footsteps sounded. Bane crouched next to me, and I could imagine the concern creasing his face behind his helmet's dark visor.

"You alright?"

"I think so," I coughed out. "Why are you back here? We need to move."

Bane helped me to my feet. "I thought you might need an

extra set of hands. This place will be crawling with first responders soon."

We walked to Dove, who had pushed himself upright. He looked to me, then at Bane with a combination of fear and awe.

"Your friends left you in there to get crispy," Bane said, his Shadow voice a gravel echo in the dark.

Dove pushed his hair out of his eyes, the flames' reflections catching on cracks in his glasses. He turned his face to me. "You saved my life."

I crossed my arms. "It's part of the job description."

Bane crouched before Dove and snapped his fingers, demanding his attention. "Here's the deal. You're coming with us, and you're going to tell us everything you know about what Kavoh's up to, then we'll decide what to do with you."

Murder wasn't on the table, of course, but you wouldn't know it by Bane's tone.

"Are you going to cause us any trouble until then?" he finished.

"No, sir," Dove said, his face solemn.

That received a snort from Bane. "Sir, my ass."

Meanwhile, my heart ratcheted up to a hectic beat. What could we possibly do with him? Keeping my face stony, I reached a hand down to the doctor.

His hand dwarfed mine, and radiated unexpected warmth through my glove. I hauled him back into my arms and took off, Bane mere steps behind us.

In a flash, we reached Bane's proposed meeting spot from earlier, and I set Dove on the forest floor with a relieved sigh.

"Don't move," I commanded. "If you bolt, we'll catch you."

Dove's face was as innocent as his name. "I'm not going anywhere."

The response made me grind my teeth as I motioned Bane to the far end of the clearing.

"What do we do with him after he talks?" I wasn't thrilled with the whine in my voice.

Bane rubbed the forehead piece of his helmet. "If we drop him somewhere, Kavoh's folks could find him and kill him. I don't love that idea."

I shook my head. "Me either. And we don't know what he knows about me. About us. How much did you get from the security tapes?"

Bane fished a thumb drive from his hip pocket, scattering jelly beans over the forest floor. "Not as much as I'd like, but we'll see."

I crouched, resting my elbows on my knees as Bane paced. On top of everything, it had begun to rain, and icy drops peppered my head and shoulders as they filtered through the leaves. "What?" I said, letting my eyes wander the maze of bark on the closest tree. "So, we just take him home? Leave Kavoh's second-in-command tied up in the Den and hope he doesn't touch anything until we figure out a better plan?"

Bane rubbed his neck. "We could keep him in the guest room."

I blinked, letting the slow movement relay my many reservations.

"We could fit a lock on the door, only talk to him with our helmet and mask on."

"Braveheart and Beacon will be thrilled."

"They actually might. They can ask him about the bacteria and memory serum."

I snapped my fingers. "The memory serum. We could replicate it and dose him if we need to."

"This plan is only slightly more baked than our usual," Bane mused.

"We don't have a lot of options, and I want to get out of this damn rain."

"Alright." Bane nodded his assent.

We returned to Dove, who I hauled back into my arms.

To his credit, Dove stayed mostly quiet during our awkward jog, though I'm sure I jostled his bag leg plenty. We couldn't go very fast, and one particularly rocky patch of woods halfway home had me stumbling. I nearly dropped Dove, and catching him with my wrist that I'd landed on funny caused me to hiss in pain.

Bane steadied me, then held out his arms. "Here, give him to me." I helped Bane haul Dove over his own shoulders, like some handsome, haggard sack of flour. "Sheesh, you're tall."

Dove laughed weakly.

Bane stepped forward, and his boot caught on a fallen branch. He kept himself upright, barely.

"This isn't gonna work," I sighed, massaging my wrist. "Why don't you go grab the car? We can wait." We'd only just crossed one of the smaller roads leading back to the Leo house.

Bane set Dove down with a huff, and glanced between us, indecision etched in the set of his shoulders. "I'll be quick," he said finally, and sped off.

I stood in the quiet forest, the only sounds the nighttime rustling of trees, rain plopping through leaves, and Dove's stilted breaths. An unnatural light snagged my attention. It glowed from Dove's wrist, where one of the activator bands for the FR-10 bacteria was wrapped. Faint trails of dried blood leaked from the underside. I crouched before him, gently taking his wrist and tugging back his sleeve. I examined the eerie blue light with a shudder.

"They injected you with your own bacteria?"

He didn't say anything, but rubbed a hand up his arm, his closed mouth rolling around unsaid words. He wondered what I knew. How much I remembered.

I pursed my lips. "What's the bacteria's purpose?"

This, Dove didn't seem to mind sharing. He had to try a few times before words came to him. "Coercion. To subject someone to so much horror they'd do whatever is asked of them in order to make it stop."

"Charming. What did they want you to do?"

Dove's eyes darted to the forest floor. "Suffer."

Thankfully, an SUV's headlights shone through the trees, and I helped Bane quickly maneuver Dove, half-conscious from pain, into the back seat.

Bane shut the door and held out a hand to stop me. He withdrew his visor. "Are you okay with this?"

His silver-blue eyes searched my face.

"It's the right thing to do. Amidst a sea of bad options."

"That's not what I asked," he said, not unkindly.

I huffed a long breath. "It's hard already," I admitted. "But he has info on Kavoh. I think he's the key to my memories. I want to know what happened more than I want to stay away from him. Not by much, but enough."

Bane studied me a moment longer before climbing into the driver's side. I hovered my hand over the passenger door's handle, then shifted to the back. Dove's considerable height took up most of the bench seat. He had one foot on the floor and the other propped at a diagonal over the seat's back. I slid in carefully, nudging his head with my hip. It occupied most of where I was supposed to fit.

Dove looked shocked. If being around him was going to trigger my memories, I needed to get used to it. Bane didn't comment on my seating choice. Feigning nonchalance, I slipped off my gloves and ran my fingers through my hair.

Dove tilted his head to the side so it hung off the seat in an attempt to make room for me. "Sorry," he murmured.

"It's fine."

I lifted his head so it rested on my thigh. Wisely, he didn't resist. No need for him to be any more uncomfortable. Bane pulled onto the road in silence.

Dove's hair was soft, the dark locks slipping between my fingers before I withdrew my hands, though it looked like it hadn't been washed in a few days. I really looked at him for the first time, using my hood to hide it.

I felt the now familiar nudge of memories wanting to emerge, but nothing solid had showed up since we left the facility.

"Why did they turn on you?"

He scrubbed his palms over his pants, but he said nothing.

"You know," I drawled. "Usually, when you're the captive, it's your job to give up information. It must be hard for you— to be the one at a disadvantage for once."

His hands curled over his stomach like he was going to be sick. Silence stretched the length of the darkened car. All the while, I glared down at him, refusing to relent.

Just as Bane made one of our final turns, Dove swallowed. "They were certain I helped you escape."

My heart stopped. A last-minute thought made me place my hand gently over Dove's eyes. It seemed unlikely he'd be able to catch a glimpse of a street sign from his angle, or that he was conscious enough to keep track of our route.

"Did you?"

Dove's lashes fluttered against my palm.

Had he blown the hole in the wall for me to escape through, or had I?

"I—" he stammered, then clamped his mouth shut again, slamming an iron door on the tiniest bit of faith I offered.

Rage sparked bright and hot in my chest. It roared up my throat and took my mind captive, blinding me with the demand to punish this man who had hurt me.

I scoffed and glared out the window, uncomfortable with unfamiliar wrath hijacking my reasoning. "It doesn't matter. You're the one who dragged me into that hellhole in the first place."

I told myself I imagined Dove's lashes suddenly feeling wet as we passed through the gate to the Leo property, but he didn't dare say anything in his defense. He took something that was mine—that he had no right to—and we both knew it.

"You can't hate me more than I hate myself," he said, barely above a whisper.

We pulled into the garage, and as its door closed behind us, I withdrew my hand from his face. "You have no idea what I'm capable of." A memory flashed through me, fleeting but clear. *"Monster,"* I finished with a hiss, firing the word at him like a swift punch to the throat.

He flinched, the pain in his eyes fathomless. A twinge of sympathy swam across my heart.

My wrath quickly devoured it.

CHAPTER
TWELVE

M‌ERE MINUTES AFTER WE HEFTED HIM ONTO THE D‌EN'S medical table, Dove was asleep.

As his breath evened out and the deep lines of concern smoothed from his forehead, I sagged onto the bench beside our cubbies, needing space between us.

Bane eyed the LUMA, examining—or pretending to—some data our suits had sent back during the night's adventure. He kept his thoughts to himself as I stared at my palms, counting their lines and trying not to think.

Eventually, Bane strode my way. He read my expression and didn't ask if I was okay, instead rubbing his arm. "Let's get him situated, yeah? Then we can change."

I gave a weak nod and trudged to Dove's side.

He woke as I approached, confusion crossing his face. I peered over to remind him where he was, and he jolted.

Terror.

"You're safe," I told him.

It's all I felt like offering. He tried to sit up with a wince. I reached for his elbow to assist, but he managed to hold himself up. After all he'd been through, his strength was impressive.

Bane's face pinched in frustration as he ransacked Chezza's carefully organized medical cabinet.

"Where are we?" Dove asked over the sounds of Bane's pillaging.

"Not telling you that," I said, crossing my arms.

Dove blinked at me. Fear and something else blended in his gaze.

I shifted my attention to Bane, who had what looked like a tangled catheter tube between his teeth.

"YES!" Bane held up what he'd been searching for, a thick binder labeled: "How To Not Bleed To Death: For When Shit Hits the Fan and Beacon's Not Here" in Chezza's neat handwriting.

I snatched it from him, and Bane rubbed his hands together. "Okay, doc, what needs fixing?"

Dove gaped.

"We're the best you're getting," I said, flipping pages. I was crashing fast and wanted to get to bed.

"Uh—" Dove stammered. "I don't think anything's broken. I've got lacerations I should clean, but otherwise, it's just my leg. I'm pretty sure it's dislocated."

"Oh!" Bane pumped a fist into the air. "I know how to fix that! I dislocated loads of stuff before I had any help."

"I'm sure," I drawled. "What do you need me to—"

Then, something happened very quickly.

Bane lifted Dove's wrist, where the bracelet rested, its blue light still glowing. "I assume you want this off?" he asked, at the same time pinching the plastic band between his fingers so that it broke. The bracelet remained firmly lodged in Dove's wrist. The light flicked to ghastly orange, and my breath disappeared.

What little color was left drained from Dove's face.

"No," I gasped.

Dove's chest rose and fell in severe bursts, and white became clear all the way around his eyes.

"The failsafe," he spoke quickly, searching around. I realized he was looking for me for some reason. His eyes met mine, and his voice was strained. "In case an asset tries to take it off. It activates."

My eyes darted to the wristband. My pulse ratcheted up at the memory of orange light's meaning. A harbinger of your worst fears.

Dove's eyes remained locked on mine, desperate and fearful. Alone.

The glimmer of recognition disappeared from his eyes, signifying his vision had gone dark.

"Oh, shit." I growled.

Dove thrashed on the table as some invisible monster came for him. A howl caught, strangled, in his throat. He jerked violently. Without thinking, I threw myself over him, holding his arms and torso against the table as he whimpered and thrashed. I couldn't look away from his terror-stricken face. He screamed.

I tore my eyes from his. Bane was frozen, guilt paralyzing his features.

"Fix his leg! One problem at a time," I demanded.

"I didn't mean to—I thought he'd want it off."

"I know, I know. We'll fix it!" I shouted over Dove's unintelligible cries. He was much stronger than I expected. I pressed him down harder, his chest straining against my arms.

My focus pulled back to Dove's face like a magnet. Recognition flickered there for a second. Maybe he was able to see every few seconds like I had been able to. I held his gaze, perhaps the only person who could offer him solidarity for having suffered the same agony. I wondered what he saw. Some compulsion deep inside called me to speak.

"It's not real."

Bane grabbed Dove's leg in one hand and braced the other against his hip. Bane counted quietly to himself before wrenching Dove's leg in a way that nearly made me gag. Dove yelled again, this one distinctly different from the cries of whatever he saw in his mind.

"Trade me!" I shouted.

Bane banded his arms over Dove. I grabbed his flailing arm and trapped it beneath mine like a vice. He writhed, and I knew my grip couldn't feel good. Excruciatingly slowly so as not to rip Dove's arm to shreds, I withdrew the prongs of the bracelet and dropped it on the ground in disgust.

Immediately, Dove's panic lessened, if infinitesimally. I rifled through the drawers until I found the vials of the antibiotics we'd replicated as a precaution. I snatched one and pulled the stopper. Bracing Dove's chin, I dumped it down his throat the next instant he cried out.

He choked and jerked out of my grip, but he seemed to understand what I'd done. He swallowed and calmed a fraction, knowing his suffering would end.

Bane drew back, but I instinctually laid an arm over Dove again, for fear he'd accidentally throw himself off the table. He was soaked through with sweat, and he still twitched and gasped. Dove's eyes flicked back and forth beneath the lids, his dark lashes slick with tears.

I leaned close and spoke gently, "It helps if you open your eyes."

Slowly, he heeded my advice. His irises glowed a glorious blue, surrounded by a small explosion of bloodshot lines. "Thank you," he whispered, and there was such weight in the words that I stepped back.

My arms felt cold where they no longer touched him. Dove's battered form slumped on the table, shaking intermittently. Blood from his wrist flowed across the sterile paper cover. I hadn't noticed he wasn't wearing shoes. His feet and the hem of his pants were both torn and muddy. Bane had stepped back, hands pressed against his mouth, eyes wide in horror. This was the first time he'd seen the bacteria in action.

Seen how it had decimated Dove's grip on reality. How it must have affected me.

Dove prodded at his hip socket and winced. "You weren't kidding. I'm impressed." He laid back, looking up at me again, his breathing nearly returned to normal. "What now?"

Quick as a viper, I struck out at the pressure point in his neck. Dove's eyes rolled back and closed, finally giving me peace.

"What was that for?" Bane asked.

"I need a minute," I said shakily, grabbing one of the many blankets I kept stashed around the house and draping it over Dove. "Several minutes."

Bane's footsteps drew close, and he squeezed me gently against his side. "The Ellos are gonna be so confused when they get back."

I croaked a laugh. "Seriously, what do we do now?"

"I think you should go to bed."

"And leave you to deal with this—him?"

Bane set his stance to stubborn, a move he learned from me. "You said you need a minute. I bet you need more. How about an entire evening's worth of minutes? I'll get Dove situated, and you get some sleep."

He made a great point. My posture slumped. "I'll be in a better position to comprehend all this in the morning."

Bane nodded sagely. "Promise I'll shout for you if I break something."

I removed my mask and raised an eyebrow.

"Fine, if I break something major that can't wait until tomorrow."

"Deal," I waved him off and headed for the stairs, stopping only to shed my suit and leave it in a sweaty, smoky heap inside my cubby. I'd deal with it tomorrow, alongside the confusing mix of anger and excitement I felt that Dove was here.

THE TELLTALE SOUND OF BANE MAKING A MESS IN THE kitchen hauled me from muddled dreams. Glaring at my clock, I considered staying beneath the covers for five more minutes.

At the third sound of ringing metal, I growled and abandoned the warmth of my bed for whatever shitstorm of a morning awaited me.

Dawn's light blared through the windows. I felt a little less volatile than the night before, my emotions less sharp around the edges. After brushing my teeth, I tugged on leggings and a sweatshirt before I stepped into the hall and shut the door quietly behind me.

"He's down the hall."

I jumped. Bane leaned against the banister at the top of the stairs, looking exhausted and splotched with splashes of flour. From my sense of smell, he definitely hadn't showered since our excursion, and he was also making bagels. The door to the rarely used guest room at the other end of the hall was fitted with bulky tech that must have been Bane's attempt at a lock.

Dove was in there. My stomach turned.

"Have you even slept?" I asked.

Bane looked like he could topple over.

I pointed down the stairs, and Bane followed me to the kitchen, where he collapsed on a bar stool as I headed for the pantry.

"Did you sleep?" I repeated.

He had his glasses on, which was a bad sign. He only wore them when his eyes got tired. He had great vision thanks to our powers, but also astigmatism that wouldn't quit. He pressed knuckles into his eye sockets. I set a sandwich that was more peanut butter than bread before him.

"You are a miracle sent from the heavens," he told me somberly.

"Don't you forget it." I started on coffee.

"I did sleep. Not for long, even for me, but I did," Bane said after a few huge bites. "There must have been an insane dose of bacteria in him. He said one of Kavoh's other high-ups did it." Nicklai's face flashed through my mind, sending shudders down my body. "He was still panicky when he woke up, but the antibiotics kicked in fast."

Remembering the side effects they warranted, I winced. I poured myself a cup of coffee, adding a dash of cinnamon to the top. I took a sip before voicing my question.

"Did he . . . tell you what happened during the period of time that my memories are missing?"

Bane stared out the window at the sun washing over the stones of our driveway, the lion statue casting a deep shadow in the early morning. "I didn't ask. I want to follow your lead on that piece, Mel. Whatever you determine is best for you, I'm game."

"I have no idea how I feel." I took another shaky sip.

Bane squeezed my shoulder. "You can take your time."

I snorted. "The mad scientist sleeping in our guest room would suggest otherwise."

Bane pulled at his hair. "Excellent point."

I jerked my chin toward the doorway. "Get some sleep. I'll . . . handle Dove. Keep an eye on him or whatever. I'll shout if I need you."

"Liar," he said, but he didn't argue as he meandered stiffly off to his room, his too-long cow print pajama pants whooshing over the floor.

I pondered over my coffee for five minutes, then ten. I knew I shouldn't delay and leave Dove to his own devices. I sighed and set my now-cold coffee in the microwave and dashed downstairs for my mask.

As my coffee finished reheating, I affixed my mask to my face, absently pulled out another mug and filled it.

The microwave beeped, and I looked down at the cup whose intense heat seeped comfort into my hands.

No cream, no sugar.

I stared blankly as realization struck. The second coffee— the steaming, perfect cup I'd poured without thinking—was for Dove.

My brow furrowed, I carried the drinks carefully upstairs. The gentle sounds of someone waking reached me at the landing. Suddenly nervous, I ducked into my own bedroom and dove further into the bathroom. I set the cups on the counter and glared at myself, prepping a mental pep talk.

"You are *intimidating*," I insisted.

My scowl deepened as I applied some eyeliner. With a stern squaring of my shoulders, I headed for the other room. Taking both mugs in one hand, I typed the code Bane had programmed and twisted the handle, announcing myself with its loud creak and waiting a moment before pushing inside.

Think of it as guard duty, I thought dismissively.

Dove was seated in bed with his back against the pillows. His eyes turned wide and hesitant upon seeing me. He'd bathed, and his dark hair was pushed back from his face. His glasses had been cleaned, though there was still a small crack along the bottom of one lens. He wore clean clothes—some things of Bane's judging by the way the sweatpants stopped a few inches above his ankles and the T-shirt stretched tight across his chest. His bad leg was propped on a pillow, and a discarded ice pack lay at the edge of the mattress, perilously close to falling.

He looked domestic and, alarmingly, practically darling, especially with sleepiness softening the carved lines of his face.

I reminded myself what this man had done to me, envisioning hulking, shadowy beasts over Dove's shoulder.

"Monster." The breathless word escaped my lips before I could think it through.

He gulped. "Terror."

I narrowed my eyes. "You still think that?"

His chest heaved. I made him nervous. "Shouldn't all superheroes be a bit terrifying?"

"Hmph." I settled into the armchair situated next to the bed. At Dove's proximity, the fizzle of a memory tingled but didn't materialize.

He tensed as I offered the mug.

"Relax. I don't enact retribution before noon. It's just coffee."

He reached out, nostrils flared, and took the cup carefully, his fingers never touching mine. He stared down at the dark liquid, his eyes veiled behind his glasses in the glare from the lion-shaped bedside lamp.

"Thank you." He took a tentative sip.

One of the memories I had was a cup of black coffee steaming at his elbow as he questioned me in my cell. It was fuzzy and not long before my memories trailed off into the gloomy nothing that took up so much extra space in my head.

"What was your job for her?"

Dove didn't drop my gaze as he answered. His eyes were much clearer than the night before, when they were clouded with fear and pain. They looked an even brighter blue now than they appeared in the prison, but that could have been due to the dingy lighting there. "To keep captives alive and compliant, while she assessed their capacity to potentially become enhanced by experimental infusions."

Kavoh was making Extrahumans. We knew that.

"To become Extrahumans," I murmured.

Dove tilted his head.

"That's what we call people that she gives superhuman abilities."

Dove tightened his long fingers against the mug, seemingly mustering courage to voice a question.

I cut in before he could. "The bacteria helped with your work?"

"The FR-10 Bacteria is basically a psychological long island iced tea." Dove massaged his forehead. "As you know, it'll seriously mess your system up. Besides working as a means of control, since fear of the bacteria's activation coerces someone into doing whatever their tormenter says, it also helps determine tolerance under stress, how one's body adapts to additions to their system . . ."

I swirled my coffee. "You engineered it?"

He slumped like he wanted to disappear, and nodded miserably. "I—I was prepared to die there last night . . . Thank you again for saving my life. There's nothing I can say to thank you enough."

I cocked my head. "You know how you can pay me back?"

Dread washed over Dove's face, draining the little color he'd gotten back with sleep.

"You clearly know some of my memories are missing." I scoffed. "You must have a hunch at what a trigger could be. Give them back."

His returning stare was immovable as a glacier. "I won't."

Heat flared across my face, fury a stone pit at the center of my heart.

"Well"—I shrugged—"sounds like you and I are settled." I turned on the TV and glued my eyes to it.

"Listen—"

"Do *not* tell me what to do. I'm free of your sadistic micro monsters, and you have no authority here. Unless . . . Did we become friends somewhere along the way of that epic nightmare you caused me? Because if we did, I. Don't. *Remember.*" My words were acid. Dove looked like I'd struck him. "I'm your keeper, not your friend, so just behave while we decide what to do with you."

Dove studied me for a long time. I felt his gaze tracing my face, but I refused to look his way.

Eventually, he gave up and pretended to watch TV too.

We stayed like that for what felt like an eternity, until Bane trudged in looking slightly better than earlier. He still wore his pajamas, and he had simply added his Shadow helmet to the ensemble. He balanced a tray full of enough bagels and cream cheese to feed ten people. Dove looked like he'd been handed gold when Bane passed him one on a napkin. I focused on devouring mine.

Bane leaned against my chair, since eating would necessitate withdrawing his visor and revealing a portion of his face. While I noshed, Bane simply angled his head toward Dove and gave him his most intimidating Shadow stare.

It certainly worked, as Dove swallowed far more than was warranted for a bagel.

Finishing mine, I took my time primly wiping my fingers on a napkin, then glanced at my uncle, happy to play this game of merciless vigilante duo with him.

Bane propped a chin on his fist. "How's our captive this morning?"

"He was just saying how he refuses to help restore my memories." I sniffed.

A sigh of disappointment reverberated from Bane's helmet.

Dove held up his hands. "Melbourne, I—"

The instant my name left Dove's mouth, I was on him.

I knocked him backward and straddled his chest, pinning his shoulders to the mattress with my knees and wrapping one hand around his throat. I squeezed enough to let him know the threat was real.

"Silhouette," Bane cautioned just as I withdrew my fist, holding it like a guillotine above Dove's face. He gasped, his throat bobbing against my palm.

"You know my name," I accused, deathly quiet. "How?"

"I didn't tell anyone," he gasped.

I pressed harder, dropping my masked face close, crowding out everything in his field of vision except me. "Is your word supposed to mean something to me?"

Bane cleared his throat. "I know I'm not one to talk, but maybe we should discuss this calmly?"

I didn't move for several moments. Then, with a resigned sigh, I climbed off Dove and smoothed my clothes to hide my shaking hands. Bane steadied me with a touch to the shoulder. "I've only combed part of the data we retrieved from the complex, but I didn't find evidence they knew who you were, which means this one"—he nodded at Dove—"didn't tell his friends."

Dove rubbed his throat. "I didn't, and they're not my friends," he said hoarsely. Realization struck across his pale face. "I'll tell you everything I know. But I can also help as you track down Kavoh and stop her. If you let me."

My eyes narrowed. "We have no reason to believe you."

"I'm inclined to, nonetheless," Bane said. "Think about it. If anyone else knew your identity at that place, they'd use it against you while you were there, or come after me. They would have done *something*." He pulled off his helmet and ruffled his hair into random angles like he'd been electrocuted. "Crown's Prince of Chaos, terrible to meet you. You've already met my niece." Bane's smile was sharp, letting Dove know he was safe for the moment, but standing on *terribly* thin ice.

I pulled my sweatshirt's hood up and over my eyes and groaned. "Heir to the throne, yeah."

"She's basically acting Prime Minister. I'm only here for PR stunts," Bane finished with a wink before ripping into a bagel with absolutely no decorum.

"That metaphor went off the rails quickly," I muttered, holding my masked face, hesitant to abandon the shield it provided.

Sucking in a breath, I pressed the buttons. It released and dropped to my lap as I massaged the lines from my face.

Dove gaped. It occurred to me he'd never seen me without my mask before.

"Hi," I said flatly.

Bane took a final, massive bite, tried to start talking, and nearly choked. He chewed for a few seconds, pulling faces until I smacked him on the back, forcing an aggressive coughing fit.

"Thanks," he gasped. He cleared his throat multiple times and pointed at our guest. "So. Dove. Our options for what to do about you are limited. Kavoh Labs made a statement this morning after news broke about the facility—one of their "auxiliary labs"—burning. They claimed it was an electrical fire based on unsealed wiring from the recent explosions. Since the building was 'uninhabitable' as they claimed, the only one there last night was a staff member attempting to retrieve salvageable research." He took a dramatic pause before delivering the last tidbit. "The doctor, one Mr. Ian Dove, sadly perished."

I started, remembering Dove had a first name. Disguising the movement, I snagged the remote and clicked to one of Crown's news stations, and sure enough, the Kavoh Labs fire was the top story. Dove's ID photo that I'd seen so many times accompanied it. It didn't list his name beneath, just: FREAK FIRE RESULTS IN TRAGEDY

Bane handed me his phone, and I read the excerpt from

the article he had pulled up there and summarized. "Per a statement from Doctor Kavoh, the loss of life was needless, tragic, and due entirely to your 'undying commitment' to your work."

Dove tilted his head sharply to one side. "I died?" The news didn't stop him from taking another bite.

"You're *dead*," I clarified.

Bane's head bobbed. "For all intents and purposes. We don't think she'd declare you dead unless she really believed it. The fire left nothing behind. Kavoh had probably arranged for minimal remains to be found anyway, since the state of your body would be suspect."

"Not to mention whatever other evidence was there," I added.

Dove didn't look the least bit sad.

Bane leaned forward, meeting Dove's gaze. "You can't be Ian Dove anymore. You know things they don't want out in the open. I can't imagine the lengths they'd go to to keep you quiet. Do you have somewhere to go? Friends, family?"

"No," Dove and I said in unison.

My face reddened. "We've been keeping tabs on Kavoh and her people. I've researched you."

Dove blinked rapidly.

Bane rubbed his chin and rescued us from the stretching silence. "I don't want to leave you out to dry, but we can't send you out into the open knowing our secrets. Our team can build you a new identity, and help you start life wherever you like."

My stomach squeezed at the thought. But if I didn't want him here, or for him to leave, what did I want?

Bane continued, "We'll do that, but in exchange, you have to help us take down Kavoh first."

My thoughts ground to a halt. Bane's ability to understand me really impressed me sometimes. Keeping Dove around for a little while would help with my memories, but also set an end date on his time here, so I wouldn't be stuck around him indefinitely. Dove got to do some penance and leave at the end, if he earned it.

"I think you should stay," I said finally. Dove opened his mouth to ask something, but I interrupted. "We need to stop Kavoh, and you're our best shot."

Bane rubbed his hands together. "Do we have a deal, doctor?"

"I'll stay," he said, sounding breathless. My heart squeezed as I recognized the tone in his voice. The desperate longing for a family when you didn't have one. "I'll tell you what I know. I'd do that regardless. I—I was part of something terrible. I can't be excused, I know, but I can help you stop them from doing further harm."

Bane pinned him with an unforgiving glare I wouldn't want to be on the receiving end of. "Good. Now, remember this; your safekeeping is a gift in exchange for good behavior and assistance in bringing down Kavoh. One step out of line, and I'll wipe your memories back to the instant you decided to nab Silhouette and dump you on the doorstep of a prison with copies of all the data I pulled from your facility. This family's safety isn't a game."

Dove nodded wordlessly. The whole room had gone icy.

Bane blew a sesame seed off his sleeve. "Great! Now that that's settled, you should rest. Mel and I have very important, busy lives to lead."

I dropped my head into my hands. "Could you have phrased it any lamer?"

"What?" he demanded. "It's true."

"You have a desk job, and I'm in college. Lions, Uncle Bane."

He scrubbed at the back of his head, mussing his already snarled hair. "I probably could have."

"Please don't try." I eased to my feet. I held out a hand to Dove, who stared at me blankly. A smile hinted at the corner of his mouth. "I can take your coffee mug," I clarified.

"Right." He scrambled to hand me the now-empty mug, which I tugged from his grip with a hint of attitude, so he knew he was still on my list.

"The rest of our team will be back later today. They're the masterminds that can build your new life, and we still need to convince them you're worth it."

I turned on my heel and left.

Bane followed silently, though he searched my face after closing and locking the door behind us. "Are you all right?"

I considered before answering, squaring my shoulders. "This is the right thing to do, but it doesn't make it any less difficult."

Bane frowned, shoving his hands deep in his pockets. "How do you think he knows your name?"

"I have no idea." I leaned against the wall, tossing my mask from hand to hand. "Do you mind if I get out of here till Chezza and Vennie are home?"

"Do what you need. I've got your back."

"Thank you." I handed him the coffee mug, suddenly adamant to be rid of it, like it was electrified.

Snagging Bane's helmet in exchange, I speed-walked to the Den, and once safely inside, dialed Gem.

She picked up on the first ring. "Queer royalty speaking. What appeal do you have for me, my loyal subject?"

I snorted. "Are you free right now? I need a friend date. I have lots of stories."

"Sold!" Gem crowed. "Give me half an hour. Let's meet at Red Ramen."

🔥🔥🔥

I CHASED AN EGG AROUND MY BOWL WITH A SPOON. GEM EYED me, her hazel gaze surely reading every thought of mine through my posture. We were tucked into the corner of our favorite ramen shop, shielded by tall potted plants.

Gem whistled after I finished telling her all that had gone down since my disastrous solo trip out as Silhouette. "That is a *lot.*"

I nodded, my mouth full of broth, and swallowed. "Thanks for waiting for me to be ready to talk about it."

"Of course . . . And to process a kidnapping? Any time, girl. Especially since I wasn't there to suffer through this one with you."

I snorted into my soup. "I can't believe how angry I am about my missing memories."

Gem slashed her chopsticks through the air. "It totally makes sense. It's a complete violation of your mind, on top of the fact they kidnapped you and violated your actual physical freedom. Any idea what this Dove guy wanted you to forget?"

I offered a noncommittal grimace, and Gem took the cue that I wasn't ready to share. "At least show me a photo of him?"

I pulled up Dove's old headshot from the news headlines and slid my phone across the table. Gem's shriek rustled the wall of leaves around us. "You're living with a *hot doctor?!*"

"Gem! What the actual hell?" I frantically scanned the restaurant for anyone looking our way.

"I'm sorry," she hissed in an impressively loud whisper. "But even when you were keeping tabs on him before, you never thought to tell me he was sexy?"

I balked, at a loss for words. "He's—His face is busted." I hedged, refusing to look at her.

"Aren't you the one who busted it?"

"Enough, enough, enough." I snatched my phone back and stuck my tongue out at her. "Unhelpful. You've heard about my luxurious spring break getaway," I deadpanned. "Tell me about Cancun."

THE FOLLOWING AFTERNOON, MY EYES CRACKED OPEN AFTER an intense post-class nap to brighter light than when I'd fallen asleep. I crawled to the edge of my bed, trailing blankets. A few blinks and I figured out why it felt like someone was shining a spotlight into my room.

The descending sun was bouncing off of lots and lots of snow.

It had flurried while I slept. A light blanket of it covered the grass, with only fistfuls of the most robust tufts sticking up out of the snow. Fat, cheerful flakes drifted past the window, mocking me. With a groan, I shoved out of bed and added slippers and a hoodie to my already cozy ensemble of leggings and a fitted, long-sleeve tech shirt. I'd sped through homework before my nap, so the rest of the late afternoon was fully my own.

The house was quiet, which meant Bane was still at work. A good sign, though it meant I was down a sparring partner. I zipped downstairs and stuffed a delicious but poorly shaped croissant, Bane's latest baking endeavor, in my mouth and slipped to the hallway behind the kitchen. I passed my fingerprints over the sensor behind the lioness painting and opened the door.

At the foot of the stairs, the Den echoed with the soft whirr of machines from the locked safe room and the frantic clicking of Vennie's fingers on keys. A complex string of code ran across the LUMA. I didn't even pretend to unravel it as I swallowed another monstrous bite of croissant.

I checked the weather on my phone, not wanting to interrupt Vennie's no doubt much more important use of the LUMA's expansive curved screen. "Ugh. It's supposed to snow all night."

"Yet another point in favor of my 'leave the house as little as possible' lifestyle," Vennie said without looking away from his work.

As I got to know Vennie better, he shared with me what Chezza and Bane already knew. Vennie really did prefer to stay inside the Leo house as much as possible. He cited several reasons, from PTSD from his time in private security (he never denied one of his old job titles was 'mercenary') to his general preference for introversion. I envied that Vennie knew himself so well. He knew the exact amount of social time he needed to feel whole. It amounted to a dinner or two a month at a dive bar with his handful of friends that weren't Chezza, Bane, and me. He got his fulfillment from his work—with us, with freelance gigs from private entities and non-profits, from his online gaming community.

"This had better be the last snow of the season," I grumbled, stepping to our practice mats to stretch. "Where's Chezza?"

"Well, after you sprung the news on us last night about our new roommate, most of the alterations we could handle in-house. Not all of them, though," Vennie said, finally looking up. The LUMA's light gilded his black hair with streaks of blue. "She took Dove to get some sketchy Lasik."

I snorted, but my follow-up question was interrupted by

the elevator's soft ding. Chezza and Vennie had greeted Dove with healthy skepticism but complete agreement with our decision to keep him on board to help us take down Kavoh. When asked if they could help build Dove a new identity, they'd jumped at the chance like they'd been given a holiday present.

"'Sketchy?' Please." Chezza emerged from the elevator, helping a wobbly Dove maneuver on Bane's crutches to ease the pressure on his leg. "The building is nondescript, and Dr. McDowell knows how to be discreet. The surgery itself was perfectly respectable. But we needed to avoid a paper trail," she said, shooting a look at her brother. She guided Dove to the couch. "Take it easy for a little while."

I forced myself to not stare, instead shifting my focus to loosening the knots in my shoulders.

"That one guy you got to close the gap in my teeth was definitely not board certified," Vennie accused.

"Oh, for sure. But the price is right, and I like the hotdog stand next door while I wait. You've got a great smile, so it's fine."

Vennie grumbled and returned to his code.

As they bickered, I settled into a routine of push-ups and crunches, ignoring the magnetic pull toward the man on the couch—the "hot doctor" as Gem had called him. I moved into planks, directing my heated face toward the floor.

Chezza and Vennie huddled together, speaking Tagalog and finalizing Dove's forged documents. Dove reclined on the couch, seemingly content to listen to the soundtrack of our lives. It wasn't long before Bane's familiar shout punctuated our productivity from the top of the stairs. "It's snowing . . . It's snowing . . . It's snowwwwww-ING! Also, just saw spoilers for *Drag Bonanza*. Apparently, they sent Sparx home. Can you believe—"

I eased out of the mostly-there split I was in as Bane hit the bottom of the stairs and pressed my hands against my ears. "Aw, come on! I thought we agreed to stay off social media until we watched it together."

Chezza cut into our banter. "Let us show you what we did today," she interrupted, motioning for Dove to get up from the couch as Vennie pulled up a bunch of different documents on the LUMA.

It was then I got a good look at him. Dove rose and stood awkwardly next to the LUMA, revealing the results of the Ello's long day of work.

Impolite as hell, I stared.

Chezza hadn't simply changed Dove's look. She'd used her damn gift to improve upon his natural features. His already dark hair was dyed night black and cut back a few inches into a tidier style than what he'd sported before. He rubbed a hand over it absently, like he already missed it. My insides certainly missed the way it had curled around the nape of his neck. I smothered those feelings with a gulp. His nose was less straight than in his old photo, thanks to my punching it in. Chezza had changed the shape of his brows entirely, and it looked like she'd tattooed the base of his lashes dark. His glasses were gone, making his intense stare even more captivating than before. Clare must have sent over some clothes in his size. A simple cobalt sweatshirt hugged his strong shoulders, and his jeans fit perfectly. His feet were bare, as he'd kicked off his shoes and socks the minute he made it to the couch.

All this coupled with the improved posture, since he no longer answered to his old employer . . . It was like we'd lifted an anvil off Dove's shoulders. He looked entirely different. Happier. More full of life. With his posture unweighted, his height was even more evident. He easily dwarfed us all.

He looked incredible. Handsome and strong and shy.

I shifted from foot to foot and chewed my lip in an effort to remind myself I HATED THIS MAN.

Then he smiled at me. It was devastating. *He* was devastating.

It didn't make me angry at all, and that made me furious.

"You're welcome," I said.

Dove balked. "Um, thank y—"

"For fixing your nose," I cut in with a wicked smirk.

On the LUMA next to him, Vennie had pulled up Dove's old picture from the Kavoh Labs website. Chezza lounged at her brother's station, eyeing me. Bane was somewhere behind me, no doubt watching my reaction too.

Suddenly uncomfortable, I turned my back on all of them and headed to my cubby to start dressing in my Silhouette suit.

"A standing ovation is what's warranted, Mel," Chezza called flatly.

With a wince, I faced her and Vennie. "You guys are amazing, really."

Chezza raised an eyebrow, but she accepted it. She was one of my closest friends, and I feared she was reading my mind.

Vennie cleared his throat. "We decided after much back and forth that the easiest route was the least obvious. Dove still looks like Dove, so let's make him a Dove." Clearly, he was pleased with himself, and I couldn't help but be intrigued.

I slipped my suit pants over my leggings, keeping my Crown City FC hoodie on over top. I gave Vennie my attention as I sat on my bench and pulled on my boots.

"I'm confused," Bane said, shrugging the jacket of his super suit on.

"Standard operating procedure," Chezza and I chorused in unison.

He flipped us off as Dove explained.

"I'm not from Crown City originally. Kavoh relocated all her staff here. I don't have any family." He rubbed his arm. "Thankfully, in this case, I guess? No one's going to disagree with my new identity."

"So, what's this new identity?" I demanded.

I shimmied out of my sweatshirt and pulled my jacket on. Tugging up the zipper, my fingertips skimmed the edges of my flame emblem.

Chezza clapped her hands, and Vennie gestured to the documents on the LUMA. "Leos, may I introduce you to Caleb Dove? Older brother of Ian. Long estranged, but he flew to Crown upon hearing of his younger brother's untimely demise. With some of our more brilliant tech, we altered his fingerprints, and Mel, you actually did change the shape of his face with your punch."

"And," Chezza continued, "once he's been properly fed for a few weeks and spent some time in the sun, you'll see a familial resemblance, but people won't believe they're the same person."

Dove—Caleb—reached up as if to adjust his glasses that were no longer there. The gesture made my lower insides go all twisty.

Bane broke my reverie with a slow clap. "Well done. It's genius."

I tied the front of my hair back as I looked at the screen, surveying Caleb Dove's new, immaculately forged records. There was a driver's license, school records, résumé, and work history. No doctorate anymore. His fake past seemed utterly ordinary. They had aged him up a few years to twenty-eight years old.

A deeply confusing soup of emotions roiled inside me. I didn't want to unravel or understand them, so I stuck my mask to my face, using it to hide my features as I searched for a distraction, for some way to fill my time and delay having to figure out how Caleb being around impacted my life.

I could be civil for a little while, if nothing else. I knew what it was like to start fresh here. How hard it could be if you felt alone. I walked up to Caleb, my face flat, his hesitant, and surveyed him up and down. Chewing on my thoughts, I looked for remnants of the old Dove in his new face.

Finally, I stuck my hand out. "Nice to meet you, Caleb."

He took my hand. A disbelieving smile completed his transformation into someone else entirely, and the heat from his palm seemed to dwarf that which radiated from my glove. He found his voice, and though it was still slightly hollow, it sounded happier than I'd ever heard him.

"Silhouette?" he asked. There was a light in his eyes now. Small, flickering, but there.

Unable to peel my eyes from him. I dropped his hand like a normal person would drop a hot coal. "Mel's fine, really." I tugged on the ends of my hair. "Are there many people in this city who would recognize you?"

"Besides some of Kavoh's people, no. I hardly ever left the facility."

"In how long?"

"Years."

Bane whistled. "Talk about a thorough brain-washing."

Caleb shrugged. "I didn't have anyone. I was overconfident. It made me easy to manipulate. I'm sure Kavoh saw that when she scouted me."

The sympathy working its way through my bones made me squirmy, so I headed toward the LUMA. "Did you have a nice weekend with your folks?" I asked Chezza and Vennie. The night before had been too hectic to get the details.

Chezza's eyes lit. "It was wonderful. They fed us so much good food, and they only pried into our personal lives for the first night, which isn't bad for them."

"They're into this game show now, where contestants have to sing karaoke while suspended over a giant fish tank." Vennie added, "I didn't get the point, but it was fun to laugh at."

"I wish they hadn't turned my old room into a gym, though." Chezza sighed. "Last time, Ven and I had to fight over who had to sleep on the couch, but their solution this time was to put bunk beds in Vennie's old room. Like, full on children's bunk beds."

Vennie laughed. "Ugh, yeah, and you snore."

"You recite computer code while you sleep!" Chezza shot back. "That's not a relaxing lullaby, either."

Bane sidled up to us, fully dressed as the Shadow. "I've been told I practice stand-up comedy."

"By who?" I rubbed my forehead. "Never mind. I don't want to know." I turned a glare at Caleb, who wisely gulped. "It's time to tell us what you know."

BANE PULLED ME ASIDE. "I THINK WE SHOULD SLOW OUR ROLL, Toasty. I know he's got some penance to do, but maybe we can let the guy rest for more than a day?"

I pursed my lips. Bane's tone wasn't judgmental. We made decisions together; he was simply suggesting a pause in my rampage to stop Kavoh. Usually, I was the one to keep us from charging ahead unprepared. The role-reversal jarred me.

"And . . ." His eyes darted away. "I wouldn't be upset if you took a bit of a rest, either."

I blew my hair out of my face. "You're right. Thank you for pointing that out." I raised my voice. "Chezza, Ven?" The Ellos turned our way. "Family meeting?"

They helped Caleb to the couch, then we gathered around the LUMA. Chezza crossed her arms. Vennie pulled his chair over and perched on the edge.

After quick deliberation, we settled on providing Caleb with a blank notebook—he hadn't earned internet rights in our minds yet—and tasked him with listing everything he knew about Kavoh. The slowness of it all made me grind my teeth, even though I knew taking down someone as dangerous as her warranted careful planning.

In the meantime, Bane and I headed into the night.

"You good?" Bane asked as we paused along the lakeshore and reviewed live surveillance footage Vennie pushed to our suits' screens.

My nastiness must be bad if it was apparent to Bane. I shook the tension from my shoulders. "Adjusting to our new circumstances. Give me time. I'll get there."

He rested his chin on a fist, but didn't ask anything further.

Vennie's recon revealed the Gold Guard was on the prowl through most of downtown testing some new tech, so Bane and I kept to the city's outskirts, keeping an eye on people walking home alone in the dark. The night was quiet, and I didn't appreciate it. It allowed my thoughts to race as my heated boots melted the small layer of snow to puddles around my feet.

"We still need to figure out a story for why Caleb's sticking around Crown, and why he's with us," Bane mused.

Vennie grunted his agreement over the line. As the only one of us with a rigid work schedule, Chezza had gone to bed.

I kicked at the sludge, then looked up to watch the moon gild the choppy lake, how its light bounced against the distant skyscrapers. "Why don't you hire him? To help with the philanthropic side of Leo Optics."

"You want him to work for the Foundation?"

"We need a grant writer," I mused. "We could sell it to the media like this—he

came to Crown to grieve his brother, and being sympathetic to loss, you took him under your wing. He could be your protegee."

Bane's brows came together. His withdrawn visor allowed the icy air to blow on his face. "That's you."

I grinned. "Duh. But this is for show." I looked away again. "Might as well be useful if we're stuck with him."

Bane chewed over my words as Vennie cleared his throat.

"Speaking of . . . He, uh, can hear you. I've got you guys on speaker like usual. Should I switch to an earpiece?"

I coughed and recovered. "Well, it's the truth."

Caleb's voice came over the line. "I'd like to be helpful. I like the idea. Of working for your Foundation."

Bane's eyebrows disappeared beneath the top of his helmet. "Well, that's that. Great idea. I'll get the paperwork started tomorrow."

Slightly bashful, I changed the subject. "So, if the facility's destroyed, where has Kavoh moved her operation?"

Caleb's voice sounded again. "I know she has other facilities, but I was never told where. If she's doing anything illegal at her public lab, she's definitely hiding it well."

"That matches what we've hypothesized."

Bane rubbed his chin. "Can we use any of what we've learned about the first facility that might help us locate the second?"

"That's actually a great idea," I said.

"*Actually?*"

I stuck out my tongue. "How about a compromise? You want me to rest? I can rest and research. Look for other properties with the same qualities as the first facility."

Vennie piped in. "I can dig to see if she procured any other property via the same method. A shell corporation or whatever."

I nodded enthusiastically, surely giving Vennie a dizzying view through my bobbing mask cam.

"She's good at keeping things above-board. None of us could leave if we wanted to. Her control extends so deep . . ." Caleb's voice trailed off.

"She'll slip up eventually," I said. "She has to."

Bane grimaced. "This isn't what I had in mind . . ."

An echoing crash tore through our conversation. Bane and I snapped toward the direction of the noise. Bane's visor slid closed.

It sounded again, this time a louder crunch. Based on my enhanced hearing, I estimated it to be coming from a quarter mile away.

I jerked my head toward the sound and sprinted off, Bane following close behind.

As we approached, the sounds continued but had quieted to the faint bouncing of metal. We were in one of the more rural parts of town, and the sound's source was slowly moving. I trailed it through dense woods, seeing the flash of lights through the thinning trees. I poked my head out to survey the dirt road. A pickup truck went flying down it, trailing a mailbox as it swerved back and forth across the gravel.

"Drunk driver," I said, the words a curse.

Bane added his own profanities.

"You want the driver, or pedestrian safety duty?" Bane asked.

"I'll take the driver," I growled, itching for a challenge.

"Shout if you need help," Bane called, already loping toward the single stoplight a mile down the road and the scant businesses huddled around it: a gas station, a tattoo parlor, and a small pub with a raucous group of patrons out front, braving the cold for a chance to smoke and stare at the stars.

Taking a moment to compose a plan, I vaulted from the tree line and chased down the truck, carefully pulling up behind its erratic swerving. The mailbox dislodged, and I dodged as it tumbled down the middle of the road. Putting on a burst of speed, I launched myself and landed in the bed of the truck with a thump the driver was too inebriated to notice.

Through the comms line, there was a sudden hitched breath. Caleb wasn't used to seeing me in action.

Fighting the whipping wind, I braced my hands on the cab. Once I was sure of my footing, I leaned over to thump my knuckles against the driver's window. He gasped and jerked the wheel. Gritting my teeth and barely keeping my balance, I punched through the glass and grabbed the steering wheel to keep us on the road.

The driver hit the gas.

"Moron," I grumbled.

Gripping the truck's body so hard I left dents, I leveraged my way around the truck's side and shimmied feet first into the cab, smashing the man's face back against the seat. I crawled into his lap and kicked his feet away from the pedals until I was finally able to press my boot against the brake.

The man fought me weakly, spitting and growling, but I had my hand over his face and he couldn't wrangle his arms around me in his inebriated state. As soon as the car slowed to a reasonable ten miles an hour, I put his seatbelt on him and pulled the parking brake. The truck spun, and I launched myself back out the window.

I landed with a gasp and rolled into a ditch as the car ground to a halt, half off the road a few yards away from me.

Allowing myself a moment, I whispered, "Lions, I hate driving."

I shoved upright and pulled grass from my hair. I strolled up to the broken window, where the man's head lolled and leaked a thin trail of blood. He groaned, in a daze.

"Neutralized," I murmured to Bane.

I quickly searched the man's pockets for a wallet. I held his license up to my eye level, so Vennie could see it through the camera in my mask.

A beat of silence, and Vennie whistled. Caleb made a disdainful sound, almost like a growl.

"This guy's done time for domestic violence," Vennie said.

With a grunt, I reached in and jammed his seatbelt, then clamped the door shut, so he'd have to be cut from the vehicle, doing the same to the other door so he couldn't run.

"Patch me through to CCPD, please?"

Vennie acquiesced, and a ringtone sounded in my ear.

"9-1-1, what's your emergency?"

"Hi. A drunk driver crashed on Old Linden Highway right before it meets Clementine. Whatever his punishment, can you try and get him paired with an addiction specialist?"

I hung up before the person on the other end could get a question in, making a mental note to track if my instructions were followed later.

Bane jogged out of the trees to meet me. "Nicely done! I didn't even have to talk to the barflies, which is kind of a bummer. They usually buy me drinks."

I shook my head. "We've got plenty of booze at home. We need to go. The dispatcher might report the odd call to the Gold Guard."

It wasn't the first terse, anonymous call we'd made to the police department.

"After you," Bane said with a flourished bow.

"Race you." I flashed a wicked grin. I slammed my max heat button and took off.

Bane didn't reply, but I heard the press of his own max cold button and the whoosh of him sprinting through the trees in pursuit.

🔥🔥🔥

"So . . . Call it a tie?" Bane proposed as we walked through the garage. He'd removed his helmet once we cleared the boundary wall to expose his face fully to the falling snow. He shook his hair, showering me with wet flakes.

Throwing up my hands as a shield, I snorted. "Yeah, right. I had three tenths of a second on you, at least."

He shoved me playfully. "I dunno, Toasty . . ."

"Should we ask Vennie to check the cameras?" I challenged, leaning against the elevator's back wall as it descended beneath the Leo house.

Bane chewed the inside of his cheek and backed down. "Now, no need for that."

"That's what I thought."

When the doors cracked open to the Den, my eyes tracked straight to Caleb, who was perched on the arm of the old couch. His head lifted, and his eyes snapped to me. The way the movement accentuated the lines of his neck was immensely distracting.

I cleared my throat and headed to my cubby, shucking my suit as I went. I hung it up carefully and drew my hoodie over my compression top, then gently wiped the inside of my suit with a disinfectant cloth. Finally, I removed my mask, pressing my fingers to the hidden buttons that released it from my face.

"Glad that's over," I started, ready to lament my distaste for drunk drivers.

As the words left my mouth, a surreal mist frothed across my eyesight as a fragment of memory resurfaced. I was swamped with the feeling of fading panic and the sterile scent of fresh-cleaned tile.

"It's over," Caleb said.

We were back in Kavoh's facility. I'd only known him as Dove, though I couldn't divorce his new name from his identity in my mind.

I managed a shaky laugh. "This particular moment of horror, maybe." My voice was raw and cracked on the words like I'd been strangled.

I wiped moisture from my mask. My hands came away red. I'd scraped myself while Nicklai tortured me. My vision shuttered black again, and I gasped. A sob erupted from my chest.

Nausea swept in next, and I retched, hacking phlegm all over the tiles. Caleb eased me forward with a firm hand around my upper arm, so I didn't choke.

Caleb swore, and the pressure of his arms encircled me. I snarled and tried shoving him away, but he was stronger than he looked, and I had been cold for too long. My sight returned for a second and his arms withdrew, but his face was close to mine. His nose was swollen from where I'd punched him, the bruise going yellow around the edges. His cheekbones were high, the skin beneath them sunken. Up close, he looked less intimidating and more . . . exhausted.

"Listen," he said.

I blinked. That was the best he was getting from me.

He continued, "I know you can't trust me, so I need you to just tolerate me for . . . fifteen minutes." He looked desperate; the calmness he wore up until this point clearly a mask.

"Why?" My eyesight flickered a few times in rapid succession. From blackness to those eyes and back again. I couldn't stop shaking, and blood or tears or both ran along the edge of my mask.

"You don't want to meet who's coming."

"Kavoh," I breathed.

"How do you know her name?"

I bit my lip and shook my head, refusing to answer.

"Nicklai will come back with a vengeance, eventually. I can help you now, but I don't know about later."

Whatever his motive, could I afford to not take this chance? Debilitated by the bacteria, I was in even worse shape than when I arrived. I'd lost track of time, and I didn't know how close my family was to launching their rescue.

I nodded stiffly, the motion barely discernible amidst my shivering.

Caleb shrugged out of his suit's jacket and draped it around my shoulders, his hands' pressure light through the fabric.

He hesitated, as if bracing himself. Something sparked in his eyes when he slid his arms around me. One under my knees, one behind my back. He lifted me in a shockingly smooth movement. The room spun, and my head lolled back, too heavy to lift. Dove hitched his shoulder, nudging my head to roll against his chest.

It felt strangely nice to simply be tired and terrified. I promised myself it was only for a minute. Caleb smelled like a crisp breeze through tree branches at midnight. Blood from my face smeared across his shirt. Good riddance.

He swept from the room, carrying me easily. I memorized the route we took. A sharp right, then through a door at the end of the hall. He kicked it open. I squeezed my eyes shut, fighting sudden nausea.

Caleb somehow unlocked another door, though I didn't wobble in his hold. He shoved through into warmer air than I'd felt since waking up in the facility.

Before I could make sense of where we were, my vision went black again. I sucked in a breath. There were shadows before me, but less agitated and violent than before. Caleb shifted, and I was set somewhere soft. His arms gently receded. I reached out, blind, to clamp down on some part of his arm. He froze. I panted as the shadows roiled, gathering their nerve to onslaught me once more. He was my tether to reality.

"It's not real. Whatever you're seeing, it's not really there." Caleb's hoarse voice floated through, and light broke through the blackness.

As the room drifted into focus, I pried my fingers off him.

Caleb receded, and I turned my head to track him. He stalked to the only door and turned a number of impressive locks. I was sure we hadn't left the building. What else was here causing him to need such measures of protection?

He'd brought me to a room much like the one I'd been trapped in, though the bathroom area had a curtain for privacy, and there were the makings of a sparse but functional kitchen in the corner. A yoga mat covered the scant free space, and a dated TV sat on a dresser. There was a half empty bottle of red wine on the counter, alongside a loaf of bread and massive jar of peanut butter. A single plastic chair and a card table were to my right. I rested on a bed twice the size of my cot, though just as low and stiff. My blood dripped onto the pillowcase.

I dug my fingers into the comforter, grounding myself in reality.

Caleb glanced over every few moments as he made his way around the . . . apartment? His dark brows were furrowed. He paced to the kitchen, opened a drawer, and withdrew a long, sharp cooking knife. I stiffened, but instead of brandishing it at me, he stretched and easily stowed it atop the wall's single cabinet.

I nearly snorted, realizing his actions were so I couldn't reach it. As if a knife would do me much good in this state. As if I would need it once I got my strength back. Caleb checked the locks on the door again, strode back to the kitchen, grabbed a glass, and disappeared to the bathroom. There was the brief sound of a faucet. Finally, he came my way. He withdrew the chair a healthy four feet from me before sitting, and held out the glass in my direction.

In my defense, I had just endured a violent physical and psychological attack from bacteria trying to devour me from within my own body and was more or less saved by someone who had injected said bacteria in me in the first place, so I peered at the glass like it was full of poison. I stared at it, shaking. Eventually, Caleb gave up and set the glass on the table.

"Why are you helping me?" I demanded, my voice raw.

Soft, uneven footsteps pulled me from my reverie. I set my mask on the shelf and turned with a frown.

Caleb stood sheepishly before me, leaning heavily on one crutch with a wisp of dark hair fallen over his forehead.

Blinking rapidly, I tried to remedy the man in my present with the one from my recent past.

"What you did was incredible." His voice was tinted with awe.

I squinted. *What did I do?* The returning memory had me off balance.

"Thanks," I said, covering my confusion with confidence. *Oh, right, the careening pickup truck.* I crossed my arms. "Did I not do a lot of acrobatics back at the facility? You'll have to fill me in, because, you know." I tapped my head like an asshole.

He stammered, cocking his head. "Erm, no. I saw a little of it . . ."

"The night you captured me at the shipping yard."

"Yeah." He shifted from foot to foot. "Can I ask you something?"

"Sure."

Maybe we were finally getting somewhere. I knew he'd helped me, and he seemed marginally more forthcoming with information.

"How does the suit work?"

This question, for some reason, burned rage straight up my spine. Of all the things. All the questions. This was what he elected to say across the strenuous tether of our truce?

I let my rage take the lead, enjoying its fierce tide coursing through my veins.

Like some trap snapping shut on an herbivorous animal, I whipped my arm out and snatched the crutch from under his arm.

Caleb fell on his ass, shock contorting his face. He hardly flinched as his tailbone connected with the concrete floor.

I twisted the crutch, the aluminum splitting with a crack as I easily ripped the thing in two, then four. Part of me knew I was being awful. I ignored it.

Tearing it once more, I gathered the pieces in one hand and squeezed until they were a sad melted mass in the middle, bound by my handprint. I dropped the mangled crutch at Caleb's feet.

"The suit's got nothing to do with it."

Caleb's angelic mouth hung open. I turned with a sniff and walked away. I'd made it to the stairs before the rage morphed into shame.

"'Nothing' is kind of an understatement. The suit helps," Vennie muttered.

Shit. I needed to apologize to Vennie. Profusely. But I couldn't turn back now.

Halfway up the stairs, I heard the shuffling of Bane's feet behind me. He tailed me to the foyer. I spun to face him, but kept my eyes rooted to the marble beneath my feet.

"I know this is hard, Mel," he started. "I'm sorry. I hate to see you uncomfortable, but . . ."

I scuffed a foot over the Leo family seal patterned on the floor and met his blue gray gaze. "Don't be sorry. I know helping Caleb is the right thing to do. Part of me also hates it. I'll try to be less of a jerk."

He grinned and ruffled my hair, though the smile didn't reach his eyes. "You're never a jerk, but this was the closest I've seen you come to it."

I twined my fingers together, sudden tears pricking behind

my eyes. "He bested me, Uncle Bane. Him and Kavoh's people . . . They had me completely under their control. I was helpless. How can I forgive him?"

Bane shook his head. "You don't know what another day would have brought. You would have found a way out of there, or we would've rescued you. But do you think Caleb randomly decided to grow a conscience? Why did he choose to help you? He likes you, obviously, but that's because of who you are. Something about you made him question his own choices. You could have swayed any number of people in that place. Of course your soul sought out the other aching person there. Here's what you need to remember, Mel. I've been in a lot of seemingly hopeless situations—inside the suit and out. You're not hopeless until a lot later than you usually think. Something you did made him help. In that way, you got yourself out."

I couldn't bring myself to say anything. My brain was overloaded.

"Try to cut him a break?" The look on Bane's face nearly killed me. He was disappointed.

I nodded glumly. I wanted to dart past him, to hide in my room and pretend my temper didn't have consequences, to continue telling myself Caleb didn't deserve kindness. But I stayed there across from my uncle, waiting for the scolding I deserved.

What followed was much worse. Bane gave me a final, forlorn look and walked away, calling to me over his shoulder as he did.

"Try to cool off."

CHAPTER
SIXTEEN

I put on a movie and waited until I heard the click of Caleb's door closing before I padded back to the Den.

Vennie was perched at his worktable, flashes of light illuminating his face in bursts as he soldered pieces of one of my Silhouette suits. Wringing my hands, I moseyed his way, watching in silence as he deftly maneuvered the delicate components of a circuit board.

Given that my suit's bulky material presented an awkward angle, he had to reposition it every few seconds.

"Can I help?" I offered.

He acquiesced with a dip of his chin, and I steadied the section he worked on.

"I'm really sorry, Vennie," I said after a few quiet moments. "I lost my temper earlier and was way out of line discrediting the suit's role in my abilities. I wouldn't be Silhouette without it—without you and your genius."

He pushed up his safety goggles. "Don't you forget it. But there's something else you should feel sorry about. Something to do with your actions." His face was expectant.

I reddened, thinking. "Oh, *shit*. The crutches. They're an

accessibility tool. Caleb needs them to get around. I took his mobility away from him."

"Knew you'd figure it out."

"I'm such an asshole."

Vennie shook his head. "No, you *were* an asshole for a few minutes. So . . ."

"I can listen, learn, and do better. You shouldn't have to be the one to point things like that out to me."

"Exactly. Apology accepted. Move your hands for a second."

"What are you working on?" I asked, doing as he requested.

"Just some repairs and hopefully improving the reaction time for when you issue temperature changes." He pointed to where I should brace the suit for him next. "It seems like you and Caleb can't help how much you like each other, and that makes fireworks—sometimes the bad kind."

"I don't think that's it," I sputtered.

He gave me a flat look, but didn't push.

I cleared my throat. "After I behaved like a brat, did someone fill Caleb in on our powers and how we got them?"

An absent nod. "Bane gave him the entire rundown. We should make a movie about it. It would go much faster. Okay, you can let go." He sat back and rubbed his eyes. "Regardless of what you think, Caleb does seem to want to help you . . . er, us. He started his notes on Kavoh for us already. Didn't seem to want to wait. I scanned what he got down if you want to take a look." He gestured at the LUMA.

I stepped into the embrace of the curved screen. Its soft blue light brushed against me on all sides.

Caleb had listed what he knew of the structure of Kavoh's operation. They divided her staff into three units and kept them separate. Caleb didn't know the identities of anyone beyond his teammates. He, Cellina, and Nicklai made up the Vine Unit. There was also the Thorn Unit and the Spore unit, one of which he believed to be housed in Kavoh's public lab. Beneath, Caleb had scribbled:

I think she keeps her staff small and separate so no one has a full picture of what she's after.

He suspected each team was small, including at least one scientist and someone who served as "muscle."

I rubbed my chin, lost in thought. "Caleb was listed on her staff directly for her public lab. Anyone else listed there might be part of one of the other units."

Cellina and Nicklai were definitely not on the website.

There was the subtle tap of Vennie's footsteps, and he was beside me. "That's a good hunch. Let's look into it. Caleb might know more to help us find her." Vennie shifted his weight. "I think it's good he's here."

I pressed the heels of my palms to my eyes, trying to hold back the quickly approaching headache. I needed to get to bed *now*. "I do too," I admitted quietly.

Vennie held out a closed fist. I bumped it with my own and headed upstairs.

As much as I was a good influence on Bane and he now averaged three days a week where he made it into the Leo Optics office on time, he had the reverse effect on me.

For example, on this particular morning, I found myself sprinting down the stairs with one sneaker on, untied, and the other tucked into my armpit because my hands were busy juggling a granola bar and a hairbrush, respectively.

I dashed out the front door and nearly tripped into Max. I managed to stay upright. Max's arms were crossed, his brows knit together as he scowled at the house's second floor windows.

The guest room windows, I realized with a string of silent profanities.

"Good morning," I said breezily, tugging the brush through the last of my hair's tangles and shoving it in my backpack's side pocket. I bent to tie my shoes. "You'll never believe it—Bane found us a new roommate."

As I straightened, I caught the tail end of Max's eye roll. "You know I heard about it already. I watch the news."

"Oh, good," I huffed. "I don't have to explain it to you."

Max opened my door before heading to his side of the car. "So, some stranger lives in your house now?"

I stared out the window. "I was a stranger when I first moved in."

"It's temporary, right?"

My fists clenched. "I don't know, Max. Why do you care?"

Max ignored me and started the engine. Halfway to Camden, he spoke again. "Let's get dinner."

I frowned. "It's ten o' clock in the morning."

He flapped a hand. "You know what I mean. This weekend. Like old times. I can get us a table at Tepeéé."

"'Like old times?' That sounds . . . date-ish. We talked about this. Boundaries. 'Just friends,' remember?"

Max's hands tightened on the wheel as he pulled into a parking spot.

"Lions," I said, sitting fully upright. "Are you asking me out because Caleb's living in my house?"

Max met my eyes, looking frustrated. "I would have asked you every day for the past month if I thought you would've said yes."

My mouth went dry. I scrambled out of the car.

"Mel, wait—"

I whirled on him. "That's not fair, Max. We've both been dating. We both agreed to try and be friends!"

Max stepped close, his voice low. "And we both admitted how hard it would be with what used to be between us. Especially when you never really told me why you wanted to break up in the first place."

I clamped my mouth shut. I still couldn't tell him. Max hated Silhouette, Shadow, and all we stood for. It's not that we literally *couldn't* be together. Instead, Max's attitude toward Silhouette had broken something in how I loved him. I couldn't love him like I wanted to, and it tore me up because everything else about us had felt so right.

But I wasn't willing to tell Max any version of that, for fear of him learning my secret and spilling it to the mayor. Any other excuses I'd made were flimsy, and Max knew it.

In almost every aspect of my life now, I didn't know what to do. "I'm going to be late for class," I said finally. I spun on my heel and walked away.

AFTER CLASSES AND A SILENT, AWKWARD RIDE HOME WITH Max, I spent the latter part of the day in Sydney's office—my favorite hiding spot.

"Studying inflation rates?"

"Gah!" Sydney's AI seemed to care less and less whether I activated it or not. "I asked you to add some sort of welcome chime."

Sydney's projection shook its head. "You're a superhero, for god's sake. How can you be startled by things appearing out of nowhere? You're supposed to incite fear, not feel it."

"I'm not a superhero at this exact second," I argued, one palm pressed to my racing heart. For whatever reason, bickering with the echo of my grandfather always provided me comfort. "Can you put on my study mix, please?"

Sydney's program processed the request, but kept the volume low as he mimed peering out the office's small window. "I hear we have a new houseguest. Why don't you talk Brisbane out of another one of his terrible ideas?"

I sank deeper into the armchair with a groan. Not this again. What I wouldn't give for someone who found the topic of Caleb's arrival boring. "We make choices together. You know that," I chided. "Why could you possibly disapprove?"

"Housing one of Kavoh's old lackeys under our roof? Surely, I don't need to list all that could go wrong."

His level of sarcasm was impressive for a computer program. I raised an eyebrow. "I take it Vennie backed up all the info on Caleb's arrival to the Cube last night?" The blocky mainframe hidden in the Den housed all of our vigilante data. It was also where my grandfather had hidden his program before he died.

Sydney nodded solemnly, and I cut him off before he could complain more. "He's going to help us stop Kavoh."

"And have we figured out what exactly we're stopping her from doing?"

"I—" I stopped. We were stopping her from creating Extrahumans. We knew that. But we didn't know why. I leapt to my feet, sending my textbook flying. "You're a genius, Grandpa!"

He tugged at his perfect, digital lapels. "Perhaps the next time you visit you'll tell me why." He deactivated as I was halfway down the narrow staircase.

🔥🔥🔥

CALEB DIDN'T ANSWER HIS DOOR WHEN I KNOCKED, SO I RAN downstairs and slid into the kitchen. Not checking my speed, I careened toward the dining table and nearly took out two chairs in an effort to slow myself.

A very startled Caleb looked up from the coffeemaker, where he was reading a battered paperback with one hand and held a mug in the other.

"I have a question for you," I said, batting my hair out of my face.

"You are your uncle's niece, for sure."

His comment made me smile against my better judgment. "Thank you."

He set both the book and mug on the counter. "You had a question?"

"Right!" I leaned against the counter's opposite side, facing him. "Do you know why Kavoh is making Extrahumans?"

Caleb deflated a little and rubbed his neck. "Because she can? Because she's the *only* one who can. I suspect she wanted a personal army so she could do whatever else she wants."

"That can't be all it is, though, can it?" I mused. "She experimented on my grandpa because she wanted to become invincible, immortal. Like, literally to live forever, right? That's why your ex-boss may look under forty, but she's twice as old, at least."

Caleb's jaw dropped, and I pressed on. "I assumed Bane told you that already. Process it later. I'm on a roll. Given how she looks these days, she's reversed her aging somehow . . . We assumed she achieved immortality. But she hasn't made a bigger, more specific move yet. Just these Extrahumans she seems to make for no reason."

"Usually to help steal a piece of equipment," Caleb said.

"Maybe she didn't succeed. Maybe we're wrong, and she's made moves toward immortality, but she hasn't cracked it. That's what she's still trying to do," I said triumphantly.

"And that's . . . good?"

"It means we still have time to stop her before whatever her master plan is *after* the invincibility. And we can try to theorize where she'll strike next, depending on what materials she needs."

Caleb's eyes stared, unfocused, at something far off. "The animals. *That's* how she decides."

I waved a hand in front of his face, startling Caleb back to the present. I crossed my arms, and he mirrored the move-ment. "What are you talking about?"

"Kavoh imbues people with enhanced abilities by merging them with animals—kind of. She kept the specifics of how close to her chest, but . . . Hey, Shadow and Silhouette fought with Rhett Fannon, right?"

It took me a moment to remember that Rhett was the real name of the Extrahuman we called "Redzilla," a terrifying mix of man and bright red dinosaur-like features.

"That was *you?*" I caught myself. "I mean, Kavoh made him like that?"

"Yes, she's been fixated on reptiles recently, and knowing what she's after now, it makes sense why. Many of them have significantly longer lifespans than humans. I suspect Eleni Brooks was merged with a reptile too, though with none of the physical side effects Rhett had. That shows Kavoh's making progress, unfortunately.

"It takes her months and months to find success with making these people Extrahumans, based on how rarely she would instruct us to bring new patients to the facility," Caleb mused. "She must try new methodology on each patient, gauge what works, make changes and try again on someone new. Knowing that, I might be able to surmise if there's some tech in the city she'll go after next. I'll think on it."

It was at precisely that moment I realized I didn't have another conversation topic prepared for my adversary-slash-housemate. Caleb seemed to be on the same wavelength, so we both stared out the window. As we stood there, his shoulders dropped.

"What have you been up to this afternoon? Studying?" he ventured.

"Yeah." I played with the ties of my hoodie. "With the whole superhero side-gig thing, I try to stay ahead on my homework however I can."

"Have you declared a major yet?"

"Economics."

He drank from his coffee, piercing eyes searching my face.

"Why not something to do with film? Does Camden not offer cinematography?"

Hardly a week with us, and he already knew I loved movies. He paid attention to how I spent my precious downtime.

I chewed my lip. "They do," I hedged.

"But?"

"But that felt risky. Selfish. I wanted to pick something that would result in financial security, so why not the study of money and how it affects our world?"

"You want to be wealthy?"

I shook my head. "Clearly, I lucked out with Uncle Bane and all the privileges we have, all that comes from Leo Optics. But when I first came to Crown City, I wasn't sure I wanted to stay. So, I wanted to set myself up for success as best I could."

"That's admirable."

"It's boring, is what it is." I scrubbed at a coffee ring marring the counter. "Maybe I'll add a film studies minor."

Caleb gave his private smile. I found myself staring.

His gaze drifted to the fridge; his head tilted in intense focus.

The tiniest twinge of guilt turned my stomach. Caleb wouldn't get an apology like Vennie, but maybe I could spare a scrap of kindness.

"Hungry?"

He looked sheepish. "I'm okay."

My stomach growled in response. I glanced at the clock. "Well, I'm hungry," I said, shoving off the counter. "And it's time to make my second lunch, so you might as well join."

Caleb's smile widened. "Second lunch is almost as good as second breakfast."

I rolled my eyes. "Don't get excited. I only know that reference from the movies."

Our silence wasn't unpleasant as I focused on cooking. Caleb wisely kept his mouth shut until I set a plate with a grilled cheese before him. I snatched mine directly from the hot pan.

I caught him glancing at me.

"This looks incredible."

I shrugged, taking a large bite.

We ate in silence. "You seem to dislike me much less than normal today," Caleb said finally.

I coughed, hacking crumbs into a napkin and wiping my suddenly watery eyes. Regaining what composure I still had, I piled dishes in the sink. "I realize this can't be easy for you. Starting over. I've done it. I empathize. I do. You don't need me making your new life any harder."

"Let me, please." He came around the counter, and I backed out of his way as he continued my work on the dishes. "I'm listening."

It took me a moment to find my train of thought. "I'm angry with you," I continued. "Like, monumentally pissed. Don't get me wrong. I don't like it when people keep things from me. What you've done . . . what you're doing. I hate it. But that doesn't mean I should make you miserable in return. I'm not a—"

He stilled, surely guessing what word came next.

The door from the garage banged open. Bane stumbled in, seemingly in a fight with his tie.

"Hold still," I commanded, going to his rescue. "Important meeting today?"

"A full day with the Board," he groaned, slouching and half-strangling himself. "I'm exhausted. Are you up for a healing movie marathon and pizza party tonight?"

"Always," I said, returning his extremely rumpled tie.

"Can I pick the movie?" Bane ventured.

I snorted. "Absolutely not."

Bane conceded easily. "Of course, my most esteemed cinematography emperor."

I shoved him and made myself meet Caleb's eyes again.

The blue was so vibrant a shiver passed over my skin like sparks. I mumbled a few syllables of nonsense.

He leaned down to hear me better, and I blushed at the reminder of our vast difference in height.

"Care to join us?"

Caleb stammered. "Um. Uh, yes. Yeah, I'd love to."

CHAPTER
SEVENTEEN

I didn't see Caleb again for a few days, until he quietly brought his notebook down to the Den and sat on the couch. He peered over to watch Bane and I train every few moments. We didn't stop him.

Bane cut a glance my way. I gave him one of our looks. We'd become adept at reading each other during my time in Crown City. This look had a clear message: *I'm fine, really.* I'd come to terms with the situation; part of me loathed Caleb. He knew it. He knew he had the power to change it. The rest was up to him. For the time being, part of me could tolerate him and be polite.

There was an additional part that felt differently than the first two, but I refused to give it attention.

Which wasn't too difficult, since my focus was sorely needed elsewhere. Bane and I were working on airborne twists. We both lacked the feline grace of our namesake, and harsh landings were leaving us injured. We took turns heaving each other over our shoulders, or leaping backward from each other's hands, trying to turn in midair to land on our feet.

Bane tossed me over his hip with a little extra oomph, so I had more time in the air, but I didn't manage a full rotation. I smacked the mat on my side, rolling ass over heels before landing on my back.

"Lions," I swore as I sat up, nursing my wrist against my chest—the one I'd wrenched while rescuing Caleb.

"Maybe we should cut our losses and just add more padding to our suits?" Bane mulled.

"Or we could pay a professional acrobat to teach us. Bribe them to keep it hush hush," I offered, checking the bubble-braided ponytail Chezza had taught me to do in the wall of mirrors.

"I did date a clown from that Vegas acrobat show once . . ."

"Ballet would help with that."

Both our heads snapped to Caleb, whose eyes met ours over the top of his notebook.

"Really," Bane said, thoughtful.

"How so?" One of my eyebrows took a skeptical slant.

Caleb stretched, and I couldn't help but appreciate the quiet grace in his long limbs as he unfolded from the couch. He strode to the mat and . . . posed. I recognized the position, but I couldn't name it. Caleb set his posture and took a few pointed steps to the side before leaping into the air and spinning twice before landing lightly on the ground.

"You were a ballerina before you were a criminal?" I asked flatly.

Caleb flushed. "Till I was sixteen, yeah. I loved it. It helps with flexibility and fluidity. I could show you if you like."

Bane held out a hand. "The mat's yours, if this will keep my back from aching."

"Is that a gray hair?" I teased, picking at his scalp.

He batted my hand away and clamped both hands over his head. "Stop it!"

"So," Caleb said, standing in the middle of the mat and eyeing us. "When you're falling or being thrown, try to orient yourself toward the direction your momentum is going, and twist your body into the movement." He took a less graceful jump to the left and spun once in midair. "It helps to try and do it while standing first."

Bane stepped up. I receded another few feet, fearful of his chaos. As he worked, I turned into myself and tried to visualize the movement, how it would feel. As Caleb helped Bane, I took steps along the edge of the mat, gradually faster, until I leapt and turned in the air, keeping an eye on myself in the mirrors. Surely not as graceful as Caleb, but I felt more control in my body, and I saw how it could transfer to being airborne.

After a few tries, I felt confident. I took a few running steps, launching myself to spin in the air. I landed mostly on my feet, tripping a few steps to brace my hands on the lion mural with a triumphant, out of breath smile.

Warm hands gripped my hips. "Try to brace here, and always have your pelvis facing where you want to go." Caleb's voice was soft against my cheek.

With my enhanced hearing, I heard it vibrate through his chest, and the way his heartbeat stuttered when I spun to look at him with wide eyes. I twisted out of his grip.

His hands snapped back to his sides. "Sorry—you can pull up through your core to tighten your body." He fisted his hands together in front of his stomach, illustrating.

Caleb looked slightly mortified, and I'd fully forgotten how to speak.

Bane was too focused watching himself in the mirror, fixing his hair.

"Uh—" I stammered.

"Who's ready to cause a *ruckus*?"

"EEP!" Bane jumped even higher than I'd thrown him as Roger barreled down the stairwell.

I crossed my arms, warm and confused and extremely grateful for a distraction. "You're not supposed to be here until tomorrow."

Roger tousled my hair. "Awe, c'mon, Toasty, who doesn't love a surprise?"

"Toasty?" Caleb asked.

"Who's this?" Roger looked Caleb up and down. Caleb had an inch on Roger, even.

"This is Caleb," I offered.

Bane leapt in to explain the rest. After he finished, Roger whistled and shook Caleb's hand.

"Boy, you really do like to take in the strays, don't you?" He raised an eyebrow at Bane.

"Hey!" I snapped.

Roger flapped a hand. "I came early to make sure you two are prepped for the match tomorrow."

"Prepped? What kind of prepping do we need to do?" I demanded.

"Exactly," Roger said, pointing a finger gun my way. "You were both going to head into the Shadow-Silhouette Smash-down Throwdown half-assed."

"We had shirts made," Bane said with a pout.

"Yeah, yeah. I'm talking about practice, kids. Besides using mobsters as punching bags, have either of you formally boxed before? Like, with rules?"

"Bane hates rules," I said, jerking a thumb his way.

He nodded somberly.

Roger rolled his eyes skyward, running a hand over his dark hair, which was long enough to be tied back in a bun now. "What the hell am I gonna do about you two?" He eyed the Den. "Doesn't make sense to get drunk the night before anyways. I wanna see this play out at your full potential. Let's move up our schedule. Are the Ellos here? The ropes came in already, yeah?"

Bane pointed toward a pile of long boxes in the corner and pulled out his phone. "I'll see if they can make this work with us tonight."

Roger nodded. "Then get started on the ring, and don't

get 'em tangled. At least you know the rules, even if I have to make you follow them. Mel, do you know anything about boxing?"

"I know how to punch a man so hard he won't open his eyes until the next day."

Roger took my shoulder. "And as tempting as that would be to do to your uncle, you still gotta know the rules." He eyed Caleb again. "You're fit. You can spar with her."

"Sure," Caleb said before I could protest.

My skin still tingled pleasantly where he touched me.

"Your funeral," I murmured.

"That was last week," he said.

I glanced up, gaping. Caleb's eyes glittered with mirth. It was true. He had to tell the press he held a private memorial for his "younger brother" Ian.

I burst out laughing.

"Enough cutesy cutesy," Roger grunted, digging in his bag. He tossed a pair of boxing gloves to Caleb. "Mel, can you boil the new guy a mouthguard, please? Unless you promise not to punch him in the face."

I narrowed my eyes at Caleb and flashed a too sweet grin. "I'll get the mouthguard. Just in case."

Caleb gulped.

With a laugh, I rifled through the cabinets for my gloves and mouthguard, as well as a fresh one. The sheer amount of miscellaneous athletic equipment we'd accrued in an attempt to become the ultimate vigilantes was comical.

A few minutes later, properly outfitted to meet his safety standards, Roger walked Caleb and I through the basics of a boxing match, then let us at it for a practice round. We hovered our hands near our faces, stepping in and jabbing whenever we saw an opening. Caleb landed a hit on me about half the time I did on him, his punches solid against my shoulders and torso, but nothing I couldn't handle with my elevated pain tolerance, even without Tempatches on to assure I didn't accidentally break one of Caleb's bones.

"You're pulling your punches," Roger called out.

I crinkled my nose. "You're not going to hurt me."

"I'm not talking to him, Toasty. I'm talking to you."

I balked and glanced at Bane in disbelief. He was in the corner helplessly tangled in the boxing ropes. He raised an eyebrow pointedly as if to say, *well, are you?*

Caleb rubbed one glove along the back of his other arm. "You're not going to hurt me," he echoed.

I scowled and lunged for him.

EVER QUICK TO ADJUST TO A CHANGE OF PLANS, VENNIE procured a mountain of snacks and set up an impromptu buffet on the outskirts of the boxing ring. Chezza brought the T-shirts from where she'd hoarded them in her room, including ridiculous satin robes for all of us. Mine was scarlet and emblazoned with "Silhouette" on the back. Bane's was royal blue. Chezza's was pink; Vennie's was yellow.

We checked ourselves out in the mirror wall.

"Not shabby at all," Bane mused, turning to admire his own calves from where they peeked out below his boxing shorts.

"Yes, you'll look fabulous while I kick your ass," I said.

His jaw actually dropped. "We'll see."

I shrugged and examined my nails. "I was trained by the very best."

"Well, I was—wait. You mean me, right?"

"Alright, remind me of the bets," Roger called from his spot in the middle of the mats, dressed in a skintight striped ref's jersey with the sleeves cut off and spangled with crystals. He'd brought it from home.

"What is happening?" Caleb asked for the tenth time. He

wore one of the extra shirts Chezza always ordered when we did things like this. It was definitely a size too small, and I fought to not ogle how it hugged his chest.

"Just go with it," I advised, my eyes slipping to his torso again. I cleared my throat and looked away.

Vennie pulled the bets up on the LUMA. His and Roger's shared love of shenanigans apparently landed them in a truce for the evening.

Bane whistled. "Really, guys?"

Though the bet placers' names were removed for right now, most of our family had put money on me winning in the match against Bane. Odds were split evenly between Vennie and Chezza for their match.

"Do you want in on this?" Chezza asked Caleb.

"Absolutely not."

"Smart man," Bane murmured at the same time I said, "Diplomatic. Won't win you any money, though."

"Most of the money I have belongs to all of you, so . . ."

"Let's do this," Roger said, gesturing us over as he recited the rules.

We'd settled on the best of three rounds, with points being scored to the person able to knock their opponent down first. Our Tempatches were placed identically. Vennie had them set to his best approximation of what would match us at equal strength.

Roger chucked a bundle of cotton wraps at Caleb, who caught them easily. "Tape her up, will you? I'll help Bane."

Caleb approached me hesitantly, and I held out my hands. He tucked the roll beneath one arm. "Here," he offered, holding out both hands with the first two fingers pointing toward each other. "Let me see how your wrist is doing, so I know this isn't a terrible idea."

"Most of ours are," I muttered, but I slipped my fingers around his.

He had me tug them gently, then push back to try and

move them. He kept himself incredibly still against my enhanced strength.

"Does any of this hurt?"

I shook my head, determined to look at our hands rather than his suddenly close face or chest, or any part of his body, really.

"You're sure?" He kneaded my wrist between deft fingers, then bent it forward. The look on his face was of pure concentration. So much for not looking up. The fearsome Silhouette was making googly eyes while Caleb was trying to provide me medical care. "No pain there, either?"

I pulled my wrist back. "I'm sure," I said, hating the heat I felt rising on my face. "We agreed on no headshots, right?" I asked Roger, turning my back on Caleb and shrugging out of my robe.

Chezza perched on one of the ring's corners, serving as a secondary ref to keep Roger unbiased. I had a sneaking suspicion he was the one betting on Bane. Vennie walked across the mat, waving a tablet he'd scribbled "round 1" on and doing his best attempt at a sexy model walk.

Bane and I entered the ring and bumped our gloves together.

"I'm gonna freeze you out," Bane said, with an exaggerated serious face.

"Um, get ready to feel the burn?" I countered.

Chezza groaned and played a bell sound from her phone. "Just fight already!"

I dashed forward, shocking Bane and forcing him a step back. He easily dodged my first two jabs. I shot a wicked grin his way, and he must have realized my plan to toy with him. With a scowl, he darted toward me. With our enhanced speed and reflexes, I was able to truly appreciate my uncle's incredible fighting skills. Clumsiness aside, his slapdash approach was an impressive and intimidating whirlwind. I sidestepped his punch and couldn't help my small laugh. We quickly devolved into a wild, poor execution of boxing that might as well have been charades.

Per Roger's discretion, I won the first round. Bane took the second.

"Alright, kids, best of three. Let's do this." Roger signaled for us to go on the attack again.

We punched and weaved away, trading blows that rarely landed. When they did, we easily shook them off. I got one solid punch to Bane's shoulder. When he stepped back, I drew that hand in, cradling it against my chest for a second before shaking it out.

Out of the corner of my eye, I saw Caleb's mouth open, surely to protest me using my wrist again.

I shook my head slightly, and Caleb shut up. Bane eyed my wrist, and a twitch of his body revealed his plan to focus on my weaker side.

Caleb's brows furrowed. I glanced his way, shielded my face with a glove as I wiped my hair from my face, and winked at him.

That dropped his jaw again.

Bane went for my 'bad' side, raining a flurry of blows. I took the brunt of them with gritted teeth, waiting for the perfect moment. At the peak of his momentum, his body tilting to one side as he threw his force behind his attack, I withdrew my free arm and punched him square in the chest through an opening he left.

Bane stumbled back several feet before landing on his ass with a satisfying thud.

"Victory to the smaller of the two Leos!" Roger bellowed, pointing my way.

I punched the air as everyone cheered. Even Bane gave me rueful applause before I helped him up.

"Joke's on you," he said, ruffling my hair with his glove. "I had Vennie put money on you on my behalf. It's never a smart idea to bet against you."

"Yeah, yeah." I shoved him, bashful at his high praise.

I retreated to sit at the edge of the couch, chugging from a water bottle Chezza handed me.

She hopped from her perch and air-boxed a few punches. "Our turn, our turn! You're going down, bro."

Vennie shook his shoulders loose at the ring's opposite corner. "You frighten me," was all he said. He kept one eye on her warily as they warmed up.

Caleb came over, tugging his hair in disbelief. "You were faking it when you acted like your wrist still bothered you."

I grinned. "Sorry to waste your medical expertise."

He shook his head and shoved his hands in his pockets. For some reason, I didn't want the look of him comfortable in our house to go away.

"It was cool, though," I offered. "To see you in action as an actual doctor. Helping people."

I must've said exactly the wrong thing, because Caleb's face fell, a shadow crawling over his features. "I—"

A scrap of memory roiled over me, turning my stomach. Staring up at Caleb from a dingy cot, spitting some sort of vitriol at him. *Doctors help people. That's not what you do.*

I blinked. "We've had this conversation before."

Caleb's voice was strained. "A version of it."

I dropped my head into my hand and twitched as I was flooded with the phantom sensation of how the fear bacteria felt. What it did to me. What *he* did to me.

My stomach churned as my heart raced.

Caleb crouched, concern clouding his face. "What's wrong, Mel? What do you need?" he asked quietly, though the darkness behind his eyes suggested he knew what was happening.

"They dosed you with the FR-10 bacteria too," I said.

"They did." His eyelids fluttered.

"What did you see when the bacteria made your vision go away?"

Caleb glanced down, twisting his hands together. "The walls closing in," he said finally, so quiet I wouldn't have heard had I not been warm from the match.

"You're claustrophobic."

He nodded.

"Then you know," I said shakily. "You know how much it hurts. How terrifying it is to have your worst fears thrown back at you. I just had to relive it. The bacteria's gone, but the shadow of the memory is there. Because of you."

"Mel, I—"

"Make my memories come back, so I can make sense of this."

Caleb glanced over his shoulder. When he faced me again, I knew what his answer would be.

"Can you leave, please?" I asked, though it sounded like a demand. "Say you're tired. Go to bed. I want to be with my family."

I made my intention clear. With people I love and care about. *That does not include you.*

His mouth drawn, Caleb made his goodbyes. Bane stopped him at the stairwell.

"If you help her remember, she might forgive you," Bane said as I shamelessly eavesdropped.

Devastation lined every inch of Caleb's body. "I blew my chances before I even saw her for the first time."

As Caleb mounted the stairs, Bane halted him with a hand on his elbow. "You're underestimating her. Especially her compassion. That's a mistake. Trust me, it's one I've made."

Caleb's only reply was a weak smile before plodding upstairs.

After his footsteps receded across the floorboard above our heads, we all focused on Vennie and Chezza's match. It escalated relentlessly until Roger nearly called it a draw before Vennie got in a good punch and sprawled Chezza on her ass.

Bane watched me as we celebrated and cleaned up. He

clapped me on the shoulder and said to the others, "Why don't you all start on the cocktails? We'll be up in a minute."

I watched warily as Bane sent Vennie, Chezza, and Roger up the stairs. There was no fooling Bane, not after all we'd been through. He strode over, his fingers flicking in a nervous tick.

"What?" I demanded.

"I need to show you something."

I collapsed into the couch. "It's insanely stressful when you say things like that."

He winced apologetically. I let him tug me up so I could follow him to the LUMA.

CHAPTER
EIGHTEEN

Both of us bathed in the light of the glowing blue screen, Bane pulled up a single, nondescript digital folder. I crossed my arms as he tapped it open to reveal two files—unnamed video clips with tiny screenshots, but I would recognize the miserable cell anywhere. Though my memories weren't fully intact, the place had made an immovable imprint on my psyche.

My breath caught. "This is the surveillance footage from the facility."

Bane watched me out of the corner of his eye. "You haven't asked about it, so I assumed you didn't want to see it. I didn't want to see it either, honestly. I was worried how I'd react. Scared of how it would make me feel to see you at their disposal." He heaved a sigh. I hadn't realized how high his shoulders had climbed as he spoke.

"You watched them?"

Bane chewed his lip. "The other night and . . . I think you should see them."

The suggestion pushed my stomach off a cliff. "I don't think I can."

He placed a tethering hand on my shoulder. "If you

decide to, I'll be right here with you."

"They hurt me." My voice shook like puddles in the path of some furious beast.

"I know. We've got to try to make sure they don't hurt anyone else."

I stepped closer to the glass, standing right in the middle of the LUMA's curve. "Go ahead."

Bane tapped the first clip and stepped back.

It enlarged to nearly fill the LUMA's massive screen, encompassing me on both sides. I eyed the timestamp. This clip was late in my stay at the facility, the footage grainy and the sound not much better. I hardly recognized myself as the shaking, tiny ball of gray fabric and greasy hair curled on the cell's floor as Nicklai prowled my way.

My own garbled screams in my ears, I gripped myself tight to remind me of reality—that I was safe.

On the screen, my eyes were wide and vacant as I scrambled backward across the tiles, careening into the wall. My mask was secured to my face, hiding my features.

Nicklai took threatening steps closer, the fingers of his free hand curling menacingly as he reached for me.

The cell door slammed open. Caleb towered there, his hair disheveled, his face a brewing thunderstorm. There was a stark difference between the hollow version of him on screen, and the healing one I knew now.

"Who authorized these tests?"

Nicklai flinched, and I didn't comprehend the words they exchanged as I beheld Caleb's face. Beneath the wrathful mask, he looked terrified.

Whatever he said sent Nicklai scurrying out the door with a curse. I stepped closer to the screen as Caleb—his old self as the disheveled doctor—crouched before me.

He murmured, quiet enough that the camera didn't pick up his words. His tone was low, crooning, as he tried to tell me something, ease me out of my terror. I watched as he helped me lean forward and I threw up over the tiles, not moving when it soaked the knee of his pants.

Though I remembered this, witnessing it as cold technological reconnaissance added new flavors of terror. And even though I knew what happened next, I held my breath.

I watched myself argue with him, defiant even as I was terrified, like an idiot. And eventually I acquiesced to whatever he said. On screen, Caleb wrapped his jacket around me. Then, gently, he lifted me into his arms.

I swore I could feel the ghost of his cheek against mine as I watched my head fall forward to lean against his.

Caleb eyed the camera, and something settled in his gaze. He clenched his jaw and carried me from the room.

The churning mental sensation I'd come to associate with a returning memory shifted.

"Come on," I whispered, screwing my eyes shut. "Show me something."

"Why are you helping me?"

It's what I'd asked Caleb next, once he'd set me on his bed.

Dove's lips pressed into a tight line. We were at an impasse, and I was at a severe disadvantage.

"I'm invested in your survival," he said simply, not giving me time to follow up. "Can I look at your abrasions?" He lifted his hands, his fingers flexing in the direction of my temples.

I nodded once sharply, his sparse explanation enough to buy a few minutes of my patience.

He disappeared into the bathroom.

A moment passed, and he poked his head out. Pale face, gaunt features, a shock of dark hair. The top few buttons of his dress shirt were undone, his tie loose. "Can you promise me you'll wait fifteen minutes into whatever this truce is before cooking up a scheme?"

I frowned. Maybe this was some sort of adrenaline-fueled self-defense dream my brain had invented to give me a break from the bacteria's attack.

I considered him, my eyes narrowed. "Ten minutes."

Dove snorted and disappeared into the bathroom. He emerged quickly, a plastic kit in one large hand.

He'd changed his clothes, and it confused me. He wore a T-shirt with a pocket and sweatpants. He looked like me five minutes after getting home from class. The intimidating mad scientist I'd come to fear had shed his armor. His glasses were crooked and his hair tousled, as if he had yanked his shirt over his head with them still on. He returned to the chair and opened his kit. I kept my eyes locked on him the entire time, wondering if there was anything sharp in it I could snatch. He withdrew a small tube and turned his attention to me.

Though I braced myself, I wasn't prepared for the onslaught of those eyes again. I sat up a little straighter. He stared at me, almost expectantly.

"Go ahead," I said.

Bane's voice pulled me from the memory's mist. "This is the only footage of you at the facility."

I furrowed my brow. "That can't be right."

"I suspect Caleb attempted to delete it, but they caught him before he finished."

"Why do you think that?"

Bane jerked his head towed the LUMA and started the next clip. I watched Nicklai drag a badly beaten Caleb into my old cell and drop him on the floor. His head lolled against the tile. Blood dripped from his nose, his lips, his hairline.

Nicklai crouched before Caleb, depraved glee setting his eyes alight. "Tell me what you did."

Caleb remained silent.

"Doesn't matter," Nicklai huffed, withdrawing something from his belt. "You'll be talking in no time."

He plunged the injector pistol into Caleb's arm.

"How about you sit with the consequences of your own actions for a while?" Nicklai said, mashing an activation bracelet into Caleb's wrist.

The spurt of blood drew a mirror of bile up my throat. I swallowed and forced myself to keep watching.

"And," Nicklai drawled, "don't even think about pulling your party trick. I gave you a heavy dose."

Caleb shoved Nicklai, who laughed and pulled out a remote, then activated the bacteria.

The result wasn't instant. Caleb crawled to the cot and hauled himself up, sitting upright and fisting his hands in the mattress. He muttered to himself, too quiet for the microphone to pick up.

For a handful of heartbeats, the only sound was Caleb's heavy breathing. It hitched, and he slammed his eyes shut, his jaw clenched sharp as a knife's blade. His first startled cry was muffled, like he tried to hold it back. He jerked sideways, dodging an invisible threat.

But the dam broke, and Bane hit fast forward as Caleb began to scream.

I made a noise of protest, but Bane held up a hand. "The next hour or so of footage is all the same. He doesn't talk." Bane moved the video ahead. Things had changed drastically. Caleb sagged against the cell wall, looking dehydrated and underfed. He had a puffy black eye and new bruises along his arms. His clothing was filthy, and he shook. Blood had dried in tracks down his chin, some trails darker—fresher—than others. His head rested against the wall, and his eyes pointed, unfocused, at the ceiling.

The cell door creaked open. Caleb didn't budge. My breath caught as Cellina entered the room. Her hair was flawless, and a deep frown weighed on her purple painted lips.

"Feel like talking yet?"

"Get on with it." Caleb's voice was like flaking rust.

Cellina sneered at the remote in her hand. "This is stupid. You've always been good at your job. You can fix this. Tell me where—"

Caleb was shaking his head before she could finish.

"I didn't think you were stubborn or stupid," she said quietly.

"Just press the button before you get in trouble too."

"I can take care of myself," she hissed.

It seemed Caleb had hit whatever mark he'd aimed for because Cellina jammed a manicured nail against the remote's button.

Caleb's suffering was instant this time.

His voice was so wrecked, his screams were more guttural howls. He batted his arms around his head. I knew he must be trying to fight his way out of some dark, invisible prison constricting tighter and tighter. His breathing became panicked and he choked.

"Damn it, Dove. Who was she?" Cellina demanded.

Caleb threw himself forward, cowering. *"Her name is Mary!"* he screamed finally, his voice breaking on the name.

Cellina took her finger off the button. She planted shaking hands on her hips, but her voice was steady. "You better hope Kavoh finds that helpful, or you're a dead man."

Cellina swept out of the room. Caleb remained prone, his face pressed to the floor, but it seemed like his shoulders sagged with relief.

The video ended frozen on Caleb in his broken and reverent posture.

At some point, my hands had landed over my mouth, and tears pooled along my fingers' edges.

I shrunk, crouching, barely keeping myself upright as I processed.

Bane sat on the cold floor next to me, his face a mirror of my dismay.

"He kept them from finding me," I whispered.

Bane laid a tentative hand on my back and ran a soothing course along my shoulders. "Does it outweigh that he took you in the first place?"

"I don't know."

He sighed, the frozen video frame drawing our eyes back to the LUMA. "Me either."

CHAPTER
NINETEEN

I PULLED MYSELF TOGETHER BEFORE WE HEADED BACK UPSTAIRS where Chezza, Vennie, and Roger had already begun the afterparty with a round of midnight margaritas. Caleb mercifully listened to my request and stayed sequestered in his room the entire night, leaving me to get drunk, so I wouldn't have to think about him at all.

It didn't work of course, but the tequila shots were fun while they lasted. I even convinced Roger to arm wrestle me. After, I owed him an apology and a wrist brace.

I barely slept and bolted to Camden extra early to avoid running into Caleb. The sun was setting outside the student union's broad windows when Bane texted.

Got a lead on an arms deal going down tonight. Feeling up for it?

After getting home, the speed with which I changed into my suit was a personal record. No sign of Caleb.

The third time I glanced over my shoulder at the stairwell, Bane raised an eyebrow.

"So . . . Your plan is to avoid him forever?" he asked, not ungently.

"I have no plan. Let me flounder."

Bane acquiesced and steered clear of the topic our entire run to the dive bar where the deal was to take place.

Hidden behind a rusting roadside sign for the Wheat n' Greet—which apparently had the hottest pool tables in town —Bane won our traditional game of rock, paper, scissors to determine who got to bust the deal, and who had to play lookout and catch anyone who made a run for it. He assigned me the usually less risky lookout duty, which was probably for the best. My mind was occupied with a constant replay of Caleb writhing on the ground, protecting my secret with every ounce of his willpower.

I pressed my back against the pickup I was using as cover in the bar's parking lot, my only company a large, determined squirrel rummaging in the dumpsters.

For the first time since it happened, I thought about the scruffy dog whose bark had alerted Eleni Brooks to my presence on that fateful night. It wasn't the dog's fault, of course. I'd insisted on going out alone. My actions alone are what landed me within reach of Caleb's grasp.

The hot well of anger within me grew dimmer every time I thought about it. I rubbed my chest, scrubbing a hand over my flame-shaped emblem uneasily. My mouth dried as a question floated to the forefront of my brain. Did I regret it?

And if I didn't . . . what did that mean?

The crash of splintering wood echoed through my earpiece. "Everything okay in there?"

"Eh," Bane's voice was breathless. "I mean, specify the parameters of 'okay.'" There was a reedy snap that could only be Bane walloping someone with a pool stick.

"Do you need backup?"

"No, no. I've got it. *Give me that!*" Bane grunted. I could just make out the sound of unspent bullets hitting linoleum.

I chuckled quietly, sinking lower to the ground. There was

a bubble in my chest—joy—floating above the hurt too. I squinted, reflecting on all that had happened recently.

I was . . . I was glad.

"Silhouette!" A shout sounded in my ear.

I jerked upright and darted from my hiding spot.

I'd been so lost in thought I'd missed the back door slam open. A tank of man barreled toward me, shocked at my sudden appearance across his escape route.

This was all wrong. I wasn't prepared. I shifted as fast I could to take him on—he seemed sure he could run right through me. I adjusted my arms to catch him as he flew by, making to slam the pressure point on the back of his head. I succeeded, but not before he slashed out with a wicked looking knife, jerking a gash straight through the suit and across my collarbone.

He collapsed, still as stone. I kicked his knife into a ditch, then swore, pressing my hand to my wound as pain beat through the adrenaline.

"One attempted escapee," I announced, "but I got him." I couldn't suppress the groan at the end of my sentence.

"Mine are all down. Are you hurt?" Bane appeared in the back doorway and ran to me. He glanced at my hand over my slice and peeled back my hand to inspect it.

"It doesn't look too deep," he said. "It's been a while since you let a sour get you."

I swore at the blood leaking down the front of my suit as Bane sent an anonymous tip to Crown's police department so they could round up the unconscious sours. We'd hoped to trace them to their source, but I couldn't fight further. I'd be a liability. With a resigned curse directed toward the night sky, I followed Bane home.

🔥🔥🔥

Wooziness came for me by the time we rolled into the Den. Bane headed straight for Vennie to share the information he'd gotten while eavesdropping before busting the meeting. One of the sours had mentioned Sprinkles. It might mean the crime boss was expanding his drug ring.

"I'm getting Chezza," I called over my shoulder. "I need her help with this."

Bane nodded absently from where he and Vennie already pored over a map on the LUMA.

Keeping a firm grip on the railing, I made my way carefully up the stairs. At the top, I stumbled and fell against the kitchen island with a curse, the blood loss finally catching up with me.

A head of dark hair poked out of the living room. "Mel?"

I rolled my head back and closed my eyes. "I'm fine. I just need Chezza."

Caleb came around the counter in a flash, with a swirl of mint and woods scent that did nothing to help my light-headedness. "She said she had to work an earlier shift tomorrow, so she went to bed. Oh shit, are you okay? What happened?"

I looked down. Though the pain was minor compared to other wounds I'd suffered, the thin sheen of blood dripping over my emblem was startling. "I'm fine. A sour got a lucky shot with a knife. That's all."

Caleb held out his hands, and they froze an inch from me. "Can I help you?"

My head swam. I told myself I didn't care as long as I stopped bleeding soon. "Fine."

With a curt nod, he reached down and hooked his hands beneath my thighs, hoisting me onto the counter. "Don't fall off, okay?" His face was a perfect blend of serious and sweet. He was starting to get freckles on his nose from his jogs through the property on days the sun came out. Not that I'd paid attention.

"No promises," I said dumbly.

Then he was gone, quickly and quietly down the stairs to the Den. With a groan, I slipped off my hood and unfastened my mask, setting it gently on the counter beside me. The sting of the slice grew stronger.

Caleb vaulted his way up the stairs, his arms full of supplies. He eyed me, his serious doctor face on.

"I'm still upright," I said with an unconvincing thumbs up.

"Mmhmm," he said, stepping close. He pulled on a pair of gloves and sifted through the pile he'd set on the counter.

I swallowed and unzipped my jacket one-handed, my entire chest throbbing.

"Let me," he offered. His hand stilled on my suit's collar. He waited for my permission.

"Thanks," I murmured.

I let him hold the jacket as I shimmied out of it. The dripping blood had dyed the upper half of my white tank top pink already. Caleb braced my good side, wrapping his hand firmly around my upper arm.

With me on the counter, our faces were level. But he wasn't looking at my face the way I stared dumbly at his, want and hate swirling through me. Caleb held a pen light between his teeth and patted the blood away with a wipe. His cool skin beneath the gloves felt good on mine.

Thankfully, the sharp antiseptic smell helped me focus.

The man who so intently tended to my wound had saved my life. He had forfeited his own so I wouldn't be found by those who wished to harm me.

My throat burned with the question I couldn't muster the courage to ask.

Why did you do it?

"It looks like the bleeding has nearly stopped. I'd like to do stitches, if that's okay with you," Caleb said, arching a dark eyebrow.

"I'll be fine." I set my jaw. "Chezza's done them on me lots of times."

The corners of Caleb's mouth turned up in the smallest smile—the one he rarely gave. It made my stomach flip, which only got worse as he prepared the needle and other tools he needed. I tilted my head toward the ceiling and closed my eyes against the bright kitchen light, kicking my feet back and forth.

I held as still as possible as Caleb began on the sutures. Gentle tugs on my skin, and I peeked down. His face was peaceful as he worked. I matched my breaths to the rhythm of his hands. "Almost done."

I bit my lip against the pain of him securing the final knot.

Suddenly, the fog in my head shifted in full force. A memory swam before my vision. What it showed me was stronger and clearer than any I had seen so far. Caleb, before me, just like this. Me, wounded. His hands assessing. Fixing. Healing. His head bowed before me, focusing on his work, his hair longer and messy and a little lighter.

It was him from the most recent moment I remembered. Further details swirled, but they failed to solidify.

I reeled back as the vision faded, moaning because I wanted it to show me more.

"Mel?"

My eyelids fluttered, and I saw the real Dove before me. Caleb now. Healthier looking, but no less a mystery.

"Mel, are you alright?" He grabbed my elbow to steady me.

Caleb watched in silence as I blinked, his eyes carefully roaming my face. I bet he knew what was happening.

How could I have forgotten what he'd done? What he'd stolen? What he refused to tell me? I'd lulled myself into complacency. It was a secret he wanted to keep clearly, so how could it be anything other than bad? And when had he become comfortable saying my name like that?

His face was close to mine, cloaked in concern. I jerked back, determined to look anywhere but his eyes. I gingerly touched my chest. The spindly stitches lined up in a neat row, my skin covered with some sort of silky salve.

"Are you done?" I asked quietly, not looking up.

He took a step back and handed me a sterile bandage to cover up the line of sutures.

"Yes." He looked like he wanted to say more, but then, of course, he didn't.

"You can relax," I snapped. "I didn't remember anything clear. Just scraps, like usual. Nothing that explains anything that happened between us."

He snapped backward at the venom in my voice.

I slid from the counter and staggered. Caleb reached out to steady me, but I jerked away.

"I'm going to bed."

I swiped a brownie from the counter and devoured it on the way to my room, shutting the door firmly. After its click, I sagged against it. My chest throbbed, and wisps of unclear memory drifted in my head. A gaunt Caleb looking up from taking my pulse, deactivating my arm band, saying something I couldn't hear. Over and over. I heard his steps come down the hallway. He stopped between our doors. I counted for a full minute. Then he went into his room. I didn't hear him shut the door behind him.

I dragged myself to the closet to change, cursing that I still had my suit on. We never brought them out of the Den if we could help it. I shucked off the pants and hung them up with my jacket. I'd clean them tomorrow and see about sealing the slice with some of Chezza's SuperSeam. I dragged on yoga pants one-handed and dug in the drawer for a shirt. There was only one left crumpled in the back of the drawer. I withdrew it and my body went rigid.

It was Caleb's. The one I'd been wearing the night I fled Kavoh's facility. It still gave off the relaxing, minty smell of him, underneath the faint whiff of smoke and sweat. Old blood stained one wrist's cuff. Mine or his?

At precisely that moment, I became entirely fed up, or determined, or desperate. Blood roared in my ears. I pulled the shirt on, the edges of my vision threatening me with darkness as I lifted my arms over my head and my stitches pulled. I was dangerously close to overexerting myself. Thankfully, stubborn, idiotic recklessness runs in the Leo family.

I stalked to the room across the hall and shoved through the door.

Caleb looked shocked to see me. He turned from the window, already dressed for bed in gym shorts and a black T-shirt.

His face was unreadable as he took in what I was wearing, the desperate look on my face.

"I—" he began.

I staggered then, falling against the chair we hadn't yet bothered to move from his bedside for "guard duty." He rushed to my side, helping me sit. I didn't have the strength to fight him.

All the fight, all the fire, all the speeches and accusations and lectures I'd imagined disappeared from my head. I wanted to demand my memories back, but I failed to muster the will.

"Doesn't it bother you how much this hurts me?"

Caleb sat at the edge of the bed. He took one of my hands in both of his smoothly, like he'd done it before. His palms had warmed as he'd stitched me up. He didn't ask what was wrong as I fought to take a steadying breath. He knew. We both did.

"Can't you see what you're doing to me?" I said. "Not knowing what happened . . . It's driving me crazy." Pain frosted his eyes, the rest of his face a mask of concern; his body tilted toward mine. "I can't go an hour without wondering what happened. Or without panicking that other parts of my memory somehow disappeared. What if you had erased an entire month, a year? That's longer than I've had

Bane, longer than I've had this home! This is my *life*, and you took some of it from me.

"The void—it's a space I can feel in my head, taunting me every day. And when you're around, it starts to come back. But only flashes. Only hints of what happened, and that makes it worse. I feel like I should hate you. Logically, that's what I should feel, but I don't, and I don't know why. If I hated you, how did I end up at home in this shirt? How?" I stared into his eyes, adding every ounce of conviction I had. "I need to know. Whatever it is, I can handle it. The longer you wait, the worse I imagine those memories must be. But they can't be worse than this. Please, please, tell me the trigger. . ." I swallowed, then gave one last plea in just above a whisper. "Show me why I'm so happy you're here."

"Okay," Caleb said, not a trace of anger or resentment in his voice. His face immediately changed to determined.

He shifted his weight, situating his long legs on either side of mine.

He took my face in his hands, sending electric sparks up my cheeks. "I'll do it," he spoke with urgency. "I didn't realize keeping it from you would upset you this deeply, I swear. It makes it worse because everything I've done since—I don't know, not long after we met—I've done because I thought it would protect you."

I was confused, but I didn't question it, fearful he would change his mind. His eyes were all I could see, glowing and magnetic.

Very slowly, Caleb leaned forward and pressed his lips to mine.

CHAPTER
TWENTY

No wonder I'd been such a wreck lately. Somewhere along the line, Caleb had become my oxygen, and in hating him, I'd kept myself from breathing.

I scooted closer. My hands found his face, tracing across his cheeks to twine in his hair.

He stiffened in shock, then the glorious sensation of his warmth melding with mine was interrupted as my memories returned.

Part of me thought my remaining lost memories would appear all at once, like a magic trick. Suddenly back and full of sense, wiping the mystery away in an instant.

Instead, the fog filled my entire mind. I slowly relived those missing hours. In fits and spurts, some of the memories flew by, and some replayed like a movie in perfect detail. I couldn't see beyond the memories—what was actually before me, but I was unbothered. My mind urged me to patiently wait this process through. There was a pressure on my lips, but Caleb had pulled back, I was sure. I didn't feel his heat. His scent was faint. It was my own fingertips resting on my lips, forlorn at the loss of Caleb's touch.

"Go ahead."

Caleb leaned toward me, all focus, and used a pen light to examine my face. I jumped a bit when he touched my chin to turn my head to the side. We both froze, then both pretended we hadn't. Briskly, he used a sharp-smelling wipe to brush away the blood from the edges of my mask, his hands gentle though the liquid stung. A frown twisted his mouth. I dropped my eyes and let him work. He was too close for me to survey the room much. I examined the faded leaf pattern on the bedspread, the way his chest moved beneath his worn shirt. There was a hole near the collar, exposing more of his skin. He was slender, but lean muscle was there too.

His calloused fingers continued to brush my cheeks.

I swallowed, determined to keep my muddled thoughts focused on learning more, buying time, and getting out of here. "Do you live here?"

"Yes." Caleb's voice was devoid of emotion. He stood, noisily gathering the trash into a pile and disposing of it. He faced the wall when he spoke next. "Who was that . . . shouting for you? Across your earpiece. In the alley."

My blood froze. Uncle Bane. He couldn't know.

"When you took me, you mean?" I shot back.

Dove squared his shoulders, swallowed, and dropped it.

With every passing minute, the bacteria's effects lessened. I finally caved and swiped the glass of water off the table, cradling it between my hands and drinking deeply.

"You have somewhere to go," he said finally. It wasn't really a question.

"Yes." The water gentled my broken voice. My situation was precarious. In bringing me here, Caleb had made a choice, or began to. "What's the plan?"

"I don't know yet," he said simply, returning to the chair.

He withdrew a familiar stethoscope. I eased aside my shirt's collar, and he pressed the cool metal to my skin. I lacked the strength to hold back a shiver. This close, there was nowhere else to look but his face. The look in his eyes reminded me a little of how I looked on my worst days before I came to live with Bane, back when I felt stuck.

Caleb sat back with a sigh; his shoulders caved in like he was shielding the center of himself. He rubbed his eyes beneath his glasses, then clasped his hands.

"I haven't seen someone subjected to the bacteria at that intensity for that long a duration before. You're still shaky, and your pulse is all over the place, but strong, and slowing gradually. I suspect you'll be back to normal within twelve hours."

I cocked my head, grasping for any measure of bravado I had left. "Where will I be in twelve hours?"

Caleb opened his mouth, hesitated, then tried again. "Home. My goal is to get you home in twelve hours, wherever that is."

Air whooshed from my chest. This is what I wanted and had suspected. But why?

"I thought you stopped Nicklai because I'm your experiment, not his."

"You're no one's experiment." He tugged a hand through his hair, which now flowed back wildly. He spoke haltingly. "In the past, we've only grabbed . . . villains, usually. Rapists, murderers. People I've witnessed commit violent crimes. I haven't been . . . assigned . . . to someone good before. You shouldn't be here. Nicklai was just the beginning . . . I don't have a lot of control, but I can do this."

I almost didn't dare to speak if my freedom hung here so easily. I couldn't trust him, though. My mind kept returning to the stove in the corner. Possibly the only access to heat in the small room.

I licked my lips, thinking fast. "I need my suit."

Dove seemed a little disappointed at my first thought after his speech, but he chewed his lip before nodding. "I'll get it, and I'll think of a distraction for you."

"It's not as easy as opening the front door, then?" My joke hardly landed.

He grimaced. "I'm afraid not." He headed toward the door.

"Are you a prisoner here too?" I blurted out as his hand touched the knob.

He paused, considering me. "Technically. Please consider not devising a way to knock me unconscious when I get back." He disappeared through the door before I could think of a response.

I waited a full minute before ignoring his request. I leapt from the *bed, getting lightheaded in the process. I staggered against the table and righted myself, my hand instantly going to my head. I winced as my fingertips brushed my still-open wounds. I shoved Caleb from my mind and raced to the stove, scanning it quickly before turning the two burners to their highest setting. There wasn't even an oven beneath the stovetop. How had he ended up here?*

I rubbed my hands over the burners, anxious for the heat. As they warmed, I nearly moaned. I splayed my hands over the stove, my strength returning for the first time in what felt like an age. My hearing turned a little sharper, and I listened for Caleb's return. He could be back in a matter of minutes, and I was still mostly freezing. My frenzied eyes darted around the apartment again, finding nothing and more nothing to help me, until they settled on the dresser.

Keeping one hand on the stove, I reached for the top drawer. I rifled through, trying not to make a mess, until I found a long-sleeved shirt. It was well-worn and dark gray. I tugged it over my head, sighing in joy. The paper-thin ensemble I'd been trapped in was driving me mad. I hunched over the burner, getting as much of me as close to it as I could. The edges of the spiraling metal glowed red.

I forced myself to breathe deeply. I couldn't trust Caleb, though some part of me wanted to. Even if he didn't change his mind, someone else could come along and incapacitate us both. If I was granted fifteen minutes with this stove, I could get warm enough to bust out of here. If the quickest way out was right through this wall, I would do it. There was a small window set high in the ceiling, and I could see the dark sky through it. All I had to do was knock out Dove, grab my suit, climb out. Once I hit the ground and started running, I would be warm too fast for anyone to stop me. Hope sparked in my chest. I dug through the dresser for another pair of socks.

Steps sounded on the stairs. I swore and turned off both burners, pressing against them one last time. As quietly as I could, I stepped back to where he'd left me and crawled onto the bed. As an afterthought, I yanked back the covers and slid under them as he opened the door.

He stepped into the room, my suit like a limp body in his arms. His eyes searched the room and snapped to me. He stopped in surprise, like he was shocked to see me where he'd left me, like he truly had expected me to ambush him. Smart man. I stared impassively. I realized his eyes were locked on what was different about me. That I was wearing his shirt and snuggled into his bed.

"I'm fucking freezing." It wasn't technically a lie, and my stammering was genuine.

He swallowed, an odd look on his face. "Of course. I—I should have thought of that. I'm sorry."

Though it sounded sincere, the apology rang hollow given the circumstances.

He set my suit on the foot of the bed, and we both stared at it. With the front facing up, you couldn't see what a mangled mess I'd made of it. It almost looked impressive, with the scratches and scuffs, and the faint sheen on my emblem still intact. He reached down and touched the unmoving flame.

"I didn't figure out how it worked, so whatever secrets you have are still safe."

"Good." I wouldn't thank him. I hugged my knees to my chest, trying to retain the heat I'd managed to steal. "What now?"

Caleb was more antsy than he'd been upon leaving. "Cellina noticed I moved you." My stomach dropped. "You need to get out of here now. I set up a distraction."

I grabbed my suit and stuffed my legs in. Without the brick, it wouldn't work, so it didn't matter if the lining had contact with my skin. Dove set something on the table and fiddled in his medical kit. My breathing evened a little as I zipped it up and was embraced by the familiar compression. It was a little tight over the strange array of clothes I wore, so I didn't zip it up the entire way. I pulled up my hood and instantly felt more at ease.

Dove faced me and held something my way.

It was the remainder of my glass of water. An odd priority, but maybe he wanted me hydrated, given he was a doctor and I was about to run for my life. Maybe it was the final gift he could afford to give me. I took it from him warily and gulped it down.

The water's off taste was obvious the instant it passed my lips. The liquid felt full, like wine or a sports drink, with a warm, acidic aftertaste. I gripped the glass so hard it shattered. Caleb jumped, eyes wide, but he didn't look entirely surprised at my reaction.

I sat on the bed, hard. "What did you put in here?"

"It's harmless." He spoke quickly. "It's a serum that makes you forget things. Blocks memories. You won't remember the last day and a half very well. It'll kick in in a minute."

My body heaved against the idea of having my experiences stripped from me. "Why?"

Tentatively, Caleb kneeled in front of me, so our faces were level. "It's safer."

"Safer for who?"

"Please." He grabbed my hand. His was wonderfully warm.

I tried a different question and hoped it was the right one. "What's going to happen to you?" And why the hell do I care?

The corner of his mouth pinched. He leaned his head close to mine, joining me beneath the shadow of my hood. I realized I'd expected him to since that damn alley, for no good reason. So, I leaned toward him, ever so slightly, showing him I felt the urge too. That he was like a magnet to my metal, and for whatever lions-forsaken reason, I felt drawn to him too.

Caleb kissed me.

Of its own volition, my hand lifted. I set it against his neck, holding him close. His pulse surged beneath my thumb.

In a moment, one more instant, I'd find a pressure point and knock him unconscious, and bolt for my life. Just one . . . more . . . second of his lips on mine, before I forced the world to make sense again.

An echoing boom shook the room. My thoughts grew fuzzy around the edges, unable to keep up with the speed of what happened around us.

Caleb pulled back, gently removing my hand from his neck.

Why . . . Why had I been touching him?

As my thoughts crawled in nonsensical circles, he withdrew an angular key from his pocket and inserted it to the band on my wrist. My stomach roiled as he gently withdrew the prongs from my skin. With a few hurried motions, he wrapped my wrist in gauze.

He helped me up. "Are you able to run?"

I jerked from his grip and glanced down, disoriented to see I wore my Silhouette suit.

Caleb moved to the far wall and pressed a small bundle there at shoulder height. It stuck, small and round and gray. I'd seen a similar ritual of motions in action movies. The doctor was rigging explosives.

A red light glowed. He leapt over the bed and hauled the mattress over us.

He threw himself around me like a cage, my head tucked against his neck. He smelled like sweat and my favorite blend of calming tea.

With his mouth somewhere near my ear, Caleb spoke softly.

"It was nice knowing you."

The room exploded.

Debris careened everywhere as we were thrown sideways.

The mattress caught the worst of the blast. I slid down the wall, fine dust coating my suit and mask. I coughed and tried to catch my breath. Tried to make sense of what was happening.

Had I just woken up? It felt like it. It felt like that searing, nameless pain that rips across the front of your brain when you have to get up long before sunrise. A groan drew my attention. That doctor—Kavoh's lackey with the scary intense eyes—was next to me, and in his pajamas, for some reason.

He was yelling at me. I couldn't make sense of the words. He gave up his frantic gesturing and grabbed me by the arm.

My reflexes stalled. I stared blankly at the contact between us, needing a moment to piece together what I needed to do.

I ripped out of his grip and backed against the wall. Knowledge slammed into me. Where I was, how I'd gotten there, and why my suit wasn't emitting any heat. I'd broken it to protect my family.

Uncle Bane.

The doctor set his jaw. I heard yelling from far away. Other rooms, maybe. Was this the room I'd been kept in? The size was right, but it didn't look quite like mine. There was too much stuff in this one.

Caleb grabbed my arm in an iron grip this time, and he dragged me to my feet.

"Get off me!" I fought him, but he towed me to the hole he'd blown in the wall.

Any questions I had disappeared at the touch of cool night air on my face. Whatever was going on, this was my chance to escape. My toes kissed the floor's edge. I eyed the empty two stories to the street. Sirens howled somewhere in the distance.

The words Caleb kept yelling finally sharpened in my ringing ears.

"You have to RUN!"

I caught one last glimpse of his sad eyes and jumped.

I landed awkwardly. With a gasp, I found my footing shoved upright. Staggeringly, I began to run. As I did, heat built around my body, steadying my movements. Reaching behind me, I yanked my hood up from where the wind had blown it back. Not seeing any landmarks I recognized, I made a blind dash into the woods, panting and putting as much distance between me and that horrible facility.

The heat built in my suit in bounds. I put on a burst of speed, flying along the darkened forest floor like I was being chased by wolves, getting whipped in the face by branches, and nearly tripping a few times. Guessing the right direction between the placement of the moon and the curve of Crown's ring of mountains, I eventually made it to a part of the city I recognized. Leaking tears of relief, I turned for home.

Eventually, a familiar stone wall appeared through the trees, pale in the starlight. I was too winded to make a sound of disbelief. Instead, I threw the last of my energy into my momentum and careened toward the front gate, my desperation finally allowing my balance to fail. My boot caught on the pavement, and I went sprawling against our front gate.

The memories slowly melded into the ones I already had, fitting themselves back into place in my mind. As they did, a familiar voice broke through the disappearing fog.

"How much longer will she be like this?" That was Bane.

"A few hours." Caleb's voice was hoarse, like he hadn't used it in some time. "It varies. It depends on how long her mind needs to process the memories."

"Can I move her?"

"That shouldn't be a problem."

Bane spoke again. "I take it you feature heavily in these memories?"

A pause. Then, like an admission of guilt. "Yes."

"I think you should be there when she wakes up," Bane said. The firm comfort of his arms lifted me from the chair. "She'll have questions."

I didn't escape the facility on my own. Caleb had helped set me free.

When I woke, my head was clear for the first time since my memories were stolen, like a lost puzzle piece had casually been pressed back into place.

Caleb was sprawled across my window seat, his face peaceful in sleep, his hands crossed over his stomach. The morning sun splashed over his tousled hair.

I felt completely normal, aside from the ache in my chest. No more fog where memories should be. And my feelings for Caleb . . .

I wanted to go to him. To wrap my arms around him.

Lions, I wanted to tear his clothes off.

Bolting upright, I chucked a pillow at him. "Hey!"

Caleb woke slowly, scrubbing both hands across his face before finally opening his eyes. He moved to my side and kneeled beside the bed. I reached for a thousand different words, unable to decide on one. Caleb pressed a hand to my forehead, short-circuiting my brain.

"How are you feeling?"

I released a shaky laugh as he withdrew his hand. "That's a loaded question."

His nose scrunched, close enough for me to count the faint freckles there. "How about we start with how you're feeling physically?"

I blinked. Between his proximity and the recent kissing . . . "Um."

"You're not feverish. How about a headache? Fatigue? Memory recall can have a variety of side effects."

"I'm fine. I'm just . . . confused." I searched his face. "I don't exactly understand why you kept those memories from me."

Caleb leaned back. It took plenty of my willpower to not reach for him. "When I brought you to the facility . . . you were so obviously good. A real-life superhero, right in front of me. Your light shone upon all I'd done wrong, for all my time working in the lab. By the end of the first day, I knew I had to get you out." At this point, he dropped his gaze. "While I worked on a plan, my feelings toward you grew. I— I came to idolize you. To want to protect you. The force with which I suddenly cared for you . . . I think Nicklai noticed, and he targeted you to torment me. When I saw you on the floor with him looming over you, I had to get you out right then. When we spoke in my apartment, a desperate part of me thought maybe you cared for me too. But I knew setting you free meant my life was forfeit, and that was what I deserved."

"It's not," I cut in.

He looked at me gratefully and continued. "Regardless, the situation was much easier if you hated me completely. Since you're a hero, and you maybe cared about me, I knew you might come back. I couldn't risk you. Couldn't stand the thought of Nicklai putting hands on you again—or worse, Kavoh." He shuddered. "So, I gave you the memory loss tonic as a precaution, to erase any fondness you might have had, and to keep you away. But you came back anyway."

I shrugged, swallowing a smile. "Bane practically had to drag me."

He laughed then, and it was a wonderful sound.

Collapsing into my pillows, I kneaded a blanket's edge

between my fingers. "What did you think when I showed up in the cell the night we rescued you?"

"You looked like an angel sent from the only heaven I'd ever be allowed into."

"Dove. Caleb." His name was comforting on my tongue. He turned those baleful eyes on me. His hand dangled off his knee. A few inches from where mine twined in the bedspread.

I didn't know where that left us. I was saved from finding out by the sound of the doorbell.

My mind cranked into motion. What fucking day was it? I glanced at my phone.

"Max!" I gasped. I had class. I was on the brink of making us late for it.

"Max?" Caleb parroted.

Bane swore from somewhere downstairs. He had forgotten too. "Mel! MAX!"

I cursed even more colorfully than he had. "Buy me three minutes!" I shouted.

"Will do!" His footsteps moved for the front door.

Caleb tilted his head. "You two have enhanced senses. You literally don't need to shout."

I hurried out of bed, wincing at the sore tugs coming from my stitches. "Yeah, but shouting's fun. I have to go." I sprinted to the closet and yanked down the first sweater I saw and a clean pair of jeans.

Caleb coughed from my room. "Right. Yep. I'll, uh, see you later."

I whirred to the closet's door, a lock of hair falling over my face. "Yes, yeah. Yes. We'll talk more."

His departing smile was small, but there.

"Great, so nothing's resolved," I muttered to myself as I tore through the bathroom.

My three minutes were certainly up. I grabbed my school bag and stopped only to make sure my sneakers were a matching set before flying down the stairs.

"Sorry," I said to Max brightly. He stood in the foyer, listening politely as Bane explained, from what I could gather, the merits of various insulated travel cups. "Slept in."

Max's eyes darted to the upstairs landing. Had he seen Caleb cross the hall? I tugged him toward the door.

"Rough night?" he asked.

My responding laugh was manic, and apparently answer enough to keep Max silent all the way to campus and our short walk to class. My thoughts took my entire attention, though when we sat and I looked over at Max, I could tell he was annoyed.

I didn't want him to get the wrong idea of me and Caleb, at least before I figured out what exactly that idea was. "Bane and I tried to teach ourselves to box," I fibbed. "I hurt my wrist, and I didn't sleep well because of the pain."

"I'm thinking of switching my major," Max mused with a sniff.

I relaxed a fraction. He was being a dick, but it got us on a new course of conversation. "Don't switch to nursing. Your bedside manner is shit."

Max adjusted the cuffs of his sleeves. "I'm much better *in* the bed, as you know."

I opened my mouth to snap a response, but Professor Gray-Phoenix chose that moment to start class.

NOT FIVE MINUTES INTO THE LECTURE, MY PHONE BUZZED with the trademark frenetic buzzing I'd assigned to Bane's number.

You okay?

I typed back under the table.

Yes. Really. I'll fill you in later.

Goob!
    Goot.
    GOOD i mean dammit.

I could feel Max growing annoyed beside me. I set my phone down on my thigh. Not two seconds passed before it buzzed again.

I ignored it.

Then again.

And again.

I flipped it over to more messages from Bane.

Also . . . This comes as a shock considering it's me, but I may have forgotten to tell you about a commitment we have tonight.

Brow furrowed, I typed out a response.

What is it this time?

The Mayor's Dinner. Max's dad's annual fancy fundraiser gala thing?

I vaguely remembered an exceedingly thick-papered invitation arriving in the mail weeks ago.

A pointed cough interrupted my reverie, and I glanced up. Professor Gray-Phoenix raised an eyebrow.

"Sorry," I mouthed, and turned my phone entirely silent. Then I waited a few minutes to finish reading.

I called Clare. She said if you swing by after class, she has some gowns you could choose from.

When Professor Gray-Phoenix finally excused us, I turned to Max. "Would you mind dropping me off at Clare's?"

Max scrunched his brows. "Your uncle forgot about The Mayor's Dinner?"

"And by extension, so did I."

"Of course I'll drop you off. Can't have you wearing something you've worn before. That would be embarrassing."

I elbowed him, but he merely kept talking. "Don't forget to bring your checkbook. I'll be the important looking one in the tux."

"I'll write you a check right now if you agree to stop talking," I grumbled.

Max slung an arm around my shoulders with a dramatic sigh. "Thank fuck I'm rich."

CHAPTER
TWENTY-ONE

"Ruffles or a train," Clare said, brandishing her lit cigarette in my direction. "You can say 'no' to one, but not both."

"I'll take the ruffles," I said, stuffing another mini croissant in my mouth.

Arriving at Clare's warm studio broke me from my reverie. The walls, now painted a dusty rose, were covered in velvety curtains to fend off the cold, and she always had a spread of snacks ready.

We caught up over coffee, interspersed with Clare asking me harmless questions about my preferences of one color or texture over another, when Chezza pranced in from the warehouse, a garment bag in her arms.

"Is Bane dragging you to this too?"

"Of course not. I'm Clare's plus one."

"My esteemed guest," she corrected. "My husband is such a bore at these things. Chezza's going to help me catch the ear of a city council member about a grant to expand women's health resources in the city."

Chezza nodded. "One of the doctors I work with should be there too, and she'd totally be on board. I'll introduce you."

She turned her appraising gaze on me. "What are you thinking?"

"I'm overwhelmed by all my options, I think. I'm not sure what I like."

"What have you worn for things like this before? What did you wear to prom?"

"I never went."

They would have been less alarmed if I told them I'd impaled someone. (I hadn't, but I came close once. Arms dealer, a broken piece of pipe . . . It's a long story.)

Clare jumped so quickly she dropped her mug on the floor where it shattered. "Don't worry, I've got plenty more," she insisted. She and Chezza bustled me into the massive room where Clare kept her stock and battered me with questions.

"Would you rather be noticed or blend in?"

"Is there some option in the middle?" I asked.

Clare inclined her head. "Of course there is. Now, a picnic in the woods or a swim in the ocean?"

"Picnic, I think?"

"Okay, and do you feel more drawn to a jaguar or a crocodile?"

"What does that have to do with anything?"

"Please, Melbourne, you trust me with your life in your Silhouette suit. You should extend that trust to my care for your style and comfort in all situations."

As Clare pulled options, Chezza guided me to a slightly raised tier in front of some angled mirrors. She laughed at the contorted look on my face, reflected back at us from all sides. "You're normally much more chill, or even excited, to play dress up. What's going on?"

I tugged on my sweater's sleeves. "Boy problems."

Chezza patted my cheeks. "Hmm, so likely not a real problem, then. Get distracted playing princess with us." She snagged a faux-fur shawl from a hook on the wall and swept it around her shoulders, giving the mirror a runway model's pout.

She tossed me a bridal tiara from one of the displays, and I set it on my head. "Gladly. This is pretty fun."

Clare returned with a single garment bag. "What's not to love about feeling special? Or confident? Or attended to, you know? Everyone needs that every once in a while. I take myself out on a lavish date at least once a week."

"My options?" I asked.

"Option," she clarified. "Singular. I nailed it. You don't need anything else."

I reached for the bag, but Clare stopped me with a hand on my arm. "The other piece you requested last month is finished, and it's in here as well." She shooed me into a curtained off booth to change.

I was out in a matter of minutes. "Clare, you deserve the key to the city."

"Boring. I was awarded that years ago."

"Oh yes, bitch," Chezza said at the sight of me.

Clare merely looked regal and satisfied. She'd wrapped herself in an ostrich feather boa while I changed.

I hopped back up on the platform and twirled, soaking in how the sage green velvet flowed to my feet. As promised, there was no train, and Clare had spared me from ruffles too. The dress' collar clasped around my neck, hiding my stitches, and it clung to my body all the way to my hips before flaring delicately. It bared most of my back, and sported a slit up the front allowing my leg to peek out every couple of steps.

"Alright, you two," Clare said. "Time to raid the shoe and handbag room. Bane said he'd pick us up twenty minutes ago, so he's bound to show up in another ten or so."

Chezza donned a miraculous red number while Clare opted for white. They helped me fasten silver pins in either side of my hair.

"Which lip color do you like better?" I asked, holding two for Chezza's examination.

"Definitely the peach one with the shimmer."

An extremely unhelpful image popped into my head of the same color pressed to the corner of Caleb's mouth.

A stream of one note car honks sounded faintly, then Bane's shouting. "Ladieeeees, your chariot *awaits!*"

Bane's SUV idled at the curb. Caleb stepped from the passenger side, dressed in a tux.

"Keep it together, Silhouette," Chezza said, nudging me with her hip.

Bane stared at me from the driver's seat, probably thinking the same thing.

Caleb's tux fit perfectly, hugging his wide shoulders, his collar finished with a bowtie. His shoes were shiny, his smile relaxed, and of course, a single lock of his dark hair had escaped to sweep over his forehead, basically demanding I meet those eyes.

Again, devastating. Devastating in sweatpants, devastating in a tux. What the hell was I going to do?

"Are you trying to kill me?" I said, just loud enough for Chezza and Clare to hear. I knew exactly who to thank for the stunning design and impeccable fit of his suit.

Chezza snorted as Caleb opened the door to the second row of seats, and she and Clare slid in. Having made sure they both made it in without tearing a seam or scuffing a shoe, Caleb finally looked at me.

The world seemed to pause for us two idiots as we stared, slack-jawed and awestruck at each other.

Say something, Mel, anything *for lions' sake. You can't stand here on the sidewalk and ogle each other all day. You're a superhero. You take on murderers. This is nothing—*

"Did you know the T-rex in the movie *Cretaceous Carnival* is the world's most elaborate puppet?"

Caleb blinked twice. My brain had short-circuited and spouted my current favorite movie production fact.

"I didn't, actually."

"Yep," I said, hauling myself into the SUV's seat and tangling my skirt's hem in my heels. "Six women operated it. Three in the head, two in the body and tail, and one for the arms."

I pulled the door shut in his face and slouched against the seat with my eyes closed, wishing I could melt into it.

"Smooth as a dinosaur's hide, Silhouette," Chezza said, barely concealing a laugh behind her hand.

"Why. Is. He. Here," I gritted out.

Bane met my stare in the rearview mirror. "Yeah, uh. I had an extra ticket."

"Why did you have an extra—" I started, but Caleb had recovered himself and climbed into the front seat, folding his long legs to somehow fit where I usually sat.

Bane turned to survey us all. "Everybody ready for a fun night?"

"Does that mean we're having two drinks, making minimal small talk, and leaving early to get fries on the way home?"

"You know me so well, Mel." He put the car in drive and turned toward the museum where the event was taking place.

My hand was warm from where Caleb had helped me in. Blood swum close to the surface of my face. His electric stare haunted my mind even long after I'd looked away.

I glanced to the front again, where Caleb spoke quietly with Bane. It was nice seeing him relax, as he did a little more each day he spent with us. He'd found a pair of black sunglasses that he made exceptionally debonair. When Bane turned onto a main road and the sunshine lit up Caleb's face through the front window . . . *Damn, those cheekbones.* I hadn't noticed his eyelashes were so long before.

The rush of attraction had my heart pounding. Like the

very core of me was pulling toward him. It had felt like this since I first saw him in that damn alley. Why? *Why?*

Why not, really? Caleb had been drawn to the good in me. Maybe my instincts had sensed the good in him.

We stopped in front of the museum where the dinner was taking place. Caleb got my door again, and I offered him a long smile with my thanks. I swear time stopped again as the rest of our group got situated around us. Bane handed off the keys to the valet.

Chezza herded us inside. Caleb offered his arm, a question in his eyes. I wish he didn't look so disbelieving when I took it.

Finally, I realized how exhausted I was of all this questioning. The magnetism between us was real, I think. So much of me didn't want to fight it, so I stopped. Maybe my gut knew something I didn't. It had been a long time since I'd been afraid of Caleb Dove, and I decided to stop being angry with him too. I squeezed his arm. The corner of his mouth turned up, all for me.

"Ready?" I asked.

"I am."

The hall was festooned with gold and silver, from the bunting overheard to the flatware and napkins. Projections on various walls showed photos of images from projects Crown City's government had completed over the prior year.

There was a short but grand staircase leading from the lobby into the event. I didn't think about who was in attendance and what they would say about the person on my arm, focusing instead on the new sense of completeness hovering in my chest with him at my side.

And I wondered how I could entice more of those smiles from him as we were ushered into a receiving line.

"Don't suppose we can skip this formality, huh?" Bane asked out of the corner of his mouth.

I pushed onto my tiptoes and swore. Mayor Keep was greeting each of his esteemed guests personally.

"We can handle it," I said.

By the time we made it to the head of the line, I'd plastered a lukewarm expression on my face and stopped fidgeting with my dress. Bane took the lead of our little group and stiffly shook the mayor's hand.

"Ah, the Leo . . ." Travis Keep's heavy stare spent a second on Bane, skipped over me entirely, and hovered on Caleb. He narrowed his eyes, as if confused. "Family."

"Thanks for having us," Bane said. "Always happy to shell out—" I elbowed him. "I mean, donate to a good cause."

I glared daggers at Max's dad, but he did an excellent job of pretending I didn't exist. Unfortunately, even in heels, I couldn't force myself into his eyeline, so I returned the favor while Bane and Mayor Keep traded barbs thinly veiled as pleasantries.

As they finished, a flash of glitter caught my eye, and I spotted Gem waving her inch-long acrylic nails at me. Max leaned against the pillar beside her, as flawless and broody as the works of art scattered throughout the room. Gem shamelessly slurped a margarita, and I was thankful it kept her from inundating us with questions as I tugged us over.

"You two look amazing," I said. The gold thread winking from Max's suit complimented the whorls of silver running down Gem's dress.

Gem elbowed Max, breaking his composure and nearly sloshing the whiskey out of his glass. "I promised to keep Maxy here company tonight if he sprung for a dress for me."

Despite Gem's jovial efforts, Max wore a slight scowl. I realized he wasn't staring at me, but over my shoulder, to where Caleb had landed. He stayed a half step behind me, his arm slipping from mine; though he trailed his fingers across the inside of my wrist before putting a few inches of dismal air between us.

"Gem, Max, this is Caleb Dove."

Caleb held out a hand, which Gem grabbed eagerly, stepping in like the amazing friend she was, so I didn't have to think of anything else to say by way of introduction. "I haven't heard enough about you yet," she effused. "It's so great you're here."

Caleb smiled, but it was stiff as Max took his hand next.

"Welcome to Crown City," Max said, his impressing-investors voice in full effect. "Remind me where you're visiting from?"

As Caleb answered with his practiced fabricated history, Gem pulled me aside and pretended to gush about my dress.

"He's so tall," Gem accused.

"Plenty of people are tall," I muttered.

"And lions, look at those cheekbones . . ."

"Can we talk about this later?"

"Don't you kinda wanna cut your lip open on them?"

"*Yes.* Yes, I do!" I hissed. "Are you happy now?"

Gem cackled. "Doesn't it feel good to admit it?"

I grumbled.

"Wait . . ." Gem squeezed my shoulder. "You're practically *giddy*. Is that why you're mad? 'Cause you're giddy?"

"What kind of vigilante is ever giddy?"

She raised an eyebrow.

"You're right. There's no shame in it. Congratulations." I dragged her back to the boys, so I could halt Max's grilling of Caleb. "Like pretty much everything, you're right. Now I need a drink."

We rejoined them just in time to hear Caleb make a grave mistake. "Right," he said pleasantly. "Remind me of your name again? Sorry, I didn't catch when Mel said it."

A muscle ticked in Max's carved jaw, drawing strain all the way down his neck to tug at his perfectly knotted tie, stuck through with a diamond-tipped pin.

"Max Keep, good to meet you. Mel and I have seen each other naked." He took a long drink, not breaking Caleb's gaze.

I cleared my throat, contemplating if I could break one of Max's fingers without him realizing my superhero alias.

Caleb held his own, despite the flush I saw rise at the base of his neck. He cocked his head. "Is that how people greet each other in this city?" He smiled evenly, projecting calm. "In that case, as Mel said, I'm Caleb Dove. Mel and I have not seen each other naked."

YET! Gem mouthed like a psychopath as she came around Max's other side.

I placed a hand on Caleb's arm. His focus found me immediately. "Do you mind grabbing me a drink?"

"Of course. What would you like?"

"Something with alcohol," I said, giving him a gentle shove into Gem's waiting arms.

"C'mon, new kid," she said, patting him on the shoulder. "I'll show you which bartender pours the heaviest."

I watched them disappear into the crowd, then turned on Max.

"Listen, I know it's been tense between us, but we need to talk it out. I'm not ashamed of our time together, but it doesn't give you permission to say shit like that. What the actual fuck, Max?"

He at least looked cowed. "I'm sorry, Mel. But you haven't even told him about me?"

"I've barely spent any time with him! He has priorities; I have priorities. He's actively grieving, and I barely know him."

"And yet, you look at each other like . . . like . . . the northern lights," Max mumbled.

"The northern lights?"

"I was trying to think of something wonderful!"

I pinched the bridge of my nose.

Max kept his distance. "I'm sorry. Truly."

"Good," I said, and I turned to search for Gem and Caleb.

As soon as I reached the bar, Gem bailed, probably to give

Max a dressing-down of her own. Caleb slid an amber-colored drink toward me, sipping from his glass of wine.

He opened his mouth, and I held up a hand. "It's handled. I don't want to talk about it."

He nodded, and the evening's emcee called us to dinner.

Caleb used his height advantage to scout for our table through the crowd. One of his hands hovered at the small of my back as he guided me in the direction of Bane's waving arms.

"Careful, or you're going to knock over the centerpiece."

Bane toasted me with his drink. "Maybe then they'd stop inviting me."

One of our table-mates smacked his shoulder. The table was filled with people I recognized— some Leo Optics board members and higher-ups. Despite his comment, Bane played nice and was perfectly amicable, though he kept checking his phone beneath the table. With Caleb between us, I couldn't quietly ask him about it. It was always good for him to try and increase his standing in their eyes, to make up for all his unexplained tardiness or sudden disappearances that had to do with being the Shadow.

He finally set his phone aside and regaled them with a story so ridiculous, Caleb and I were allowed a moment to speak.

"You look astounding," Caleb said.

Heat rushed everywhere. "Thank you. You look happier than I've ever seen you."

Another smile, and a pause as he studied my face, which sent my heart hammering. "I am. I didn't think I would have this kind of freedom again. Or . . . friends."

"I understand," I admitted.

Bane cut a glance my way, the look so knowing and his eyebrows so high up his forehead I wished I was close enough to kick him under the table.

Caleb interrupted my scheming. "You came to live with

Bane, but not very long ago, right? I'd like to hear more about that, if you're willing to share."

And so, Bane was spared an ugly bruise on his shin as I turned in my seat to face Caleb and those eyes full-on. He settled his legs on either side of mine, as we had last night when he returned my memories, and we talked.

During our conversation, presentations were being made at the front of the room.

We talked all throughout the meal. I hardly ate anything as we traversed the tales of our own histories. Caleb lost his mom to cancer at sixteen. His dad died a few years later.

"I know he didn't want to leave me," Caleb admitted. "But I don't think he had any chance of healing his broken heart."

I laid a hand on his knee as he took a drink.

"And then—" His voice trailed off, and his fork scraped across his plate.

Kavoh's face appeared on each large screen situated around the room, stealing the air between me and Caleb. She wore a wide smile, and her purple hair fell in waves around her face.

Her mouth began to move, but all I could hear was a high-pitched whine.

"Ow."

I startled and released Caleb from the vice-like grip I'd taken on his leg. "What did she say?"

Caleb swallowed; his skin was even paler than usual as people struck into applause around us. "She apologized for not being able to make it tonight, and she announced a gift she's made to Crown City schools. Big number. Lots of zeroes."

Eyes cutting to Bane, whose face was like stone, I clapped along.

It took a few tries for Caleb and I to find the thread of our conversation again.

As our plates were cleared, I realized the rest of our table had dispersed for other entertainment offerings for the evening. Bane was on the other side of the room, speaking with the coordinator of Crown City's group of homeless shelters.

"He's very philanthropic, isn't he?" Caleb asked.

"He's the greatest. He gives so much time and money, but not everyone knows. I hate it."

Caleb seemed to catch my meaning. "But *you* know, and I think that matters most to him."

I sipped my drink, buoyed by it and the band's music that was all jazz and lovely—slow things to fit the classy mood.

"Do you want to dance?" I blurted.

"Only with you." There was no haughty tone, no hint of flirtation like there would be if this was Max, who I saw staring from a few tables away. Caleb was simply telling me the truth.

I led the way. My legs were jelly as I reached back for his hand to guide us between the last few rows of tables.

Just past the edge of the dance floor, I turned to face him, settling one arm around the curve of his neck. My fingertips brushed the skin above his collar. He took my free hand and settled his other on my waist. I stepped close.

Caleb didn't seem nervous, for dancing, at least. He still seemed a little hesitant of me, as if at any moment I would change my mind and cast him off. I studied his face, letting my eyes roam unabashedly, finally. I wanted to touch his lips. Run my fingers over the planes of his face. We swayed gently to the music, tucked back into the small crowd of couples doing the same.

"Are you having fun?" I asked.

"You make it fun. Do you like coming to events like this?"

I considered, thinking of the shenanigans I'd partaken in at various Crown galas. "They're not so bad if you have good company."

He chuckled, the sound reverberating through my chest where it touched his.

Our faces were inches apart. Inches mostly provided by our difference in height. Delicately, I lifted a finger from his collar to run it through the hair at his neck.

His eyes closed, and he leaned his head back the slightest bit, into my touch. Heat bloomed in my stomach.

I swallowed, and his eyes opened again to focus on mine. What could I say to define what was going on with us? To erase that last bit of hesitation?

"Thank you for last night," I said.

Caleb looked at me seriously. "You don't need to thank me. I owe you three apologies."

I raised an eyebrow. "You've been apologizing since we busted you out of that place."

"But never in a good enough way. You don't have to accept, but I want you to know all I'm repentant for. The first is for everything I did against your will. Kidnapping you, torturing you, and kissing you without asking. The second is for assuming I knew what was best for you in choosing to not trigger your memories. None of my good intentions mattered because it was your choice to make. I see that now."

For some reason, this made him look even sadder, so I forged ahead. "Caleb, I'm glad you're with us." I squeezed his shoulder. "I forgive you. I knew it the moment I woke up this morning. Once you told me the truth."

He didn't break my gaze; he rubbed his thumb absently against my waist. My dress suddenly felt extremely tight.

He stared down at me. "I wonder if you shouldn't after all I've done . . ."

I tilted my head to chase his gaze as he tried to look away. "Who you were led exactly to who you are right now . . . And I like who you are. More every minute I get to know you."

It seemed I'd rendered him truly speechless. "Okay," he said simply, showing some teeth with his smile.

I tucked my head against his chest, content to listen to the music coordinating to the thrum of his heart, and nothing else. After a moment, he set his chin on top of my head, and we drifted.

"What's the third apology?" I asked.

He pulled back and ran a hand through his hair, threatening to ruin the style. "I—"

Bane appeared at our sides, bouncing on the balls of his feet. "Will you two join me for a chat in the hall for a moment? It's so stuffy in here."

Bane's tone lit a fire in my spine. Something was wrong.

I fixed a bland look to my face and allowed him to lead us off the dance floor. We kept our steps casual and unhurried as we strode into a side hall leading off toward the bathrooms. We took a detour into a darkened storage room.

"What's going on?" I asked.

Caleb crossed his arms, all business, staying close to me.

Bane held up his phone, where he had a call open with Vennie. With our enhanced hearing, I could hear him fine. "Go ahead."

"All the security cameras in the southern wing of the museum just cut out. Only for a second, but I think the returned feeds are a cover."

"You've been keeping tabs on us?"

"I've had the feed up while also watching soccer."

"I did invite you," Bane protested.

"Oh, hell no," Vennie said. "I'm fine here, thanks."

Bane continued. "We think Kavoh's using the gala as an opportunity to rob the museum."

"I checked the external video feeds. A duo that looked a whole lot like Cellina and Nicklai were meandering around the building's perimeter early this morning."

"And right now, all of security's attention is focused here for the gala. Never a dull moment," I finished, bracing a hand on Caleb's arm, so I could take off my heels. "Hold on to these for me?"

He nodded dumbly.

Bane squared his shoulders and said with a mocking tone, "*Such* a shame we have to leave early."

Caleb's glance ping-ponged between us. "What are you going to do?"

Bane stretched his arms high, adrenaline already blooming across his face. "What we do best."

I cracked my neck and shook out my arms. "Stop a crime. Save some people. Have some fun. Make a mess. Barely get away with it."

"Then we get tacos?" Bane asked.

"Then we get tacos," I agreed.

Caleb watched in stunned silence as I dug into my purse, withdrawing a handful of small packets. Bane tore one open with his teeth and withdrew a wadded piece of dark fabric with two small holes. He spread it over his face as I did mine.

"Vennie," Bane said. "Can you make sure all the cameras in the exhibits have dummy feeds?"

"On it. Do you want me to stay on the line?"

Bane looked to me, and I shook my head. "Nah, we'll call if we get into trouble."

"Talk to you soon, then," Vennie said, the grin in his voice evident as he hung up.

"Can I see one of those?" Caleb asked.

I passed him the spare Minimask pack. They were another of Chezza's genius inventions.

I caught Bane poking at his. "You're not supposed to touch it for a whole minute. Let it firm up."

Bane frowned, but he dropped his hands. "What are we going to do about your dress? Plenty of guests here are in tuxes." He gestured to himself. "I didn't see anyone else wearing the same color as you. You could get recognized."

"I've had Clare working on something special for me," I said, turning my back to Caleb. "Can you get my zipper?"

I wanted to feel his fingertips trace the line of my spine. Sue me.

Bane clamped his eyes shut and covered them with his hands for good measure. "Toasty, you stress me out."

"Relax, Frosty," I hissed as Caleb deftly unzipped the dress. "There's nothing to see."

I shoved the gown to the floor and stepped out, which left me in a black bodysuit covering me from chest to hip. It was gently padded all over, so it was hard to detect as anything other than shapewear under my dress, but the beauty was in the padding. Moving rapidly, I unrolled the pads, which lengthened to reveal flowy pant legs and simple short sleeves. It wouldn't keep me particularly warm, but now I wore a nondescript but fashionable black bodysuit that could fit under any outfit. If someone caught a glimpse of Bane or me, we wouldn't be easily identified.

"You can open your eyes, Bane," I said, fighting to fold my dress without turning it into a blob.

"Let me," Caleb offered, and he made easy work of it. He tucked it beneath his arm, along with my shoes.

I pulled an impossibly tiny set of rolled up black flats from my purse and put those on as well.

Bane and I checked each other's Minimasks; they'd dried around the top half of our faces to a rubbery consistency.

"Don't you have suits in the car?" Caleb asked.

"No time," Bane said.

"You're going to go after Kavoh's people in regular clothes and a few Tempatches?"

This stopped Bane, but I'd already considered it. "It's been too long since we've had a lead. We can't risk missing this. We'll scope it out, and if it's more than we can handle, we'll stick to surveillance only."

"Exactly," Bane said. "Caleb, can you go find Chezza? Tell her we were 'craving sliders.'"

"Craving . . . sliders?"

"It's our code phrase for Silhouette and Shadow stuff. No one ever really craves sliders when you could have a whole ass burger," I explained.

Bane nodded solemnly.

I snagged a museum brochure from a tower of boxes in the corner and handed it to Caleb. "Of all the exhibits here, what would she steal?"

Caleb flipped it over and considered, eyes quickly scanning the listed exhibits. "Here," he said finally, pointing. "It'll be something from this exhibit."

"Ancient Egypt?"

A grim nod. "Some mummified people were rumored to have mystical abilities during their lives. She'll explore any route that could result in superhuman powers. If she plays it carefully enough, she could probably extract some DNA without disturbing the mummies, and no one will know anything's missing."

A chill snaked across my shoulder blades. "Okay," I said. "Don't let anyone see you've got my dress, and do what Chezza tells you. Act calm."

"Won't people think it's weird you two aren't with us?"

Bane snorted, ticking down the temperature of his Tempatches via the app on his phone. "If anyone notices, which is unlikely, they'll assume we bailed already."

I winked. "We curate our public image strategically."

"Lions, leaving the house is overrated," Bane grumbled as he twisted, drawing a series of pops from his spine.

"Be discreet," I reiterated.

Caleb spared me another small nod of confirmation, and feeling reckless, I stood on my tiptoes and pressed a kiss to his cheek. "I'll see you soon," I promised.

Caleb looked a little lost as we shoved him out of the

storage room and back toward the party, then slid out in the opposite direction. We walked quickly toward the closed exhibits. Bane's phone buzzed a text alert. "Vennie says Kavoh's team has the entire exhibit side covered with dud camera feeds, and the locks and security measures are all down."

"At least it'll be easy to get to them," I offered, studying the little map to make sure I knew our way.

I ducked left, and Bane followed down an eerily quiet hallway lined with ancient-looking pottery. We jogged down a stairwell and slowed as we reached the gold-lit entrance to the hall of mummies. The sounds of hushed voices and something like a drill echoed out. Staying low, we crept down the ramp leading into the main room. At its end, we poked our heads around a plinth holding a small statue of a deity.

There were few people I wanted to see less than the one towering over the open lid of a glass case with a mummified corpse inside.

Eight feet of blister-red scales and bulging muscle stared into the case, nostrils flared. Rhett Fannon, a.k.a. Redzilla.

Bane and I withdrew, our eyes wide.

"What the fuck?" I mouthed.

"I don't know!" Bane mouthed back.

We'd defeated the Extrahuman last summer. He was supposed to be in some sort of holding cell at Roger's security company's compound. He was all rage and brute strength, with skin as thick as a rhino's and a tail like a massive club.

To add icing on the cake, Eleni Brooks cut a dainty figure next to him, maneuvering a tool toward the mummy under his watchful yellow eyes. She had another strapped across her back and a look of deep focus on her face. The soft, sick crackle of metal through ancient bone turned my stomach. Eleni balked and Redzilla's tail lashed. He nudged her, and she gulped before continuing to drill. However Kavoh had gotten Redzilla back, it seemed he and Eleni had proven themselves enough to be trusted with a mission on their own.

Bane waved to get my attention. He pointed to himself, then held a hand high, pointed at me, and lowered it.

He wanted dibs on Redzilla. Fine by me. Last time, the Extrahuman had pulled a fast one on Bane, and I had to come to his rescue, but Bane had become at least marginally better at paying attention since then.

I gave him a thumbs up and let out a slow, quiet breath, shaking loose the tightness in my shoulders.

Bane slid from our hiding spot and burst into a sprint with me right behind. Redzilla saw us first, his eyes narrowing and flicking our way, but he wasn't fast enough to react. Bane slipped to his side on the floor and slide tackled him, taking Redzilla's jean-clad legs out from beneath him.

Eleni leapt from her work, leaving the drill buried in the mummy. She was too focused on Redzilla to notice me. As Red crashed to the floor to the accompaniment of splintering floorboards, I grabbed Eleni around the middle, jerking her sideways. She shrieked and clawed, our arms tangling as I sought purchase for a pressure point to render her unconscious. Her strength rivaled mine, and we pirouetted in a vicious swirl. She reached for something. The tool along her back blinked to life—the only warning before it fired a jolt of electricity—and sent me flying.

A vision of Bane and Red trading blows blurred past me. I crashed into the floor, barely managing to gauge my momentum and land right-side-up. Eleni stalked my way, withdrawing the tool from her back. It was the size of a baseball bat and emitted a threatening buzz.

"Giant taser," I grumbled. "*Awesome.*"

Bane delivered unforgiving blows to Red's head in my periphery. Eleni hauled back her electro-club-thing and charged me with a shout. I ran toward her and ducked her swing. The electricity from the stick buzzed menacingly as it passed an inch by my bare arm. I dropped and kicked out, sweeping her off her feet.

She rolled, keeping the weapon's dangerous end away from her, and leapt upright. I scrambled to my own feet, noticing with dread that Eleni handled her weapon with comfortable precision belying lots of practice.

She swung again. I dodged, but not fast enough to avoid a kiss from the taser against my back. I sprawled to the floor. Eleni ran to the mummy and yanked out the drill.

"Red, come on!" she shouted as she sprinted for the emergency doors tucked behind a model pyramid.

Groggily, my gaze found Bane, who had rendered Red semi-unconscious, while also somehow managing to get himself stuck beneath the massive Extrahuman.

Bane grunted, shoving a massive, scaly arm off him.

"Out of the way!" a feminine voice shrieked.

I rolled and the stun baton gouged a sooty scrape against the floor. Eleni was on a rampage straight for Bane and Redzilla.

I leapt to my feet and squared up. She hauled back, aiming for Bane. I caught the baton in my hands, crying out as the electricity stung my entire body. With a shout, I hauled the baton down and my knee up, snapping it in the middle and extinguishing the power in it.

Eleni shoved me backward with a frustrated howl. She kicked Bane in the head and helped Red to his feet.

"The doors!" I shouted.

We raced after the duo. Bane weaved unsteadily behind me. We nearly caught them before Eleni threw the doors wide.

A wall of chilly wind buffeted me, dropping me to my knees. A dust of thick white flakes flurried into the room. It had begun snowing since we'd arrived. While ogling Caleb, I'd left the faux fur wrap Clare loaned me in the car.

The toll on my strength was instantaneous. Without my suit to shield me, the bolstering Tempatch heat leeched from my body, leaving me weak and woozy. I wove on my knees, trying to stay upright.

Red wasn't in great shape either, and he slid from Eleni's grip. While she smacked his face and tried to get him upright, I dragged myself forward. With my last remaining strength, I wrapped my hand around her ankle and tugged.

With a hiss, she looked back and stomped on my hand, then seemed to realize, electricity or not, she could still use her stick to beat me senseless.

"Let us go!" She hauled back with another cry.

Bane flew past, attempting to snag the sample she'd taken and stowed in a vial clipped to her belt. While the snow bolstered his strength, he slipped in one of the rapidly forming puddles that leaked into the museum. He twisted, but his body just missed the proper angle shield me from Eleni's blow.

Though I tried to bring my hands up, I knew I was too slow. I watched the baton descend and prayed that a broken skull or collarbone wouldn't hurt as bad as I imagined.

A long, pale hand shot across my field of vision.

Caleb darted between me and my attacker. A formless noise of protest barely made it past my lips and—

Caleb caught the baton easily in one hand, stopping its trajectory through midair like it had hit a wall of stone. He yanked it from Eleni's grip and chucked it over his shoulder, far out of her reach.

He wore the Minimask I let him examine back in the storage room.

Bane helped me up. Red finally got his bearings and flashed his fangs at us, bustling Eleni through the doors. He fumbled at his waist and pulled a pellet from his belt.

"Oh, no," Caleb murmured. "Back up!"

Caleb yanked Bane and I backward as Redzilla chucked the pellet against the ground. It exploded in a flurry of sparks and noxious smoke. My eyes immediately began to tear.

Caleb got us clear of the fog, then turned to me, looking mortified as I gaped.

"You—you're Extrahuman!" I shouted. "What can you do?"

He grimaced. "You're not going to like it."

"What the *hell* is that supposed to mean?"

Bane swore, drawing our attention. The smoke had mostly dissipated, the emergency doors held open by the howling wind. He ran to the doors. I kept my distance, my arms wrapped around myself. Bane dashed into the snow, hair flying as he scanned the area outside the building.

Tugging the doors closed, he jogged back and offered his jacket, brushing snow from the shoulders.

"They're gone?" I asked, shrugging it on.

"Yeah, and there's multiple sets of tire tracks in either direction."

"At least we stopped them from getting their sample." I spun, but Caleb was gone. "Did you see . . ." I started.

"Sure did," Bane said. "Let's get out of here. Someone's sure to have heard us."

"Where'd Caleb go, though? We can't just leave without him."

Bane chewed his lip, phone already to his ear. "Hey, Beacon. Yes. No. Are you close? Yeah, can you meet Mel at the bodega on Sixth and Woodard?" Bane hung up. "Chezza's been doing laps in the SUV. Go home with her, and see if Caleb shows up. I'll search around here. He can't have gone far."

I was suddenly numb in a way that had nothing to do with the weather.

Bane gave my shoulder a reassuring squeeze. "I'll see you at home, okay?"

A violent alarm sounded from deep within the museum. Bane and I reacted like it was a starting gun and raced into the night.

Half an hour later, I sat at the kitchen table with Vennie and Chezza, sharing a pot of tea in our pajamas. I was ensconced in several thick blankets. My dress and heels lay neatly folded in the middle of the table.

"He handed me those." Chezza pointed at my dress and heels. "He said he was going to help you two," Chezza repeated, her expression puzzled. "He bolted before I could stop him without making a scene."

Vennie rubbed his chin. "Why would he leave? He couldn't have it better anywhere else."

I'd filled them in briefly on Bane and I busting the theft, Redzilla's apparent freedom, and Caleb's secret. "Does he have the records you made him?"

They shared a glance. "The driver's license for sure," Vennie said. "You'd have to check his room to see if he took the birth certificate or anything else."

"I don't like that he's out there, and he knows all our secrets," Chezza said between sips.

"He wouldn't tell," I said. "Even under duress." I picked at the remnants of my dried Minimask. Bane had only texted once, saying he had no luck, but he would keep looking.

I rested my head against the back of the kitchen chair, tugging the blankets tighter around me. My heart held an unfamiliar, heavy feeling at the thought of Caleb being gone for good.

Minutes passed. Vennie played a game on his phone. Chezza tore a napkin to bits. I battled the growing urge to cry.

At some point during the unremarkable stretch of waiting, I sensed something—some movement, a subtle shift of weight against the ground in our usually silent yard—and I stiffened.

Chezza raised an eyebrow, her posture mirroring mine. Vennie's thumbs paused their tapping.

Pressing a finger to my lips, I strode through the living room and to the doors that looked out on the backyard. I couldn't shake the disorienting instinct that *something* had happened. Something had changed in our environment. Like a loss of power in the middle of the night, or a gunshot heard from far off.

The moon's glow streamed across the grass, slick with melted remnants of the earlier snowfall. A wall of tree boughs waved back and forth in the wind. I rubbed my eyes and listened. The back of my neck prickled. I stared at the moon-bleached yard until I was at risk of dozing off and falling over.

Until I saw the behemoth shadow shift between trees.

It was too big and moving too steadily in one direction to be a trick of the light.

Horror crawled across my shoulders and pinched them tight. The perimeter alarms hadn't been tripped. Since it had slipped past our wall undetected, we were nearly out of time, if it was a threat.

"Stay in there," I called back to Chezza and Vennie as I unlatched the back door.

I toed off my socks, already dreading the icy touch of the grass on my bare feet, but I needed to be able to maneuver quickly. In my pajamas, a hoodie, and a fleet of Tempatches, I stepped into the yard. There was nothing scarier than me here, and this threat, whatever it was, was about to learn that.

A cool breeze lifted the hair at my neck, blowing strands across my face. Slowly, I pulled up my hood.

A sharp crack echoed off to my left. I dashed for the tree line, arms pumping and heat building inside me with each bound. I skidded to a halt at the first thick tree trunk I encountered.

A handful of deep, jagged lines were scored into the bark.

I peered around the trunk, eyeing the dark spaces between trees. Nothing, not even with my vision enhanced. But I heard the crack and the silence that followed. Either it was nothing, or someone made an error and then froze.

Stepping further from the trunk, I tried to look everywhere at once, while shoving back the fear brewing in my stomach.

Swearing internally, I shut my eyes and listened. The trees muttered like always, nothing too loud in the light breeze. Then I heard it. The shift of something heavy on the forest floor. Perhaps two massive feet, and the shallow, dry sound I was also making. Someone trying to keep their breath quiet. By my guess, they were within thirty yards of me.

Shifting into a fighting stance, I made the Leo family name proud and did something stupid on purpose. I faked a cough.

The monster heard me. There was the soft protest of pine needles being crushed underfoot, again to my left. I spun and darted deeper into the trees.

Within a few steps, I saw it. The hulking shadow, humanoid and much larger than I expected. I had to utilize my small upper hand and catch it off guard. I barreled toward it, leaping directly toward where I thought I could make out its middle. Had Redzilla somehow followed us home?

I tackled the thing to the ground. Its breath whooshed out in a grumbly huff. I wrapped my arms around its expansive torso, and felt . . . fur. I pushed myself off and danced away as it stumbled back. To my dismay, it didn't fall to the ground. It regained its composure with quick reflexes. It wasn't Red, but maybe a different Extrahuman . . .

Then it stretched upright.

There was a werewolf in my backyard.

"Oh, lions." My voice was barely a squeak.

Mortified, I scuttled back into the shadow of a tree. The wolf stood well over seven feet tall, covered in mottled gray fur. It was human-shaped with bulging shoulders and arms and thick claws at the end of its long fingers. A ridge of hair spiked up from the crown of its head all the way down its back until it disappeared into . . . pants.

The werewolf was wearing pants—gym shorts, actually.

A branch's sharp edge dug into my back. My feet shuffled backward of their own accord.

I was a kid again. A dog barreled toward me through the snow, ready to tear me apart, and my mom wasn't here to protect me.

My heel caught on a root. I tumbled, eliciting a small noise of panic.

Its massive ears flicked in my direction.

The monster turned.

Not only toward me, but the brick house and its inhabitants behind me. I couldn't let it hurt Vennie and Chezza. I charged again.

It spun quickly, but not fast enough to face my onslaught head-on. I saw a flash of bright eyes before I careened into the beast and sent it stumbling. In my head it was male, from its body proportions and choice of pants, which I couldn't make sense of. In the movies, werewolves always had an odd, off-balance stature t0 their feet, with pads against the ground and a long foot leading to an ankle off the ground.

He wasn't like that. His legs were long and all wiry muscle under the fur, but his giant clawed feet were planted firmly on the ground from heel to toe. It was the oddest thing I'd ever seen.

As he stumbled back, I made my best attempt to look intimidating, though I was terrified. I growled and didn't back off too far, prepared to strike.

And apparently it worked because as he processed me—the puny, pajama clad cyclone before him—he took a few steps back and glanced around. The beast was going to run, but I had no intention of letting him.

He darted to the side. I followed, beating him to the line of trees that would shield him from my view. I spun, dragging my foot through the air, building momentum to land a solid kick to his side. My heel connected with his hip. He yelped and stumbled back. My ankle throbbed, but I leapt upon him as he turned to find another escape route. I managed to loop my arms around his massive neck. My hands sought each other, grappling with fur. I clasped them and pulled tight, determined to get him unconscious before he could shake me off and shred me to pieces.

I roared as I pulled. The werewolf thrashed. Rough hands closed around my forearms, trying to pull them away. He growled, teeth snapping. His strong grip managed to free my left arm, and desperately, I swung it up, prepared to bring it down hard in hopes of getting him immobile. The moonlight glinted along his snout as he jerked his massive, angular head.

"Stop!"

My body reacted automatically. I'd spent months trusting that voice.

I dropped, putting the beast squarely between me and my uncle with a tiny sigh of relief. Bane was back. This fight was won.

Bane looked disheveled, even for him. His top buttons were undone, and his sleeves were rolled to the elbow. His hair was a mess, but not in the way he liked. The scent of cologne wafted through the trees.

He didn't look as shocked as I expected to find me wrestling a werewolf in the backyard.

The beast swung his head back and forth between us, appearing indecisive. He actually brought those massive claws together and wrung his hands . . . or paws? He risked a glance toward the mountains.

"Don't," Bane said.

The beast snapped its head back to him, and my uncle put up his hands.

"Don't you want to stop running? You don't want to start over again. We can make this work."

"Um, excuse me." They both eyed me. "What the hell is going on?"

A quiet, high-pitched whine escaped the wolf's chest, and I shuddered. This thing was my worst nightmare personified. I fought the urge to dash to Bane and hide behind him.

"Call it a lucky guess," Bane said to the wolf. "Do you want to risk lying to her again? Was it worth it the first time?"

The beast stood still for a long time. Eventually, its shoulders drooped, as well as the massive, fuzzy ears protruding directly from either side of his head. It turned to me. I had so many questions, but I was too strangled by the scream building in my throat. I couldn't move, couldn't breathe as this massive berserk dog monster stepped toward me.

In the wash of moonlight, his eyes were blue.

With each step he took through the dappled moonlight, the light and shadows played tricks on me. The monster looked less scary, less threatening, less big. I peered and blinked, trying to make sense of the form that shifted as it got closer. The snout shortened; the fur retracted. A familiar face shape took over. The shoulders shrunk, but not by much.

And then Caleb stood before me, naked except for the shorts, looking tortured as ever.

Which was a real bummer because the moment could

have been spent focusing on my first opportunity to see him shirtless.

I was definitely having a panic attack.

"How long?" I managed to gasp.

Caleb wet his lips. "Kavoh took interest in my body's 'potential' for accepting an Extrahuman procedure within six months of me working for her. I was like this before I'd been with her for an entire year."

He'd been this way for most of his adult life.

This was his third apology—for hiding this. Caleb was finally out of secrets.

The damp cold of the dirt seeping into the hem of my pajama pants was the only sensation keeping me grounded.

I nearly collapsed to the forest floor in maniacal fits of laughter. "Of course!" I gasped, my wild shrieks echoing through the woods as Bane and Caleb stared. "Of course you're the physical embodiment of my worst fear! *Of course* you are!"

"Mel . . ."

I don't know which of them said it. But I shoved my hands off my knees and wiped a delirious tear from my cheek.

"Kitchen," I demanded, my voice pitched high from barely contained hysteria. "In the kitchen right now. And I want cookies," I added to Bane.

He looked a little shocked. "I told him he should tell you—"

"I'm not mad about that. It's his secret to tell. I'm mad because you smell like decaf and cologne that isn't yours. You didn't go looking for Caleb. You had a booty call. Cookies. Kitchen. Now."

Bane gaped. Caleb gaped. I marched to the kitchen without checking to see if they followed.

"Caleb's a werewolf," I called unceremoniously as I reentered the house and wiped my feet on a mat before heading to the kitchen.

"Come again?" Chezza asked at the same time Vennie choked on his tea.

I hopped onto one of the barstools, pushing back my hood. "He's a shapeshifting Extrahuman. Kavoh made him while he worked for her. Ask him." My voice hadn't fully lost its unhinged tone as Caleb trod into the room, seemingly human and definitely still shirtless.

Bane took up a spot leaning against the doorway.

"'Werewolf' isn't technically correct," Caleb offered, rubbing the back of his head. "The moon isn't involved."

I blinked.

"Oh, you have to let me take a sample of your blood," Chezza said, already retreating toward her rooms.

I planned to aim another question at Caleb, but Bane raised his hand. "Yes, Uncle Bane?"

"Can I go first? I'm tired."

"By all means."

Bane made his way to the freezer, basking in the cold air before speaking. "It wasn't a booty call earlier. It was a date. I invited him to the Mayor's Gala but wussed out at the last minute and bailed. I gave his seat to Caleb instead."

He withdrew cold chunks of cookie dough, popping one directly in his mouth, and plopped the others into the air fryer and set the timer. "When I was running around looking for Caleb, the guy texted me and asked how my night was going. I realized I made a mistake, and I wanted to see him before I came home. I knew Caleb would end up back here. I'm sorry, Mel. I should have told you all that."

"Oh," I said. "Yeah, that's a dumb reason to lie. Just tell me next time. I'm happy for you, and I want to meet him when you're ready. Go to bed."

He sagged in relief. Vennie stood, ambling toward his rooms. "I'm out too. Give me the abbreviated version of this" —he gestured vaguely between Caleb and me—"tomorrow.

I'll text Chezz and tell her that her sample's gonna have to wait."

He shot off the text without looking, and we heard a wailed, "Oh, man!" from Chezza's room above the garage.

"Goodnight," Caleb called after them.

When he turned back to me, I fixed him with a raised eyebrow.

The silence stretched between us until the air fryer dinged.

With a sigh, I made to hop from my seat, but Caleb stopped me with a wave. He grabbed the basket and offered it to me.

I grabbed a molten cookie and dug in, using the time to gather my thoughts.

"Why didn't you tell me?" I demanded. "Not triggering my memories . . . I at least see how you twisted logic to justify that to yourself. But if anyone would understand your Extrahuman abilities, it's the people in this house."

Caleb rubbed the back of his head. It made his muscles move in a seriously distracting way. "It's . . . There's been so much going on since I got here, and bigger issues to resolve, and . . ."

I waited, licking chocolate off my fingers.

"And you're afraid of dogs," he finished.

He had me there.

He knew it too. "I saw how you reacted back there, but I acted so rashly earlier. I came back here because I knew I couldn't run. I was working up the nerve to tell you."

"Why were you out there in your wolf . . . form—version —thing?"

"I needed to get here fast, and it's too cold out there for me when I'm"—he gestured at himself and seemed to register he was half-naked—"like this. The other way is warmer and faster."

I nodded like this was a completely normal thing, then

wiped my hands and rallied my courage. "Can I see it . . .him . . .you, like that again?"

Caleb seemed hesitant, but closed his eyes. They danced in apprehension beneath his lids. He reached behind his neck again and . . . pressed something?

"She installed a switch beneath my skin. In the top of my spine," Caleb grunted, his voice tight as the transformation started.

I made myself watch. Fur sprouted over his expanding body. He ducked his head as his face elongated into a snout, and his ears grew into those hilariously large flaps. It only took a handful of seconds, and then he was before me, less than a foot away, towering over me even more than usual.

Despite my efforts, I shuddered, hating how it must have made him feel. He stepped back. My hand darted out to grip his upper arm, and we both froze.

"Don't," I breathed.

Massive and menacing, he listened, his familiar eyes set in a face that was mostly fierce, but there was a tenderness there.

"Just—give me a minute."

My body hummed like I was perched at the apex of a rollercoaster's track.

It was difficult to see his eyes in such a strange face, so I looked at my hand, settled into the fur of his upper arm, curved around the muscle beneath. He was soft. His chest was a field of more thick fur in shades of gray—slate, dark graphite, and shiny silvers. He shifted, hunching forward to bring his head closer to mine. I looked up. His nose was mere inches from mine, twitching, a sheen of wetness on it. He could probably smell my moods. That could be a problem. The part of me that could look past the fear found it fascinating.

He blinked slowly, and the muscles around his eyes shifted. I could see how he vaguely had eyebrows, how I could read his expression this way.

I reached my free hand, slowly, up to his neck, and slid my fingers into the fur there.

A grumbling built in his chest. His neck tensed.

"Scared?" he managed to ask. The syllable was rough and awkward, slightly menacing, despite his efforts.

I gulped. "Yes." My fingers roved up to his cheek, tracing the ridge of bone I felt there. He closed his eyes.

"Does it hurt? The transforming?"

"Little," he managed to mutter, and he pointed his claws toward his mouth.

"Your snout growing is the worst? And your teeth?"

A solemn nod, then a tilt of his head that I'd seen him execute a dozen times in human form. He placed one rough, massive hand over mine and gently guided it over his shoulder, to the back of his neck. There was the faintest ridge there, buried just beneath his skin, and together, under Caleb's guidance, we pressed it.

Within moments, he was back to his human form.

Delirium threatened me again, so I pulled a Leo and began blabbing. "So, you retain some of that extra strength while you're human? Like, how strong would you say you are, in either form? Have you tested it? Could you lift a large kitchen appliance? A car? Are you strong all the time, under all circumstances or . . ."

Caleb burst out laughing. "Don't worry. I'm not nearly as strong as you."

The relief on his face nearly broke my heart. I flung my arms around him, hoping my touch would prove to him that this family wouldn't reject him.

He tentatively wrapped his arms around me, then leaned, letting me take some of his weight and his warmth.

"You didn't finish your apology," I said into his shoulder.

He laughed, a brilliant thing, and his lips moved against my hair. "I'm sorry. I'm sorry. I'm sorry."

He pulled back and felt the need to put a little air between us. Too much. This night, the past few weeks, had been all too much.

"Relax," I said. "I won't make you sleep in a crate."

Caleb blinked. "I'm just realizing what a mistake it was to tell you. The dog jokes will never end."

My voice was solemn as I promised, "Never."

I could watch Goldy all day.

The large, realistically rendered lion lived on the massive screen above Leo Optics' front entrance. Someone had made a donation to the Foundation so the text "DANIELLE ROCKS" floated above the digital savannah. Goldy napped on his back beneath it, his tail flicking back and forth.

But I didn't have all day, not after accidentally sleeping past my alarm. I shuffled into the warm lobby and took an elevator to one of the central tower's highest floors. A maze of hallways later, I waltzed up to a familiar sleek black desk.

I gave my sweetest smile and slid my bribe, a piping hot dirty chai, across the counter. "Does he have a minute?"

"Melbourne." Logan hardly looked up from their computer, painted lips pursed. "He's supposed to be reviewing design concepts for next year's models, but he's instructed me that he always has time for you."

I widened my smile. "I'll make sure he's on task when I leave. Promise."

"By all means, you can try," they said, waving me in.

Bane's office was almost all windows displaying a view of Crown City I never got tired of.

He was at a wide acrylic desk that featured a wilted plant and a diffuser spouting lavender and peppermint into the air, frowning at a large Leo Optics screen suspended from the ceiling on a sleek silver arm.

He looked up in surprise and leapt to his feet, nearly sending several takeout cups of iced coffee flying over the expensive carpet. "I'm sorry about fibbing about the date and going to bed. I was so tired——"

I cut him off before he could continue. "No apology necessary. Your dating life is your business. I got caught up in the heat of the moment, and I'm sorry. I meant to apologize to you first thing this morning, but you beat me out the door."

Bane shook his head. "Also not needed. We're good."

"So . . ." I hedged. "Will I get to meet this mystery person soon?"

A light I hadn't seen before took up residence on my uncle's face. "I hope so. I don't want you to know who it is until I'm sure they're sticking around." He tapped his forehead, illustrating where his Shadow helmet would sit. "Which in turn presents an entire new set of problems I haven't had to deal with in a long time."

I grimaced, thinking of how Caleb at least already came within the confines of my Extrahuman life. It wasn't a secret I had to protect him from. "Right, but if they make you happy, I'm sure we can figure it out."

He rubbed his chin. "I know, I know. More importantly, if I was out the door before you were up, does that mean you slept in?" His eyes searched my face, no doubt assessing the tiredness etched into every inch of it. "I worry you haven't been resting enough, Mel. That you're burning out."

"Me too, honestly. I'm going to try and be better about it." Twisting to be sure I closed the door securely behind me, I shifted to the second reason for my visit. "But the longer it takes us to find her, the more people Kavoh is able to kidnap to turn into Extrahumans. Eleni and Redzilla got away with whatever they were after last night, and who knows what they've accomplished that we haven't caught. I can hardly sleep knowing what's happening. Sometimes I don't want to." An uninvited waver had crept into my voice.

"I know, Toasty." Bane patted my hand. "I know. It hurts to not be able to stop something as immediately as you want to, and the hurt doesn't stop when you take off the suit."

Knuckling the corner of one eye, I pulled out my phone. "Did you talk to Roger about Redzilla yet?"

A shake of the head. "Would you like to do the honors?"

I scrolled to Roger's number and jabbed the speaker button. He answered after the second ring.

"Mel! How's my favorite God-child?"

Bane shook his head at Roger's self-appointed title.

"Hey," I interrupted before Bane could retort. "Bane's here too. Have you checked on the status of the Extrahuman we sent home with your people last year? The big, scaly, red one?"

"Nah, last I checked they had him holed up in one of our private security apartments. It's a couple of levels above my clearance to go see him, but I can try to pull some strings."

"No need," I continued. "We ran into him last night, here in Crown City. Running with one of Kavoh's people, trying to pull a museum heist."

Silence from Roger's end. Presumably stunned.

"What in the unholy, shit-eating, ever-loving—"

"Exactly," Bane cut in. "He escaped, which means you've got a security problem."

Roger continued his string of curses, and I shrugged at Bane. "Can you let us know if you find anything helpful?"

After another minute, Roger's list of profanities ran out. "Of course. I'll give you guys a call when I know more. So sorry about this."

Bane plopped his chin on a fist, looking as tired as I felt. "Keep us posted."

I ended the call and slouched further into my seat. "Half a step forward, forty-seven Redzilla-sized steps back."

"Or werewolf-sized," Bane mused, a wicked turn in the corner of his mouth.

My flat stare made him chuckle. "Want to brainstorm this problem further over lunch?"

"Can't." I sighed. "You're my first appointment of the day, and I'm running late for the second. Please get started on reviewing those designs for Logan."

With a harumph, Bane waved me off and glumly turned his focus to workplace responsibilities.

🔥🔥🔥

"That's a nice sweater." Despite his sentiment, Max's voice was stiff.

Lions above. I tried to keep my face even. Max *would* notice the small touches of extra care in my appearance. The peach sweater I'd picked was new and shot through with gold threads. My eyelids were tinted a similar color. I had two extra coats of mascara on.

I blinked. Max had called this meeting.

"Any reason?" he asked dryly.

I knew he didn't want to know, but Max couldn't refrain from picking at his own scabs.

"Plenty," I said, clipped. "It's almost the weekend, my coffee was extra strong this morning, I slept in a little . . ."

He sighed. "I'm happy for you."

"Hard to believe you when your face says I just peed in your favorite loafers."

"You wouldn't dare," he joked, but the light didn't reach his eyes. He knew where I was going, and he didn't like it. But we were at Hardwired, a favorite spot for us both, so it needed to be neutral ground.

From our usual booth, I eyed the clock along the wall. Sparring with Max at least helped stave off my nerves.

Which weren't nerves, exactly. More like a fiery anticipation I was beginning to associate with Caleb. It wasn't bad, but it was energy I had no idea what to do with.

"Lucky for you, you're saved from more of that conversation since I don't know where Caleb is taking me."

Max winced. "About that, actually . . ."

My nerves spiked, and I scrambled to keep our conversation somewhere pleasant. "What about you? How was your date with Stassy?"

"About as captivating as a date with someone named 'Stassy' could possibly be."

I grimaced.

Max primly sipped his espresso.

I searched for anything to talk about, but Max stopped me with a hand. "I'm sorry for what I said at the dinner. It was rude."

I gulped, and he held his hand up again to stop me. "It got me thinking, though. I know we decided on friendship, but I wonder if I'm not ready for that yet, with you. Not emotionally mature enough, or fully over our relationship, or something like that."

I cocked my head, a sinking feeling took root in my stomach.

"Our friendship is really important to me, but it's been under a lot of strain the past few months. I think it's more than I can handle, especially with your new . . . person. Mel, you deserve a great partner, but I don't deserve the suffering that will come with watching it happen. I'm thinking you and I could take some breathing room—some space—that might preserve our friendship in the long run."

"Breathing room," I repeated, dragging out the syllables to give my brain time to catch up.

While gentle in meaning, the words cleaved through me.

Max had ripped out a sizeable chunk of my heart, and what hurt the most was that he was right.

He tapped his fingers against the ceramic cup in a nervous pinging melody. "Yeah."

"Okay," I said shakily, blinking what surely weren't tears from my eyes. "So, what now? What're the logistics?"

"No logistics," Max said. "I think we'll just see each other around. My dad has me doing more work with the Gold Guard project."

This jolted me—a reminder of what truly kept us apart in the first place. At least the separation from him and his affiliation with the Gold Guard and Mayor Keep would make my life far easier.

And less whole.

Perhaps it spoke to Max and me not being fated lovers when my priority shifted to getting information from him while I had the chance. "What kind of work?"

Max nodded toward the door. "Never mind. Your date's here. Tall, pale, and hauntedly handsome just walked in."

I bolted upright as Caleb stepped to our table, resplendent in a denim jacket with a fleece collar.

"Double trouble," he offered as a greeting, though he was only looking at me.

Max plastered a smile on his face anyway. "Hello," he said, as perfectly polite as warranted between opposition leaders during times of war.

"I'm ready," I told them both, shooting Max a desperate stare, which he ignored. How long until I'd see him again?

Caleb held the door on our way out. As I tucked my chin into my jacket's collar, I willed the chilly breeze to cement me in this moment. I fought the reflex to console myself; I'd worry about Max later. The terms of his proposal warranted that I shouldn't think about him at all.

But would that space expand until there's so much between us we'll never find each other again?

"We can walk from here." Caleb's warm voice banished my misery.

We moseyed along the streets, exchanging tidbits about our respective days.

Caleb kept his hands in his coat pockets, and I tried not to stare as we walked. The sharp cut of his chin and his neatly trimmed haircut made my pulse all weird.

"How do you feel about what Max proposed, then? You two were—are—close, right?"

I chewed my lip. "Max was my first friend in Crown City. My first connection here. As hard as it is that he doesn't know about the Extrahuman stuff, it's nice that he likes me for me. He's . . ."

"He's special to you." Caleb stopped on the sidewalk to face me.

"Yeah," I admitted.

Caleb tugged me close, his warm arms circling my shoulders. I basked in his minty forest scent, letting a little of my grief for Max go. "I'm sorry."

Pulling back, I shook my shoulders. "Thank you."

The corner of his mouth turned up. "I want to show you some of my favorite places. Does that sound okay right now?"

My head bobbed. "Show me, please."

Watching his shoes kick against the pavement, I listened to Caleb talk. "Before stuff with Kavoh got so intense, I could explore a little." He didn't stutter over her name anymore. "I had a few things I really liked to do. They were comforting and made me happy."

He stopped us in front of a dive bar I didn't recognize and held the door. It was nestled in the middle of a strip of college bars, but this one was smaller, with thin stained-glass windows and massive screens playing soccer on each wall, except one.

"Trivia?" I asked brightly.

He nodded, satisfied at my enthusiasm. "Every night of the week."

We wove to a high-top and ordered beers as the emcee began explaining the rules. Caleb brought over a basket of complimentary popcorn from the corner.

"How competitive are you?"

"Depends," I leaned close, conspiratorial. "Halting an opioid operation in a timely manner with no casualties? Very. Bar trivia I prefer for fun."

He grinned back. "Good. Also, because we're horrendously outnumbered and neither your brute strength or mine will help us beat any of the teams of regulars. They're hardcore."

We had a positive early showing, handling ourselves fine in the categories of color theory, geography, and animal biology. Caleb cleared classic literature and anatomy, for both of which I was no help. We were at risk of dropping out of the top five teams when the bonus round category flashed across the screen.

Female Film Directors.

"No shit," I said, triumphant.

Caleb suggested we bet all our points, putting us in second place when I annihilated the category without issue. We pocketed our prize of a gift card to come back and play more trivia. Caleb led the way to his next favorite spot, an Indian restaurant a few blocks away with staticky speakers and the best chicken tikka masala I'd ever eaten. We stuffed ourselves with veggie samosas and laughed until we could hardly breathe.

It was the easiest we'd ever spoken, since I'd dropped my pretenses and Caleb his fears. Or maybe both our harsh judgements of him. Either way, by the time we declined the dessert menu twice, I was content to look at him and focus on the pressure of his foot resting against mine beneath the table.

"Are you up for one more spot?"

The answer came without a thought. "I'm up for a hundred."

Caleb's responding smile was so powerful it rocked him back in his seat.

Part of Bane's commitment to taking Caleb in included his insistence that Caleb use the barely-used blue sports car with the racing stripes collecting dust in the garage. Bane had offered it to me, but I avoided driving at all costs.

Somewhere along the way, Caleb's hand drifted over to intertwine with mine. To my surprise, he drove us away from downtown, heading toward the few precious acres of farm-land residing just inside the westernmost mountains. Like he had made the trip a hundred times, he pulled off at a carpooling lot and turned off the engine.

"We have to walk a little," he explained.

He grabbed a bunch of blankets from the backseat, as well as my winter coat, which he'd procured from somewhere.

I giggled and accepted the coat. "I have Tempatches on, you know."

"I don't want you to be uncomfortable if I can help it."

I followed him into a field, picking our way along neat rows of dirt until a small hill rose in the twilight. Caleb held out a hand to help me up. I wondered if he had forgotten we could both see in the dark. I took his hand again and didn't remind him. Mercifully, the snow from the day before had melted and left only frozen ground in its place.

At the hill's crest, Caleb shook out the blanket and laid it across the ground. Instinctively, I sat down on it and stretched on my back, looking up at Caleb, a deep navy shadow against the nearly-as-dark sky. He squatted next to me and laid down in the opposite direction, aligning his head with mine. It took me a minute to make sense of what I saw.

The stars were stunning, brilliant this far away from the city, but the real magic was the angle of the hill and its posi-tion. Far enough from trees and the sides of the nearest moun-tains so that from one end of my peripheral vision to the other, there was nothing to see but sky and stars.

"Lions," I breathed.

"I love this view," he said simply.

"It's incredible."

There was sky and nothing else, like we swam in it. I reached over my head to press a palm to Caleb's chest. His hand found mine. We stayed like that for a while, Caleb running his thumb over the back of my hand.

The tension between us was taut and tangible again. I'd slowly let it draw us together all night, and it felt right. Fancy that, I was falling for the believed-dead, sexy scientist, kidnapper-turned-housemate, who moonlighted—I suppressed a hysterical giggle—as a werewolf.

Caleb ducked his head to kiss my fingertips. I was sure I'd combust, like I was a star brighter than all of them.

I tilted my face toward his.

He mirrored me, his eyes like neon in the dark, a telltale breath building in his chest.

"I'm sorry, Mel. I'm sorry for that night in the alley, when I took you and hurt you and made you feel small."

The stars lit up the side of his face, deepening the shadows sheltered in the hollows of his cheeks, beneath his eyes, along the line of his throat as he swallowed, waiting for my response.

I lifted myself up, leaned over him. Letting the gravity inside me do as it wanted, finally. Because the maniacal truth is I liked Caleb Dove, from the instant I met him.

My hair draped around his face, and he raised a hand to cup my cheek. I braced myself on one elbow and slid my free hand beneath his neck, pulling him closer.

"I'm not."

Upside down under a sky with no edges, I kissed him long and deep and slow. Exploring and savoring. There was a hint of dampness beneath where my thumb met the corner of his eye.

Possibly an eternity later, I pulled back and rested my forehead against his chin. "Is it okay that I did that?"

"Absolutely." I was awarded his Caleb-Ian-Dove smile, so rare and precious. It wasn't wide, but it was real, and so amazing it took my breath away.

Caleb laughed, a deep, gravelly thing I hadn't heard much, and he buried his head in my shoulder. I leaned into his chest, feeling it heave gently from what we'd done.

Eventually, we sat up. I leaned into him as we watched the sky some more. He tilted his head against mine, and I met him for another kiss.

When we broke again, he muttered, "It's just as good right side up."

He pressed his lips to my shoulder, drawing up goose-bumps beneath my layers. It was strange to shake from enjoyment, when it was something I so often avoided in the name of appearing strong.

"It took me a long time to figure this out," I began, and Caleb waited, his face close and patient, his arm wrapped around my waist. "Us . . . It's so complicated."

He nodded, and I continued as the stars watched us.

"Or it *was*. Or it wasn't, really. The events happening around us were complicated. Thank you for still being here while I figured it out."

"I don't want to be anywhere else."

"I was so *mean* to you."

His husky laugh again, against my collarbone, bled warmth through my jacket. "I deserved it."

"Only some of it."

He pressed a kiss against my temple, and I shivered. "If you're treating me with what I deserve now too, then I'm fortunate and I'm glad my behavior has improved."

I followed a plane's lights as it crawled over us, chewing over my thoughts. "From the minute you showed up in that cell"—he didn't even stiffen—"I wanted to put my hands on you. I thought I wanted to strangle you. But this is also satisfying."

He traced a hand up my jaw to pull my face to his and kissed me, every part of him warm and ready to meet me however I wanted.

🔥🔥🔥

Ending a date is weird when you live across the hall from your romantic interest. Caleb and I wound up wrapped together again between our doors, trading quick kisses and small laughs and nothing at all intelligible.

"Good night, monster," I whispered finally, in one of the moments we broke apart.

"Terror," Caleb said softly, somehow making it sound loving and slightly filthy, a trace of a growl in his voice.

I made myself enter my room and dashed to the bathroom sink, staring at myself over the mirror, comprehending. Replaying. Fighting the urge to march across the hall and continue it indefinitely.

I stood there for several long minutes, until my phone buzzed violently and blew apart my reverie.

A text from Bane simply read:

Den. NOW.

I changed into stretchy pants and a giant sweatshirt and headed downstairs, absently touching all the places Caleb had kissed over the last few hours. They were all innocuous, and I suddenly felt acutely aware of every nerve residing in them.

I stepped into the Den, prepared for a briefing on any number of criminal cases we were investigating.

Instead, Bane perched in the middle of the battered couch, holding a bowl in each hand. Brownies. His doused in ice cream, mine in hot fudge.

"So, how was *that?*" he demanded.

I grinned and leapt on the couch, whipped a blanket

across my knees, and gushing in between bites, filled him in. Uncle Bane nodded along seriously and gasped at all the right spots as he devoured his own sundae.

I was buzzing on the couch long after he went to bed, letting myself replay the evening a few more times before I went to bed. If I could fall asleep at all, I was sure I'd sleep well.

A smile came unbidden to my face. Maybe, if I could have days like this amidst the despair and chaos, things would be okay.

The thought died abruptly as an angry red news notification burst to life on the LUMA.

BODY FOUND ON LAKE SILVER'S SHORE
CONFIRMED TO BE LOCAL STUDENT

CHAPTER
TWENTY-FIVE

I didn't sleep. I couldn't.

I dropped my vigilance and enjoyed myself for one day, and Kavoh had killed someone trying to create another Extrahuman.

Dante Delorio, 20. He was a new transfer to Camden College this year, admitted on an epic athletic scholarship for track and field. One look at his picture, and I realized I'd seen him once or twice at the student union.

We kept tabs on reported missing persons cases matching Kavoh's preferred victim—early adults in good health with athletic prowess and small or nonexistent families, but she'd been extra smart with Dante. He kept to himself so much that his roommate hadn't reported him missing for over a week, and by then, it was too late. According to the news, his only family was an estranged father who lived on the East Coast and wouldn't respond to interview requests.

The floor in front of the LUMA was a mess because a Melbourne-shaped bomb had gone off, leaving laptops, papers, and empty coffee mugs everywhere.

On the LUMA, I had a map of Crown City open, featuring the neighborhoods from the lakeshore to the edges of the residential areas. I'd crossed off all the regions in which we were fairly certain Kavoh hadn't hidden another facility.

I finished my last angry red slash across the map and stepped back, taking in my work. My shoulders slumped.

There wasn't anywhere left.

"*Where is she?*" I paced away from the LUMA, turning my back on its light.

I rubbed my tired eyes until I nearly ran into the wall of mirrors. With dismay, I took in my disheveled hair and blood-shot eyes.

I needed sleep, but I couldn't bear the thought of waking up to news that someone else was lost or dead at Kavoh's hands.

Rest, my body urged.

"Coffee," I grumbled back.

I trudged up the stairs and stared at the coffee machine blankly, my eyes flicking to the digital clock on the oven every few seconds. It was late enough that a fresh pot could wake up any of my olfactory-enhanced or caffeine-sensitive house-mates. With a grumble, I poured a cup from the remaining pot, which had gone cold and sludgy. I set it in the microwave.

Over the microwave's dull buzzing, a floorboard creaked.

I spun, catching sight of Caleb as he entered the kitchen—a split second before he saw me.

"Oh."

"It's too late for coffee," I said, staring pointedly at the mug in his hand, instead of his deliciously tousled hair.

The microwave pinged. Caleb's eyes narrowed at the sad, softened scent of reheated coffee. "That's why I'm drinking tea. I came down for a warm up." He tilted his head toward a kettle on the stove.

There was an electric tug toward him deep within my bones. Every single time I was near him. His simple T-shirt. The soccer shorts. His scent that I associated with warmth and support and *home*. In two seconds, I had wrapped my arms around him. He met me seamlessly, running his hands up my arms to cradle my face before we kissed. His back muscles shifted beneath my hands as I deepened the kiss, hoping he'd be okay with it. I couldn't get enough of the taste of him as I gently included my tongue in the next pass of my lips against his.

Just a moment. I could spare this reprieve for a minute.

That simple touch, the question in my mouth, and Caleb loosened a hand to pull me closer. The faintest noise, like a growl, reverberated from somewhere in his chest. We pushed and pulled and explored, my head getting light. I braced one hand on the counter to stay upright, nearly knocking off his cup.

Caleb made to pull away, but I held him a second longer, the heat from my clothes and from being near him essentially trapping him in my arms.

The delighted shock on his face made me grin sheepishly.

"Sorry."

He pressed his lips together and shook his head, the smile crinkling the corners of his eyes.

"Nothing to apologize for. Not your intentions or your strength. I like them both."

I stepped from his arms, smoothing my hair.

Caleb tilted his head and gently hooked a finger beneath my chin, urging me to meet his gaze and hold it.

His dark brows furrowed. "Are you okay?"

As I considered how to answer, I squeezed the marble countertop so hard it cracked.

Caleb bundled me fully into his arms. "Mel, what is it? What happened?"

Sad to be the reason concern flooded his face, I took Caleb's hand and led him downstairs.

After I explained to him all that had happened, starting with Dante's death and my following frantic research, Caleb nudged me toward the Den's couch.

"Sit. I insist. You're going to fall over."

I didn't have the energy to resist.

🔥🔥🔥

I jerked awake, eyes searching for the LUMA's clock.

A warm hand touched my arm. "It's only been an hour."

Rubbing my sore neck, I frowned. "You let me sleep."

"I don't think a train crash could have woken you. I've been following the news on Dante while you slept."

"Anything helpful?" My voice rasped, and he handed me a bottle of water with a sad shake of his head.

"Not yet. They're not releasing many details."

I groaned, scrubbed my hands over my face, then kneaded my knuckles against my temples. I stood, a little shaky, and waved off Caleb's hand before heading to the medical station. I opened a drawer, pawing through bottles in search of painkillers.

"Can you tell me which of these is best for headaches?"

Caleb approached and held various bottles aloft, eyeing the labels. "What's your pain on a scale of one to ten?"

I groaned. "Eight, maybe? And it's not only my head, but my neck too."

His frown deepened. "What else?"

I shrugged. "Just general awfulness, I suppose. Can you blame me?"

"If I turned up the volume on the LUMA to play a TV show, how would that make you feel?"

I recoiled. "I might throw up, honestly."

"Mel." Caleb looped a long arm around me and gently guided us back to the couch. "It sounds like you have a migraine, which should be taken seriously. Do you usually get headaches?"

I shook my head.

He offered one of the pain pills. "Start with this. I know it sounds hard right now, but you need to rest. You won't save anyone like this."

"Want to bet?"

"With your health? No."

With a sigh, I reclined across the couch. He was right. In my mania over Dante's death, I was being irresponsible, which could ruin any chance of helping others like him. "I don't know if I can sleep," I admitted.

His voice gentled further somehow. "Maybe you should focus on something else, then? Let your mind wander, and your subconscious work on the problem for a while. Or . . ." He held up a book.

"Daydreaming it is."

He laid a blanket over me, his movements stiff.

"Were you on the floor the entire time I was asleep?"

He waved me off, but I scooted to one end of the couch and patted the place beside me. Caleb reclined, with his head near my thigh. The sigh he released told me I was right, he had gotten sore on the cold concrete floor.

Though the knot of anxiety behind my sternum remained tight as I spent moments on anything other than finding Kavoh, I settled into focused breathwork, allowing my thoughts to drift.

Against my best intentions, my eyes drifted too.

Caleb held a paperback over his head, eyes darting back and forth as he devoured it. He shirked most of what Bane offered him beyond living necessities, but he put his new Leo Foundation salary to use raiding every large, small, independent, and used bookstore in the city. I tried not to stare at the curve of his throat. The book had a woman in Victorian Era dress on the cover and a wide bar along the bottom title suggesting it was a classic, before Caleb twisted the entire cover back to hold it in one hand.

With his other, he gently traced the contour of my knee.

"How's the book?"

He turned that soft smile on me. "It's one of my favorites. Have you read it?"

I grimaced apologetically. "The movie is pretty good."

Caleb blinked. "Oh, dear."

I closed my eyes, but they seemed determined to stay open, tracing the lines of the ceiling's beams. I glanced at Caleb again. The LUMA's soft light set his eyes glowing.

"You're not very good at resting, are you?"

"It's hard to with you doing *that*."

He dropped his hand from my knee.

I sighed. "Can you keep reading if I do this?" I traced my fingers up his bicep, over his shoulder, and settled my open hand against the middle of his chest. He closed his eyes, and his heart hammered beneath his T-shirt.

"I definitely cannot focus if you do that." The deep hum of his voice against my palm made my own heart beat fast.

His sudden stillness seemed more than base attraction and physical touch. Curious, I lifted my palm to trace a single finger over where his collarbone emerged from the collar of his shirt. Back and forth. Not to arouse, but to relax. His lips parted a little, a deep breath whooshing from him. He set the book down and crossed his hands over his stomach, seemingly perfectly content to let me traverse the short trail back and forth.

"How long could you lay like this?" I asked quietly.

His eyes snapped open and fixed on mine, though no other part of him moved.

"Until I'm driven mad by the need for more tea, or until you stop."

I grinned. "You always seem . . . thrilled and surprised by physical touch. Reactive to me just touching you, gently." Pink was appearing high on my cheeks, I knew it.

Caleb glanced away for a second, considering whether to answer my unphrased question. Even I didn't know exactly what I was asking, but I could tell there was a story. His throat bobbed as he prepped to tell me, and he didn't meet my eyes again as he spoke.

"It's been a long time since anyone touched me with any sort of affection. Or without an agenda." My gut turned at the implications. "It's one of the things I trained myself to expect to never happen again, once I'd made my choice to work for Kavoh."

There. His eyes finally found mine again.

Another admission that he thought himself undeserving. A monster.

I leaned close. "I'm more than happy to prove you wrong."

His heated eyes didn't leave mine as I withdrew my hand from his chest and reached for his hand, threading my fingers through his. I swore to myself I would see Caleb healed from those deep wounds, like my family continued to help me heal every day. I'd prop him up and cheer and cajole and be patient, while Caleb traversed those deep, haunted, internal waters until the wounds scabbed over, and he learned to love himself again.

It was too early in the morning for feelings, though. "Plus, it probably has something to do with your being half dog."

That startled a laugh from him. I relaxed in the couch, and he picked up his book.

Eventually, though, he commented. "You're not wrong. If you insist on petting me, I won't refuse."

Not knowing how to respond, I did a lot of daydreaming after that.

Some time later, I stretched my legs, ready to return to scouring Crown City on the LUMA, searching for spots we may have missed.

"I'd like to show you more of what there is to do in Crown, once we get Kavoh," I said. "I'd like to take you lots of places."

"I'd like that too."

I strode to the LUMA and clicked open the surveillance software. "How did you ever find that great spot from last night?" I asked absently.

Caleb stretched his neck and reached for his notebook. "Dumb luck. Last year, I got a little stir crazy, but I knew there was no way Kavoh would let me beyond the city's borders, so I took to taking hikes in the Outskirts, or running around as the, um"—he floundered, wringing his hands before sticking them up on either side of his head like big pointy ears—"in my other form, since there's no one living out there."

"Yeah, I—" One of Caleb's words snagged in my mind. "The Outskirts?" The term referred to the thick strip of forest between Crown's habited areas and the mountains.

"Yeah," Caleb said, flipping through his pages of neat handwriting. "If you go deep enough, the hiking trails end. It was my only way to get privacy."

"Lions," I gasped. "That's why we can't find Kavoh. She's not in Crown City. She must be in the Outskirts!"

CHAPTER
TWENTY-SIX

"So," Chezza said through our earpieces, "There are a few plausible options. But I've narrowed it down to your best bet."

"Great work, Beacon. Thank you so much," Bane said.

I dipped my head in agreement. We stood at the far bank of Crown's river with Caleb. Vennie and Chezza had fixed him up with some Kevlar pieces we had in storage and a Superseam mask. I wasn't thrilled to have him out here and vulnerable, but we needed all the extra help we could get if we were going to take down Kavoh tonight.

At Caleb's insistence, I'd napped and waited for a reasonable hour to wake the team and fill them in on my hunch, then we took the day to prepare. I was by no means fully rested, but definitely in a better state than when Caleb had found me the night before.

There were the frantic clicks of Vennie typing. "It's an abandoned quartz mine west of Greenwood. The middle of nowhere. It's the only site I could find listed online that would have enough space for her needs."

Caleb's eyes flicked between Bane and I as we stared at each other, musing.

We kept our pace checked, so Caleb could keep up with us on the way to the quarry. Unease pulled at my insides.

"We can take her," Caleb huffed next to me.

"You can read my face as easily as one of your books, huh?" I fought to keep my tone light.

He blushed in the sparse moonlight. "You're far more interesting than any book."

"Focus, lovebirds," Bane chided gently. "If Redzilla's here, there's an eight-foot-tall carnivore in our future. I don't want either of you losing a limb because you're too busy swooning."

"Shh!" I shot back as we neared the spot on the map Vennie had designated.

We spread out a few yards apart and crept through the dense blanket of trees. Thankfully, the night air was thick with the sound of wind and breaking branches under the weight of melted snow. The air was crisp and fresh, a harsh foil to the noxious anxiety bubbling in my stomach.

Within ten feet, the underbrush stopped before a large man-made clearing, and at its center, I made out the fiery red back of Redzilla.

He meandered, his steps slow and tired, only loud due to his sheer size.

I kept my narrowed eyes on him. I knew Bane was doing the same, while Caleb fell into his assigned task of keeping watch behind us, using his enhanced senses to assure we didn't alert Kavoh's people to our presence.

Redzilla's steps grew quieter as he wove away from us, toward a building tucked against Crown's perimeter mountains. A square of dim electric light bled from the half-open door of a pole barn. Its sides were stained with rust the color of dried blood.

We paused as a unit at the edge of the clearing.

Rhett's steps seemed to grow slower. His shoulders dropped, and his tail dragged limply along the ground as he neared the barn. I saw what I hadn't noticed at the museum—he wore an FR-10 bacteria activation band on one thick wrist.

A man appeared in the doorway, his muscled frame and rifle backlit by the light. "There we go. Wasn't that a nice walk?" he asked Rhett, the simple words turned sour by his sneer.

Rhett grumbled and trod through the doorway. When the man stepped aside, light illuminated the scars on his face. It was Nicklai.

Without thinking, I reached for Caleb's hand. His gloved palm found mine, and I felt his heartbeat hammering through it.

Nicklai turned his back on the night, ambling back into the barn like he owned the place. I scanned the rest of the area. The only other light came from a flickering lamp hung over the entrance to a small tunnel—the mine Vennie had mentioned. Someone had hastily spray-painted a black starburst on the rock next to the mine's entrance, like some sort of marker.

My deepening dread plummeted below my feet as Nicklai emerged from the barn again, this time with a different person. She was tall and lithe, her brown skin slick with sweat in the dim light, her braids messy.

I barely suppressed a gasp. Bane's head snapped in my direction.

"I know her," I whispered.

Kaye Thatcher, my dad's ex-assistant and my de facto babysitter before I came to Crown City,

wove around the clearing on unsteady feet. She too, wore one of those wretched wristbands, the blue light a bright spot in the night. Nicklai always remained a step behind, sometimes jutting her with the butt of his rifle if she veered off course. She squinted, hands framing her face, as if to block the faint light in her surroundings.

She stumbled, falling against a boulder that chipped with a groan beneath her hand.

"I'd say that's enough for one night," Nicklai said gruffly, and he towed her back to the barn.

She remained silent the entire time, her face contorted in pain.

My mouth dropped open. She was Extrahuman too.

"Next!" I jumped as Nicklai's bark echoed from inside the building.

Bane touched my elbow and jerked his head. We retreated into the woods and hunkered down to discuss.

"Assuming Eleni is here—" A tremor crept into the last word. I couldn't bring myself to say, *assuming they haven't killed her.* "There are at least three Extrahumans here."

Bane withdrew his visor and nodded, silent, thinking things through.

"We need to get them out," I whispered.

Bane met my eyes. "You're right."

"We can't adopt them all," Vennie stammered.

"We can find them somewhere to hide. They're torturing them until Kavoh's ready to unleash them on the city," Caleb said.

"We'll figure it out," I said. "We should do some surveillance and see how many of Kavoh's people are here. If *she's* here. We need to find out how many sours are with Nicklai in the barn, as well as who or what is in that mine. We need to split up." The idea made me nervous.

Reading my mind, Bane gripped my shoulder. "I'll be okay," he said, "and you will too."

I nodded, convincing myself I believed him.

"I'm coming with you," Caleb interrupted, looking at me. "The experimentation materials will be in the mine. I need to stop what happened to me from happening to anyone else."

Bane pursed his lips. "Fine. But we all need to be extremely careful. If things start to go sideways, we bail."

"Agreed."

Caleb nodded.

We made our way back to the tunnel leading into the mountain. Bane split off and looped around the barn, easing up to the side with the deepest shadows and carefully scaling the wall to peer through the gap between the roof and walls.

I spared a glance to watch him slip inside and disappear.

Over the comms, he whispered, "Only one additional sour in here besides Nicklai. Monster, you'll have to check out the cam footage later and see if you recognize them. I'm good here for a few. There are shadows to hide in. The Extrahumans are in pens, and Nicklai and his crony are setting up to play cards. You're good to move."

With a murmured thanks, I steeled my resolve and focused on the mine. The symbol on the rock dripped still-wet paint like a tainted wound. I felt Caleb, his warmth and quiet steps a couple of feet behind me, at a perfect flanking position.

My insides clenched at the thought of entering a space so narrow with only one exit. I couldn't imagine how bad it must be for Caleb and his fear of confined quarters. His face betrayed nothing but unreadable steel.

I stepped into the dim mine, keeping as best I could to the scant shadows along the wall. I paused every few steps. I heard nothing. The walls and ceiling were a clash of rough gray and beige stone, and interspersed lights buzzed softly. The tunnel was a few yards long, then veered abruptly, a curving trail leading deep into the mountain.

Three turns in, my unease wound tighter and tighter in my stomach. The subtle scuff of our boots in the loose sand scraped at the edges of my nerves. My neck and shoulders were hard as the rock around us. At the next bend, the roof of the tunnel opened into a wider space. My Extrahuman hearing picked up the rough scraping of fabric together, the creaking of a wooden chair. Someone was in the space ahead of us.

I raised a hand. Caleb immediately came to a halt, still as the stone around us. The man was a good listener, even when it was only my body speaking.

I crept to the hall's edge and peered around the corner.

The room had a higher ceiling than the tunnel, though all the exposed rock was just as rough. The old mining space had been filled with hasty desperation. Small mountains of computers and plastic crates towered precariously between the beams supporting the ceiling. Boxes were labeled with scribbled, cryptic numbers and letters, many torn open with wires or supplies dangling over the edges. Extension cords crisscrossed the floor like a treacherous web of security lasers. The room hummed and sparked with electricity, the sound magnified by the close walls. A sad-looking cot was shoved into the scant open floor space, squished between a pair of rickety folding tables stacked with machines—microscopes and other scientific tools Chezza could surely name, but I had no clue what they were.

I knew the back of the usually pristine blonde braid that faced me, though frizzy strands had been pulled loose. Cellina lounged in the chair, facing away from us and eyeing a sleek laptop. She leaned back, easing a pop from the joints in her shoulders, then slumped forward on the table, peering at the screen as it populated. Her leather loafers tapped an impatient rhythm on the rocky floor, coating the expensive seams in dust.

Crouching behind a large metal crate, I pressed a button near my chin, and the bottom of my mask morphed, silently sliding to cover my mouth. With this tech, I could speak, and Caleb would hear me in his earpiece, but his mask didn't have the same capabilities.

"I don't see anyone here but her."

Caleb remained silent in his hiding spot a few feet back in the tunnel.

"I'm going to try and see what she's up to. Stay put unless

I need you. Communicating this way is fun," I said. "I assume you're agreeing with me."

I stepped out of my hiding place and crept up to Cellina. Over her shoulder, I could make out the closing lines of an email, signed simply with the letter K.

My stomach eased with guilty relief. That meant Kavoh likely wasn't here. Fine. I'd settle for simply destroying the heart of her operation tonight.

Straightening to my full height behind her, I slid a gloved hand around Cellina's throat.

I felt Cellina's gasp more than heard it. The shocked sound reverberated through her throat before tangling near the tip of her tongue. She coughed and fought for breath beneath my hand, one of hers scraping fruitlessly around my fingers.

"Hello again," I said, my voice eerie and guttural through my mask's vent.

Without her moving the mouse, her computer screen went dark, revealing my hooded face over her shoulder. Her angry shriek escaped past my grip.

As I shifted my thumb along her neck to find a pressure point, Cellina tensed, her arm flying. I jerked back from the syringe as it speared for my arm, but Caleb was a faster blur that knocked it completely out of the way.

It shattered against the far wall, leaking FR-10 bacteria serum down the stone.

Cellina took advantage of my instinctual fear of the syringe and slipped from my grip. She backed against a thick stack of crates, whipping an unusually shaped gun from the holster at her thigh.

She kept it aimed at me, but her eyes were locked on Caleb. "Dove?"

He wore a mask, but Cellina had always been perceptive. Who else would her missing colleague be with if not me, the person he'd sacrificed his life for?

Cellina's face turned purple, even though I no longer blocked her airway.

"You left for *her?*" She sneered.

Caleb kept his hands up as he tried to reason with her. "We can get you out, Cellina. You have options."

Cellina barked a raw laugh and cocked her gun. In the time it took the click to echo across the room, Caleb growled and took several large steps toward me.

Cellina's raised hand halted him. Her voice was shot through with disbelief. "How fucking *precious*. You never looked at me like that when you were warming my bed. Whatever this one has going on has to be good, huh?"

Despite the urgency of the situation, jealousy roared through me, heating my blood.

"Cellina, please."

I searched around us for a solution. I flicked my max heat button, hoping I could reach Cellina before she pulled the trigger.

"You know, I hoped for better for you," she said. "Now you're going to get you both killed, and that's not on me. I have to tell Kavoh you're alive."

For a brief moment, Cellina's wrathful mask dropped. A torn expression flickered across her face.

She shifted her aim to point the strange gun at Caleb.

She pulled the trigger. I roared and tackled her, but she kept her finger down, the gun making strange, hollow pops. I forced her to the ground and kicked the pistol from her hand. Once I was sure I could control her struggling beneath me, I dared a glance up at Caleb.

He was splayed against the table, the laptop knocked to the ground, arms wide as he stared down at himself. Five syringe darts full of bright orange fluid rapidly drained into his chest.

CHAPTER
TWENTY-SEVEN

Cellina stood, wiping her mouth on the back of her hand. Her grim laugh echoed around the cavern.

I tensed, stepping toward Caleb while scanning the room, checking to see if Cellina's noise drew backup.

She stared at Caleb, disgust drawing her face tight. "Lucky girl." She didn't look up, just shot her words at me like arrows. "It couldn't last, though."

Her earlier words about Caleb burrowed beneath my common sense. Jealousy roasted me from the inside, starting deep in my stomach, licking up my ribcage, wicked and merciless, shoving tongues of flame into every nook of me. I saw red. These flames weren't my friend.

I threw myself to my knees beside Caleb. He twitched, fingers flexing around the syringes. Sheer horror melted his face as his eyes met mine. He groaned, pushing me away.

"It's worse," he said.

"What did you do to him?"

"We've tweaked the serum since Dove here bailed." Cellina took long, careful steps around the room's perimeter, trying to weasel past us. "He's feeling such intense pain and disorientation right now. He's likely forgotten who you are.

He'll only understand simple things, like what I'm about to tell him . . . Dove." His attention snapped to her as his name echoed off the uneven walls. She waved a remote, tantalizing him with her ability to halt his distress. "Do as I say, and the pain will stop."

Pupils the size of pinheads, Caleb's head tilted as he listened.

"Very good." Cellina said through gritted teeth. She pointed at me. "Break the little hooded one, and I'll make it stop."

Eerily slow, his face found me. The recognition there wasn't affectionate. It was determination and rage and hate. The blood might have frozen in my veins as Caleb reared back and transformed with a roar.

"No, no, no." I held up my hands and stepped back. "Caleb, listen to me."

But there was no trace of my monster in the eyes of the beast that rose to his full height in the middle of the cavern.

I darted out of the way a second before Caleb hit the ground I'd just occupied. I dove beneath a table and rolled, crouching behind a stack of crates. His pointy face jerked around, sniffing.

He barreled through the table, sending machines flying. Frantically scaling the crates, I saw Cellina hindered by the mess Caleb was making; heavy machinery blocked her route to escape. My observation took a second too long. Caleb jumped. His claws caught my leg, driving through my suit. I yowled in surprise. He threw me to the ground.

The breath left my chest in a huff. I rolled, determined to keep moving.

I sprinted blindly, but Caleb's legs were long and my breath was short. He barreled into my back, tumbling us to the ground. The world spun. My hood flapped half in my face. The only sound was Caleb's vicious, pained snarls. He shoved me to my back, landing across my stomach.

Quick as lightning, I parried, catching his wrists in my hands and shoving his arms away. He dove for me next, snout first. His glistening, sharp teeth driving toward my throat.

With a roar, I clamped a hand around his snout, holding his jaws closed. The other I braced against his sternum, holding him so it was difficult for him to reach me. His jaws worked against my fist, and he thrashed.

As I held his teeth at bay, he landed swipes across my arms and torso. One was deep enough to gouge through my suit and draw blood. Then a second. "Caleb, *please*." The words morphed into a sob.

But there was no recognition in his eyes. They were a flat, dead blue, like the sky before rain. He slashed for me again.

With a curse, I contorted my body. I writhed to wrap my legs around him, squeezing his torso until he yelped. I flipped us over.

As hard as I tried to trigger a pressure point on Caleb, or hit him on the skull hard enough, he wouldn't pass out. Instead, he continued to assault me in a blind fit of rage. The wounds added up on both of us.

With a sob, I released my legs from around him. I threw both fists against his armored, mottled gray chest. He snarled and reared. Dizzy, I stumbled after him. I snaked my hand around the back of his neck, seeking the one thing that might help.

My fingers sought purchase through his fur for the button that would turn him human again. My vision went blurry as Caleb's clawed hands wrapped around my throat.

I searched and pressed; my teeth gritted. *Come on, Silhouette. Come on, come on!*

Black seeped into the corners of my vision. I felt the tell-tale burn of an open wound, and the eerie drip of my own blood down my neck. My eyes met Caleb's one last time.

Something gave beneath my fingertip. Caleb stilled

beneath me, then thrashed. I shoved myself away, coughing and hacking on all fours.

He writhed on the ground. His back bowed, muscles taut, and his body looked like it might snap.

But slowly, he turned human again, which paused his onslaught and afforded me a moment to go after Cellina.

"Oh, no you don't." I growled and scrambled to my feet.

I hobbled to her on unsteady legs, sifting through one of my suit's pouches. She crawled toward the tunnel, hindered by a twisted ankle. I put pressure on her back with my knee, interrupting her attempt to clear rubble.

"Always a pleasure," I said drily, and sprayed a mist of forgetting serum in her face.

Cellina's eyes rolled back in her head, glaring hateful defiance until the last moment. I snatched the remote from her limp grip and deactivated the bacteria torturing Caleb.

With a huff, I stumbled back to him, human once more, and set a hand on his arm. He jerked, but his hollow cheeks turned toward me, a sliver of recognition in his eyes.

"It's the bacteria," he managed to whisper. His eyes darted around the space and went blank in flickers.

"Shh," I swept his hair back from his forehead, then showed him the remote and its light that now shone blue. "I deactivated them. It's okay. Are you alright?"

"I am now." His voice was raw as he threaded his fingers through mine.

I tapped on the metal collar; the syringes were now empty. "They came up with a new way to inject the bacteria. Think it's safe for me to take this off you?"

He rubbed his face with his free hand. "Frankly, I don't care if it's a good idea. Please get it off."

"Gladly." I wormed my fingers under the edges and ripped the thing off Caleb's neck, simultaneously planting a long kiss on him.

If my life was going to be this big of a shitshow so often,

then I would damn well be as giddy as possible and enjoy it while I could.

When I surfaced for air, I touched his cheek. "Can you hang tight for one minute?"

He squeezed my hand again and nodded. "Are you okay?"

"I'm fine. We need to go see what Bane's up to."

In the quiet aftermath of our brawl, I finally realized our comms line had been silent since we entered the tunnel. Hundreds of feet of mountain rock had cut off our connection.

Caleb sat up, examining the wounds on his arms and chest, then his eyes turned up to stare at me. But not my face. The rips in my suit where blood oozed out. His eyes shuttered.

"I did that."

I shook my head vehemently. "Not of your own volition. I'm fine. It looks worse than it feels." I rotated my forearm to get a better look at the worst of the wounds, and hardly suppressed a wince of pain. "This is nothing. Standard hazard of the Silhouette gig."

As I helped him to his feet, he seemed resigned not to argue.

A deep, echoing groan emitted from the walls around us.

I turned slowly, eyeing all the spots Caleb and I had careened into the walls and the pillars holding the ceiling upright. The groan grew to a rumble. A smattering of dust and small rocks rained from the ceiling.

"You've got to be shitting me," I growled. "We need to move."

Staring around in a quick panic, calculating, I swiped the laptop Cellina had been working on, yanking it from its cords. I shoved it at Caleb, who was still unsteady on his feet. Then, I turned and hauled Cellina over my shoulders, her angular frame cutting into my aching arms. *Still a bitch even when unconscious.*

There was a horrific, final crack. I bolted for the tunnel, sparing one glance to assure Caleb was behind me.

As always, he was. A little unsteady on his feet and stumbling every so often, but he caught himself on the walls and kept up, the biggest sign of the bacteria's fading effects his gasping breaths.

"Good boy," I gritted out as the whole tunnel shook.

With my heart in my throat, I led the way out. "We've got this. We've got this. Almost there," I chanted like a prayer as we hobbled and slipped our way back through the tunnel. Larger and larger chips of rock and dirt rained down on us.

Bane's roar of frustration burst through the comms as we approached the outside world, spurring us faster.

As the rumbles transformed into roars, and the dust whirled around our feet from the collapsing tunnel behind us, I saw the dim night in the distance.

"Got to be—where—*come on!*" Bane's stilted voice through the line sent my heart into my throat.

We turned the final corner and leapt into the night. I gripped Caleb's arm and urged him along with me. Cellina's braid bounced against my bleeding arms.

We tumbled across the ground as the tunnel collapsed, spewing rocks and debris. With a groan, I sat up and made sure Cellina was alive but unconscious. Then I looked over at Caleb. He seemed fine, considering, but his eyes were wide as he stared over my shoulder. I snapped my head around.

Backlit by the doors of the pole barn ripped wide open, Bane was embroiled in battle with Nicklai, Eleni Brooks, and two of the Gold Guard.

CHAPTER
TWENTY-EIGHT

"When did they get here?"

"Hey, kids," Bane's voice was strained over the comms line as he hurled an uprooted stump at the guards, and their laser shots flew all over the clearing. "How was the creepy cave?"

"Bad!" I spun to Caleb, shoving Cellina's limp form into his arms. "I hit her with a dose of memory serum, so she won't remember seeing you. Stash her somewhere and lay low."

He opened his mouth to argue.

"You're too off-kilter from the bacteria. You can help us the most right now by staying out of the way."

I didn't wait to watch him obey.

I flung myself into the fray, careening into one of the Guard, wrapping my arms around their torso. We tumbled to the ground. I threw incessant punches and kicks, sending their pistol flying.

Bane fought the other Gold Guard. Nicklai seemed bent on escape, but Eleni was determined to beat Bane senseless.

Vennie's voice piped over the comms. "They showed up a few minutes after you guys went into the cave."

"Could one of Kavoh's people have tipped them off to

keep you busy?" Chezza asked, her voice tight like her brother's.

I thought of Cellina's laptop. "It's a definite possibility."

The Guard darted forward, whipping his rifle at my head.

I ducked and leapt onto a tree branch. "Let's get the Guard out of here. We're their priority. We can lose them in the woods, then circle back for the others."

"Right." Bane turned tail and not-so-gracefully sped into the woods.

I followed, not executing at my full speed, so the Guard would stick on our trail for a while. As I pulled up next to him and matched his strides, Banc's helmet cut my way.

"Eleni managed to break loose during the chaos when the Guard showed up. I knocked out Kavoh's other crony in the barn. The other Extrahumans are still in there too. What happened to you?"

"Later."

We sprinted for a quarter of a mile, the only sound our gasping breaths in our ears.

"Wait," Bane said.

I slowed to a halt with him. As our gulps quieted, it became clear there was no sound coming from the forest around us, save the rustling of the trees in the cold night air.

Bane and I stared at each other in the darkness.

A beat passed. Another. There was no whisper of the Gold Guard.

"Oh no." Caleb's hoarse voice crackled quietly through the line. "They came back."

Without a word, we sprinted to the clearing, desperation driving us as fast as possible. I outstripped Bane by a dozen yards and nearly burst back into the clearing. He dove and grabbed my ankle, tumbling us both in the dirt before the tree line.

"What the—"

Bane held up a finger in front of his visor, indicating I should shut the hell up.

Slowly, he eased off my leg, and we peered through the shrubs before us.

Nicklai was nowhere to be seen. Eleni was facing down the Gold Guard duo, standing back-to-back with Thatcher.

The two Extrahumans broke apart, stampeding toward either Guard.

Her movements wild, Eleni wove with Extrahuman speed. It was hard to determine if her blows had much impact through their thick armor, but she moved fast enough and herded them together to make attempting to shoot her too risky. Thatcher seemed to be trying to disorient her foes via evasion, rather than striking.

Amidst the sounds of chaos, Eleni screamed something over and over. Blood flew from her mouth. I inched closer, desperate to make out her words.

"Leave us alone!"

Her strength flagging, one Guard managed to wrestle her to the ground. His teeth gritted beneath his goggles as he fought to hold her wrists behind her.

The second Guard lashed out a kick, tripping Thatcher and sending her sprawling into the dirt. He straightened with a curse.

"Unnatural," he muttered, digging for something in the pack on his back. He withdrew a fist-sized lump of metal and a long, wide tube with handles attached.

"We should call for backup," the other Guard said.

Something in the air froze me solid. I knew that voice.

His partner, clearly in charge, shook his head, still fussing with his items, trying to attach them. "We have our directive."

"What are you—"

Eleni took advantage of the Guard's distress, bucking him off her. She stood and limped toward the barn. The Guard didn't seem to mind. He grinned as her sobs formed words. "Rhett! Rhett, I'm coming."

Thatcher braced herself on hands and knees, reaching toward Eleni. "Wait!"

The head Guard turned, bracing his feet and leveling the tube before him. Pointing it at the barn.

"Oh no," I said.

The taller Guard stumbled to his feet, knocking his partner askew.

Bane and I dove from the underbrush. Across the clearing, Caleb did the same. All three of us speared for the Guards and their weapon.

With a muffled curse as he tried to right himself, the lead Guard pulled the trigger.

His partner's efforts misguided his aim, and the projectile flew high, embedding in the mountain above the pole barn.

The bomb was another piece of strange Gold Guard tech, the sound of it a soft thud incomparable to the aftermath. The explosion was nearly instant. The mountain burst outward, raining rubble and sparks onto the sturdy barn below. Smaller explosions sounded, blowing through the barn's roof, sending vicious shards of metal and wood flying in all directions. A tent of fire roared over the entire space; the force of it threw us all into the trees.

My back met an ancient tree trunk. The rough bark protested against my presence. I dropped to the ground and squeezed my eyes shut against the mist of ash and debris that tainted the air. Everything smelled burnt.

I couldn't move if I wanted to. My entire body vibrated like a tuning fork, and I ached all over.

Quiet, repeated chanting tugged me to reality.

"Stay down. Stay down. Stay down."

The command was hushed, insistent, and I realized it came through my earpiece.

"Shadow?" I managed, my voice a soft squeak.

"Silhouette." Relief saturated his voice. "Don't move. Monster? You with us?"

A beat of terrifying silence, then Caleb's voice, quiet and drawn. "Yeah, I'm okay. Landed behind some rubble by the mine."

"Great. Hold tight, everyone. No moving till we can see."

Any sense of urgency to move had fled my body anyway. I wearily lifted my head, finding I'd landed in a dense pack of bushes whose soft leaves softened my landing. Gently, I pushed branches aside and glared into the clearing. A bright yellow pillar of flames highlighted what little remained of the barn's frame.

No sign of the Extrahumans.

The barn collapsed and shot more flames into the sky. It would be nearly impossible to determine if they survived.

I clamped my lips tight to avoid my sudden need to vomit.

As the dust settled, the forms of the two Gold Guard became clear against the flames. The taller one was on his knees, coughing viciously.

In between hacks, he roared at his partner. *"What did you do?"*

A sharp intake of breath from Bane, wherever he was hiding. "Is that?"

"I think so." Caleb's voice was heartbroken, but not for himself.

There was no stopping the stream of tears that started down my face as Max removed his Gold Guard helmet.

My heart thrummed painful waves through every inch of my body.

The other Guard tugged Max upright with a sneer. "Better develop the stomach for this now, golden boy. Killing these three new freaks has a bigger impact than those two vigilantes."

"We—" Max sputtered. "We were supposed to incapacitate Silhouette and the Shadow."

"Get moving," he grunted. "We have plenty more nights for that. That fire'll have the cops here in no time."

Max shoved the other Guard away, but otherwise said nothing. He gave the fire one last glance, the flames dancing a wicked reflection in his mirrored goggles.

Neither Caleb nor Bane dared to breathe as the Guard fled the clearing.

I dropped my head to the ground and let my tears and blood mingle in the dirt.

TWENTY-NINE

Bone-deep exhaustion plastered me to my mattress for three days.

An elephant-heavy weight of defeat may have helped.

On the fourth morning, Chezza made her visit to check my wounds. She prodded me, with the help of a small mountain of pillows, to sit upright.

She unwound the bandage from my forearm, brows discerning. "This one's finally looking better. I knew it wouldn't be a match for your super speedy healing." She stood, stretched, and tossed a small jar to Caleb, who uncrossed his arms in barely enough time to catch it. "Apply that to help prevent scarring, will you? I need to get to work." She ruffled my hair and left.

Caleb abandoned his post at the window seat and gingerly sat beside me. I gripped his arm, sliding my hand down till our fingers interlaced. His answering smile was sad. With gentle, practiced strokes, he smoothed the balm over the shiny pink stripe that was the remnant of where he'd cut me deepest.

Bane, the least battered of us all, paced the open floor, his chin on one fist, his scrunched-up thinking face firmly in place.

We'd never failed quite like this before. Three lives lost, and all we had was a laptop to show for our efforts. Potentially, it could clue us in to Kavoh's plan and how to stop it, but we all agreed it wasn't worth what it'd cost us.

Vennie was furiously working at the laptop, attempting to hack through its impressive auto-lockdown tech I triggered when I unplugged it. Even if he got through, the case was battered and cracked and had some damage from our adventure, so he'd have to be extra careful extracting the information that was left, if any.

The grief for the murdered Extrahumans kept us in stasis, working slowly beneath the weight of our guilt.

Bane huffed a heavy sigh, rolling his stormy eyes to the ceiling. "I need to go to work. Get some normalcy in."

"It's time for the period of moping to end, huh?" I asked.

He eyed my arm. "One more day of rest might do you some good . . . Gem's keeping you updated on your coursework?"

We all winced, knowing it was usually Max who brought my homework after stints where I was 'sick.' Of course, we hadn't spoken since he broke off our friendship, and I wasn't sure I could face him knowing he was an initiated member of the Gold Guard.

I held my uncle's worried stare. "I'll be fine, I promise. One more day of rest would do me good."

Jaw tight, he nodded and left.

I deflated into the pillows a bit deeper.

Caleb and I sat in silence, his fingers gradually working more deeply into my skin. Eventually, it turned into discomfort as Caleb rubbed incessantly at my forearm, his eyes fevered like he could somehow erase the evidence of what he did. Each pass of his warm fingers I'm sure was accompanied by the crack of the whip he was flogging himself with mentally.

He seemed to be pointedly not looking at me ever since the mine. I placed my hand over Caleb's, stilling him.

"You're avoiding me," I accused. "Not just physically."

Caleb's entire body sagged.

His eyes met mine, then dropped to my scar again. "I'm ashamed," he said softly. "There's hardly a spot on your body I can look at and not see evidence of where I hurt you."

I moved his fingers away from my scar and traced my fingers up his chest, his neck, and to cradle his cheek, making him share a look with me. "It wasn't your fault."

He opened his mouth to argue, but I cut him off. "And I beat you, anyway. So, it doesn't matter. I can handle a few scrapes."

He huffed half a laugh, turning his face fully into my palm, pressing a kiss there. "You're not angry with me?"

I shook my head. "I'm not angry with you. Are you okay?"

He traced the spot he'd kissed with his thumb. "I'm fine. Just some soreness. You landed some good punches yourself. And . . . maybe I could stop being angry with myself."

"I'd like that," I said, leaning from my spot on the bed, trying to close the distance between us from where he sat on the edge. I cursed my short stature. I wasn't close enough to him. "I wish you would. What I really could use is a distraction."

He tilted his head in confusion as I pushed into his arms, closing the distance between us until there was a hairsbreadth between our faces. I sunk a hand into his hair.

"I've experienced enough emotions lately to last a lifetime. You're my partner, and what I need from you is to stop torturing yourself and help me *not think*."

The growl in my voice was all it took for Caleb to slip his leash.

I caught a flash of understanding on his face, then his massive hands were on me, maneuvering me easily. He shifted so I straddled him at the edge of the bed and kissed me with the fervor of a man who desperately needed forgiveness. Though I'd already granted it, I wanted this intensity to last.

I lost myself in his kiss, exploring with my tongue as his hands roved from my ass and up my back to hold me tight against him. He took my request as a mission and succeeded. I couldn't think about anything except where his body touched mine. His scent, his hair beneath my fingers, and the muscles of his back beneath my other hand, roiling as he explored me. He slipped his hands beneath my shirt, his touch igniting fire along the innocuous places he touched. My middle back, the ridges of my spine, the beginning of the curve of my hips.

He pulled back a fraction and bit my bottom lip.

A quick moan escaped my lips and turned to a gasp as he stood, easily wrapping my legs around his waist and taking us to the wall. He settled me firmly, bracing me between the wall and his hips. I whimpered at the pressure between my legs, needing to wiggle closer to him somehow, to feel the contact I needed.

Caleb pressed one palm against my neck, trailing a gentle line with his thumb up my throat and across my jaw. He stared at me intensely, satisfied and hungry all at once. I was at a loss for words.

This was better than not thinking. He was leading, and I didn't have to choose. I knew I could stop him immediately with a look or a single word if he took us somewhere I didn't want to go, but I couldn't even fathom where that boundary could be. I wanted more.

"Caleb," I gasped his name.

He captured my mouth with his, pressing me harder against the wall.

I grappled at his back, trying to keep up with his kisses and somehow managing to say, "please."

Without interrupting our rhythm, he shifted so there was the slightest space between us, skating one hand gently over my stomach, then beneath the waistband of my leggings.

As he explored me that way for the first time, his breath ragged in between the kisses he trailed along my neck, I drifted. My eyelids fluttered as his deft fingers, gentle but firm, traced me slowly, reverently. I knew the instant he met my wetness because a growl rumbled deep in his chest. He spun us back to the bed, withdrawing his hand to cradle my neck as he situated me gently.

I couldn't help a petulant noise of protest at his fingers' disappearance from where I needed him. He pulled back and I glared.

This pulled a dark, delicious laugh from his perfect mouth that nearly had me orgasming on the spot. I lifted my face to stifle his laugh, and he obliged by sliding my leggings down my legs and setting them gently to the side. He returned his hand to between my thighs, teasing in circles until he finally slipped two fingers inside me.

I couldn't make sense of things beyond the moment. There was just Caleb, his soft kisses and strokes interspersed with intensity, bringing me slowly and surely to an edge I was ready to fling myself off. Every sensation was heightened, my shirt against my breasts, the muscles of Caleb's arms moving against my thigh.

When I came, it was long and brilliant and bright and unhurried. Pleasure roiled through me until I could hardly remember my own name, let alone any of my problems.

Caleb eased me back to reality, a satisfied set to his mouth that I'd never seen before that was wildly sexy. He eased me against his chest, curling my legs up over his and winding a blanket around us. He stroked his fingers through my hair, the only hint of his desire the quiet panting of his breath. I was his entirely, undone and unable to think. He'd succeeded and then some. He eased my head against his warm chest. I wanted to speak, but all I could manage was a satisfied hum.

He laughed again and began stroking my back, summoning drowsiness.

"You've been hiding this superpower too, Monster," I accused, my eyes already closed.

One more laugh like silk against my overheated skin. "Guilty. If my plan worked, you're about to have the most exceptional nap of your life. You need it, little Terror."

"Thank you," I muttered, nothing but awe in my tone. I was asleep in seconds.

CHAPTER
THIRTY

Within a week, my grief hardened into something useful. No less painful, but sharp and perfect to wedge between the spaces of Kavoh's armor and destroy her.

Vennie made slow progress with the laptop—he'd managed to hack the hard drive, but was still researching ways to crack Kavoh's top tier security keeping us out of the files without giving us away, since the laptop could still connect to her network.

"Persicaria perfoliata," Vennie said over the comms channel.

"Bless you," Bane said, nearly toppling out of his quad stretch.

"It's what Kavoh named her computer network."

I deepened my own stretch, easing the tightness along my side. "Is that Latin?"

A hum of assent and the sound of typing. "A flowering plant in the buckwheat family also known as 'mile-a-minute weed.' On many regions' invasive species watch list. It's a fast-growing vine with barbs."

"Lovely," I snorted.

"The amount of money she must have dropped on tech is wild," Vennie continued. "It's so touchy."

Done with warming up, Bane and I lined up along the midcourt line on a long-abandoned basketball court at the edge of the city. Painted purple at the late hour, tufts of scrubby grass poked through the uneven asphalt.

"One of us is going to break an ankle," I said.

"Take it one step at a time, Braveheart," Bane urged, flapping a hand to dismiss my prediction. "Take the time you need to do this properly."

Vennie grunted, likely thinking what I was—this laptop was our only lead, and we couldn't afford to blow it.

We were hopeful the disaster in the Outskirts had at least bought us some time. The explosion was all over the news, and the entire city was on edge. Crown City Police proclaimed across all the news outlets that they were working hard to find information in the scraps that were left of Kavoh's site. No one but us seemed to know her name was connected, but no missing person reports had been filed that matched the pattern of her prior abductions since the explosion, so we hoped she was laying low.

"Are we all set, Monster?" Chezza asked.

I had my small, in-lens monitor on, so I could see her perched in front of the half of the LUMA Vennie wasn't using.

Caleb sprinted across the court, claws digging into the asphalt. Nose twitching, he eyed the small drones he'd placed at Chezza's direction. "Think so," he growled.

"Perfect, looks good on my end too." Chezza tapped a button and switched the screen along Caleb's forearm armor from depicting a diagram to a split screen of the perimeter alarms we'd set. He was our security for this training exercise, as things were certain to get loud.

"Okay, focus up, kids," Chezza said.

I closed out my view of her in the Den, so I could focus

and also not get a clue at the formations she'd programmed for us.

"I'm going to set the drones to execute a random set of fight sequences. They will project simple forms to represent a sour's body movements. Remember, the goal is to not get tagged. Evasion first, neutralization second."

I gritted my teeth as the drones powered up with an ominous thrum for such small engines. This was an exercise in dexterity and reflexes, but I could guess why it was on everyone's minds. The escalation of events with Kavoh had us all on edge and reminded us of the stakes of our vigilante work. We needed to be more focused and capable than ever.

Time for brooding ran out as the drones projected glowing arms and legs and rushed us.

We spent the next hour dodging, distracting, and most importantly, communicating with each other to safely escape various numbers of faux sours. We were exhausted and sweaty by midnight, when Bane stepped too slow and was rewarded with a blaring note from the drone that had "captured" him.

He screamed incoherently at the sky, but his helmet was locked down, so it only blew out the ears of those of us on the comms line.

I started to laugh, but my own curses appeared when a second drone "grabbed" me around the middle with its fake arms and made a second, quieter alarm.

"Sequence wasn't finished yet, Silhouette," Chezza said. "Let's run it again."

I braced my hands on my knees. "Beacon, these are so—"

A voice rang from the shadows. "Sloppy. Disorganized. It's a miracle you haven't gotten yourselves killed."

Bane immediately sprang to stand between me and the figure emerging from the trees. Vennie and Chezza went silent, so they could observe and assess, ready to help.

Caleb simply gasped, "How did she do that?" over the

comms channel, which meant our security sensors hadn't been triggered.

I heard quick steps through the underbrush a hundred yards off as he headed our way.

But the voice only froze me into careful stillness. I didn't want to turn too fast because I was talking to a ghost twice over.

Turning on my heel, I stared into a distantly familiar brown face, significantly more scarred than the last time I saw her.

"Thatcher," I breathed. "You survived the explosion." My heart stuttered. Had the others?

She strode into the dim light of the lone flickering street lamp, a slight limp in her gait and one muscled arm bundled in a sling. "Hello, Melbourne."

I winced. "It's Silhouette right now."

"Right." She smiled. "You look good. This town seems to suit you better than Upstate City ever did."

Bane relaxed his stance at the same time a subtle shifting of the greenery signified that Caleb was close and kept an eye on us. "I'm sorry. Who are you?"

"My name is Kaye. I'm a scientist," she said, her mouth a thin line suggesting getting more information would be a trial.

"She worked for my dad," I added through gritted teeth. "Until she . . . you"—I said pointedly—"disappeared last year."

She shrugged. "You moved on, so did I."

I rubbed my face. "And ended up as one of Kavoh's experiments? Clearly, you're not here to tell us everything, and I get that. But my head is spinning. Please say whatever it is you're here to say, and don't make us work for it."

She considered me, and maybe she saw the exhaustion and defeat in my eyes. "You must have realized your mom had powers too, right?" Thatcher laughed. "I've never seen anyone love the snow so much. Almost knocked out the power for half of Upstate City making snow angels once."

Mentioning my mother was nowhere on my bingo card for this interaction, so I fully sat on the ground to digest.

"Your mom and I became friends after she sought me out for my research. She wanted me to cure her powers, and yours too. So, you two wouldn't have to deal with them. Your dad didn't know about them, so I needed an excuse to be around a lot. I doctored some documents, learned a few new skills, and together, we got it into Sam's head that he needed an assistant. Of course, my application was a perfect fit."

"Why didn't you just tell me?"

"Your mom asked me not to. I made her a promise."

I blinked absently at the sky, eyes stinging.

Thatcher waited a beat before continuing. "I kept tabs after you left. When I knew you were safe here with your uncle, I bailed on Sam. During my research trying to help your mom, we had a general idea of what your grandpa must have done during his work with Kavoh. I followed her movement out of curiosity. I realized she was trying to make more Extrahumans and stealing people off the street to do so.

"I came here, laid low, and snooped as best I could. One night, I got too close to one of her operations, and Kavoh's people got me. Gave me some of those half-baked superpowers she's stuck on right now."

The strength. Whatever was going on with her vision. I had a million questions.

Bane beat me to the punch, though. "So, when you made it out of the explosion, you were free again. Are you alright? Do you need medical attention? A place to stay?"

"You are sweet, huh?" she asked him, not unkindly. "But no, thank you, I've got my lodging settled."

My head spun. I caught Caleb's bright, confused stare glowing between the trees.

I cleared my throat. "Don't get me wrong, I'm glad you're

okay. But what do you want from us? Can we exchange what we know about Kavoh?"

Thatcher grinned. "Better." She held up her uninjured arm, and the starlight glinted off a flash drive gripped in her fist. "You're going to help me stop her."

To find out as soon as the next installment of Mel's story is available, sign up for the newsletter at delaneyandrews.com

ACKNOWLEDGMENTS

Writing a second book was possible because so many of you let me know you believed in the first one, and that you wanted more of Mel and Bane's story. Thank you from the bottom of my heart, sweet readers. (I have *readers!* I don't know what to wish for on my birthday anymore!) You've cheered me on, recommended my books to friends, shared reviews and photos, and more. You make my day every time I hear from you! I love the DJRmy community.

Silhouette and the Monster is also in your hands thanks to a group of incredible creatives I'm so lucky to call friends.

Mackenzie Briscoe, you're the best friend and sister a gal could ask for, and I'm honored to have you as my alpha reader and the first line Mel crosses into our world with each new story.

To the brilliant Caitlin Schneiderhan, thank you for your incredible feedback that helped me to discover the "why" of this story. I'm convinced our friendship is fate, and that's why I was mistaken for you one time on the sidewalk in Santa Monica. Thanks for tolerating me when I scream my excitement at you over the internet.

To my fleet of beta readers: Brenna, Colton, Karen, and Libby—I adore you. Your thoughts are crucial to carving out the heart of Mel and Bane's adventures. I can't thank you enough, but please let me buy you several beers as small, tasty tokens of my gratitude.

Extra special thanks to Lindsey White for being this series' #1 superfan on top of a thorough and insightful beta reader. Thank you for also serving as the intermediary between me and the ghost that lets me hang my clothes in her home. (Hi, Stevie!)

To Nichole Heydenburg and the illustrious Poisoned Ink Press, thank you for your editing prowess and making this book shine!

Erin Olds at Salt & Sage, you continue to be my formatting superhero. Thank you!

Danielle Prielipp, you are an all around badass and I'm so grateful for our friendship. Thank you for being my synopsis doctor.

Heather Hamilton-Senter of Book Cover Artistry, you've done it again. Thank you for the truly astounding cover that captures Mel at the crossroads she faces in this book.

With each book I aim to thank a few teachers, and this one goes out to Bethanie George, Dan Schneider, and Linda Learman. Thank you for working with me to build a solid foundation on which my writing continues to flourish. There are skills and exercises from your classes I use all the time. You are the real superheroes.

I'd also like to thank the three different individuals who made sure during my first year as an author that when they saw me from across the street to yell, "IS THAT DELANEY ANDREWS THE AUTHOR?!" Jim Mahony and Barb and Scott Jacques, you guys rock.

Danielle Blasingame, I love you and you stress me out. Thanks for always being there for everything, but especially to talk about spicy books.

Thank you Mom, Griffin, and Grayce, for always supporting me, listening to me rant, and tolerating my shenanigans. I love you all so much. You're each going to get a book dedicated to you eventually. Relax.

Zack, this whole book is for you. Thanks for being so cool about my many obsessions, especially werewolves.

And finally to my dear sweet trash gremlin, Atreyu. I love you so much little Florida Man Sand Dragon Potato. The trash cans in this story are yours to live in forever.

ABOUT THE AUTHOR

Delaney Andrews petitioned her parents to not throw her a fourteenth birthday party, and instead buy her a prolific fantasy authors' entire bibliography. They accepted with slight trepidation, and Delaney is now creating her own catalog of books she hopes a youngster will someday want more than a birthday party. She graduated from Adrian College and lives in metro Detroit with her family. She hates surprises and loves minor league athletic team mascots. You can be friends with her online at delaneyandrews.com and @dj_rhetoric.

twitter.com/dj_rhetoric

instagram.com/dj_rhetoric

tiktok.com/@dj_rhetoric